# Angel Eyes

Larry Pedersen

DONK
KEEP HITTING EM STRAIGHT!
7/19/12

ISBN (978-0-9840867-4-0)

Printed in USA by 48HrBooks (www.48HrBooks.com)

Private Investigator Butch Brogen is hired by a couple of friends to find a young woman who has disappeared.

Follow Butch as he travels to Tennessee with his wife, where his investigation leads him to a religious compound, a local college, and a pole dancer.

Books by Larry Pedersen


**SOUTHERN RIDGE**
**MAPLE ISLE**

# Acknowledgements

Johnson City and Jonesborough, Tennessee are real cities, but they are used fictitiously in this novel.

The same is true of certain businesses, bars, golf courses and other places frequented by Butch Brogen.

Names, characters, and people associated with these places are strictly the product of the author's imagination or are used in a fictitious manner. Any resemblance to actual people, persons living, or dead, or to actual events or locales is entirely coincidental.

All errors, exaggerations, and omissions of fictionalization are entirely the author's fault.

Thank you to my regular golf partners, Dale Prestegard, Kile Holm, Bob Hutton, John Michaeu, Tom Streiff, Jim Goodman, Brandon Weick, Darryl Thompson, Darrel Post and Duane Eckert for sharing their stories, actions, language and nick names, which were incorporated into some of the fictitious golfers mentioned in this novel.

Very special thanks to my wife, Ruth, for her always-helpful comments and suggestions on the manuscript, plus her diligence in keeping my many grammatical errors to a minimum.

# Chapter One

The delicious aroma of grilling hamburgers and frying French fries, wafted across the parking lot of Southern Ridge Golf Course, Rosecrest, Minnesota on the first Wednesday in May, filling my nostrils as I got out of my Escalade and started to remove my golf equipment from the rear of my vehicle.

My name is Larry Brogen, but everyone calls me Butch. I retired several years ago from the Rosecrest Police Department so I could enjoy one of the passions of my life, golf. I had been a lieutenant in the Homicide Department the last five years of my police career. I now make a few extra bucks as a private investigator, providing the PI work doesn't interfere with my second love, golf. I'm about six foot tall, have short brown hair, blue eyes, and am about thirty pounds overweight. The weight being attributed to two more of my loves, drinking and eating.

I don't really need the money, because I am married to a wonderful woman, Martha. She inherited half of her father's lottery winnings after he was tragically killed on Southern Ridge Golf Course. Her thirty-four million dollar share provides us with more money than we can spend.

Martha is my greatest love, even beating out golf. She has silky, flowing black hair, sparkling blue eyes, a long slim six-foot body with a slim butt, two large firm breasts and a great personality. Her habit of not wearing a bra is another one of her traits I greatly admire.

My golf equipment consists of a Bag Boy Pro golf bag filled with a King Cobra XL driver, two King Cobra baffler TWS hybrid clubs, a 2R and a 3R, and King Cobra FP irons. All the clubs have regular flex graphite shafts. My putter is shaped like a hockey stick, with the Minnesota Wild colors and logo. I removed my electric golf bag kaddy cart from the vehicle, installed the battery, and sat my golf bag on it. I then inserted my SkyCaddie SG5 GPS into the holder on the golf kaddy. I removed my loafers and put on my Foot Joy Dry Joy golf shoes. I closed all the doors to the Escalade, locked them, and started my electric golf bag kaddy cart in motion towards the clubhouse.

As I neared the clubhouse, I noticed a couple guys on the putting green, a couple walking towards the clubhouse and three just standing around, talking. I nodded and waved to each person as I passed them on my way to the clubhouse. These seven made up the group I was golfing with today, Don Pastor, Karl Houston, Burt Harold, Jim Martin, Joe Granderson, Bill Walton, and Timmy Straight.

I had met these fellows through playing softball, bowling, and golfing. As many of us who can make it, meet every Wednesday for eighteen holes of golf filled with more BS than you can imagine. Don and Joe work for the local county, while the other guys work for the State of Minnesota in various capacities. No finer group of public employees, active or retired; will you ever find on a golf course.

The aroma of the cooking food was still filling the air as I entered the clubhouse.

"Hi, Mitch," I said to the young man behind the counter as I swiped my membership card in front of the optical card reader sitting on the counter.

"Hi, Mr. Brogen," he replied as my picture appeared on a small monitor next to the scanner, with the information, *Single membership 2011, PAID.*

"Another beautiful day for golf, huh?" Mitch said.

"Sure is."

7

"From the aroma in the air, Stewart sure must be grilling a bunch of burgers," I said, referring to the fellow who operated the restaurant at the golf course.

"Yep. We have a group of forty-four golfers out on the course that will be coming in shortly and want to eat," answered Mitch.

"Wow, forty-four in a group! Must be some sort of a special outing."

"Yeah. This group calls themselves the Hackers Golf Association and they come out twice a year and have fun," Mitch said.

"Hackers Golf Association, huh? Sounds like I'd fit into that group," I replied to Mitch as I was exiting through the open door of the clubhouse to meet up with the guys.

As I neared the first tee, I noticed Karl was already standing on the tee, swinging his driver.

"Get your ass going Butch, if you want to golf with me," Karl said as me and my electric golf bag kaddy cart neared the tee box.

"Do I have to golf with you?" I asked with a pained expression.

"You can golf with me," Timmy excitedly said from where he was standing near the cart path.

"Shit, I ain't got much of a choice today," I said.

"I either get to golf with a dick weed like Karl or someone who's ran over my electric golf bag kaddy cart with a riding golf cart," I added.

On one of our golf outings, Timmy had managed to drive his riding golf cart into my electric golf bag kaddy cart, bending the rear-stabilizing wheel. I never repaired the bent rear wheel so I would always have a reminder of Timmy.

"You shoulda zigged instead of zagged," Timmy said in a pained voice as he was looking for sympathy from me.

"Ain't you lucky," replied Karl as he smiled and started waggling his driver at the golf ball he had already teed up.

"I'll golf with Nutt," I said using one of Karl's many nicknames as I spoke to Don who usually sets up the parings for our weekly outings.

"Your choice," Don replied.

"You have two balls?" I asked Karl as he was about to hit his drive. Very often, Karl hooks his first drive into the woods on the left of the first fairway.

"Hell no, he don't have two balls," said Timmy.

"Why do you think his nickname is One Nut," he added.

"I mean two golf balls, dimwit," I replied to Timmy.

Karl teed off first and as unusual as it was, managed to split the fairway with his drive.

"One ball is all I need," Karl proudly said as he walked off the tee box.

"This time," I replied as I walked to the tee markers, and placed my tee into the ground. I sat a Pinnacle Gold number 3 golf ball on which I had placed a purple dot, on the tee. Grasping my driver, I prepared for my first hit of the day.

"Don't hit it into the woods," Karl said with his fake encouragement.

"Don't slice it into number two fairway," added Timmy.

"What the hell am I supposed to do?" If I have to listen to you two chortlin magpies, I'll probably miss the ball completely," I replied.

"Hit it down the middle like I did," Karl quickly said.

I hit my drive and managed to keep the ball out of the woods and number two fairway. The ball did come to rest under a small maple tree on the right side of the fairway, about one-hundred sixty yards from the green.

Burt followed me teeing off and when he hit his golf ball, an ear shattering, deafening, glass-shattering sound echoed through the valley.

"Holy shit! Ain't you got rid of that damn glass shattering driver yet?" I asked as I covered my ears.

"Nope," Burt replied as he smiled and put his driver back into his golf bag.

"I don't think I can hit a golf ball now because my ears are ringing so badly," Joe said as he placed his golf ball on a tee.

"Why don't you try hitting it from the wrong side, like Bill," Timmy quipped referring to the fact that Bill was left-handed.

Ignoring Timmy, Joe nailed his drive straight down the fairway and over the first hill.

"Have a good round and don't give Bill shit because he's a lefty," I said to Don, Jim, Bill and Timmy as they waited to tee off.

The first couple of holes didn't go very well for me. I had a double bogie on hole one and a triple bogie on hole two, after hitting two shots into the pond abutting the fairway near the green. I did have a one putt though! My drive on the par three, number three hole wasn't a whole lot better than my other shots. I pushed my short iron drive into a stand of cattails.

As we were walking up the fairway, Joe turned to me with his ever-present grin on his face and said, "We're sure having fun today. Aren't we?"

"Fun your ass," I growled.

"I haven't had this much fun since I run the tip of my index finger through my joiner," I quickly added.

"Maybe that's what's wrong with your golf swing," Burt said.

"That was ten years ago," I snapped at Burt as I neared the cattails preparing to look for my golf ball.

The rest of the round wasn't a whole lot better, but at least I was getting some pars and bogies.

My group finished hole eighteen and stood on the knoll at the back of the green, waiting for the other guys to finish.

"Think we should move?" asked Joe.

"Might not hurt. Timmy has a tendency of overshooting this green," said Karl.

The four of us moved a little higher on the knoll as the shots from the guys following us came sailing in. Two of the shots hit the green and stopped; one came up short and landed on the front slope of the green. The fourth shot sailed over the green and bounced around inside one of the riding golf carts sitting behind the green.

"Ten to one for a five the shot inside the golf carts is Timmy's," Karl said.

"No way," said Joe.

"I didn't see who hit the ball, but I agree with Joe. I'm sure it was Timmy, so I ain't biting," I replied.

Timmy walked past the green and retrieved his golf ball from the front seat of golf cart number 23.

"Told ya so," Karl said.

An errant golf ball had hit none of us, so that was another good outcome for the day. After the group putted out, we stood around for a while comparing scores and talking about next week's golf outing. We all then headed towards our vehicles to make the journey home.

## Chapter Two

As I turned into the driveway of my house at 4527 West High Point Drive, Wolf Run Subdivision, Rosecrest, Minnesota, my thoughts were still on the terrible round of golf I had just completed. My home was a six-thousand square foot two-story dwelling with an attached four-stall garage. The house and garage were located on a twenty-acre lot that was accessed from the nearby street by a winding concrete driveway, which was lined with various shrubs. The front lawn contained three maple trees, a clump white birch and two aspens. Hostas and clematis surrounded the house.

Immediately behind the house was an in ground heated swimming pool adjacent to a flag stone patio. The swimming pool was surrounded by a tall privacy fence with a locked gate leading to the back yard. The patio contained various patio furniture, which included two tables with an umbrella pole projecting out of each one of them. Each table had four chairs seated around them. Three chaise lounges were placed at other locations on the patio. The centerpiece of the patio was a humongous six-burner gas grill.

We very seldom entertained anyone, but Martha wants to be prepared in case I ever concede to have a group of people over. I'm not unsociable, it's just that I don't like entertaining. If people would just come over, help themselves to food and drink, and not bother me, I would be more agreeable to entertaining. I enjoy the cooking, but not all the socializing I'm expected to do.

Beyond the fenced swimming pool was the back yard containing a twenty-five thousand gallon pond. Surrounding the pond was another flagstone patio. Two benches sat on the patio providing seating when we were feeding the fish in the pond. A winding stream led to a waterfall entering the pond. The pond contained various water plants, lilies, hyacinth, water lettuce, and anacharis.

Swimming among the plants was sixteen Koi of various sizes and colors.

I hit the remote door opener in my Escalade and slowly eased into the garage after the door opened.

I brought my Escalade to a halt next to a Crystal Red Tintcoat Cadillac XLR-V, two-door convertible. The convertible was my wife Martha's, so I rarely get to drive it.

I exited my Escalade making sure I didn't door ding the convertible. I then walked to the entrance to the house leading from the garage.

Entering the house I called out, "Hi honey. I'm home."

"In-here," came the response from the family room.

I walked through the kitchen into the family room to see my wonderful wife, Martha. Her six-foot gorgeous tanned body was sprawled in one of the recliners reading a book. She was dressed in light blue shorts, a hot pink tee shirt and of course, no bra. The few years we have been married, I have only seen her wear a bra on a few occasions. No problem!

"How was golf, today?" she asked as she lay the book down and looked at me.

"The same crap," I groused as I walked over to Martha and gave her a kiss on the forehead.

"At least Nutt or Timmy didn't piss me off," I added as I turned to head towards the kitchen to make myself a cold Tangueray and tonic.

"Want anything to drink?" I asked as I neared the kitchen doorway.

"A glass of lemonade would be fine."

"Are you going out onto the patio?" Martha asked.

"Sure."

"It's nice outside. The thermometer on the Escalade said seventy-five degrees when I came home."

"I'll join you," Martha said as she started to remove her lanky frame from the recliner.

We exited the house through the patio door in the kitchen. I sat down in one of the lounge chairs situated on the patio. We sat on the patio enjoying our drinks and talking about my golf and Martha's shopping trip.

"I suppose we should feed the fish," I said after about forty-five minutes.

"I'll get the fish food," I said as I rose and started towards the patio door leading to the kitchen.

"Want any more to drink?" I asked.

"I'm fine."

I entered the house; made myself another Tangueray and tonic, grabbed the container of fish food, and headed back outside. We fed the fish, watched them swim around for a while, and then decided it was time for supper.

"What are we having?" Martha asked me as we walked towards the privacy fence gate. I do most of the cooking and Martha does most of the cleaning up after me. This system works well most of the time, except for when I get carried away trying some new dish and use just about every kitchen utensil we own. Then, Martha prefers I clean up my own mess.

"I took some center cut pork chops out of the freezer this morning," I answered.

"Sounds good."

"Want yours barbequed or plain?" I asked as I opened the gate of the privacy fence and started walking past the swimming pool towards the patio door.

"Barbeque sounds good. What's with them?"

"I thought asparagus in cheese sauce would go good. I saw there was some asparagus in the refrigerator," I replied as I stopped at the gas grill and ignited it.

"Great, I'll start cleaning the asparagus for you," Martha said as she entered the house.

After finishing a great meal, Martha and I retired to the family room. Martha started to watch Wheel of Fortune on the sixty-inch high definition, wide screen television hanging on the wall opposite from where we were sitting and I grabbed the latest Vince Flynn novel and started to read. Ten minutes had barely elapsed, when the telephone rang. I quickly looked up at the television screen to see who was calling. Our local cable company has an option where you can have your caller ID show on the television screen as well as your telephone.

*Gottfried Butz 657-555-4567* showed on the screen.

"Know any Gottfried Butz?" I asked Martha.

"Nope," she quickly replied as she continued to watch television.

"Me neither," I replied as I let the telephone continue to ring.

The answering machine kicked on and I could hear the person leaving a message.

"Hello, Butch. This is Bubba Butz. I don't know if you remember me, but...."

I remembered Bubba from several years ago when I was in Tennessee investigating the death of Martha's father, so I quickly grabbed the cordless telephone which was laying on the lamp stand next to my chair.

15

"Hello, this is Butch," I quickly said after pushing the talk button on the telephone.

"Oh, hello Butch. I didn't think anyone was home when the answering machine kicked on," Bubba said.

"We have caller ID, so I don't answer the telephone unless I know who's calling. I didn't recognize the name Gottfried Butz," I answered.

"Why do you think I go by Bubba?" Bubba asked as he chuckled.

"I can see your point."

"How did you figure out how to get a hold of me?" I asked.

"Don't you remember when we met and went to Your Uncles Place for a drink?" Bubba asked.

"I sure do," I replied as my mind quickly flashed back to that night when I first met Bubba and his wife Bertha at Beulah's Diner. They were the two largest people I had ever met. Not fat, just huge people!

"When we were leaving Your Uncles Place, you handed me one of your business cards and said to get in touch with you if we ever needed an expert private investigator," Bubba answered.

"You're in the need of a private investigator?" I asked Bubba.

"Sure am."

"What for?"

There was a small pause and then Bubba answered with a heavy voice, "Bertha's kid sister, Angel has disappeared."

"Disappeared?"

"Yep, she's been gone for three months now."

"Have you gone to the local police or sheriff?" I asked.

"Yep, we have no local police department and the sheriff makes Dudley Dooright look like a flippin genius," Bubba said.

16

"He claims he has done everything possible, but he still has no answers for us," Bubba replied.

"How about hiring a local private investigator?" I asked.

"I'm a long way from Tennessee," I added.

"I know that, the only local PI we have around here makes the sheriff look smart," Bubba answered with another small chuckle.

Thinking about my golf outings with the guys three days a week, I said, "I just don't know if I can be of much service to you and Bertha. If you already have the local law involved and they can't find out anything, I don't know if I can either. Besides, this time of year I'm pretty busy golfing."

"Still chasing that little white ball around the cow pasture are you?" asked Bubba.

"Sure am. Are you still throwing that black ball down the alley?" I asked as I was referring to the fact Bubba had told me he was a bowler, not a golfer.

"Sure am, and I ain't lost a ball yet. I did get one chewed up by the ball return last year though," Bubba said as he laughed.

"We would sure be beholding to you if you come down here and see what you can find out. Bertha is just a terrible wreck not knowing what's happened to her sister," Bubba continued as he sighed.

"You did tell us you were a good investigator," he quickly added.

"Well, I just don't know," I replied as I tried to figure out a polite way not to have to give up my golf and travel to Tennessee.

"Money is no object. In fact I've already transferred $5,000 into your PayPal account as a retainer," Bubba said.

"Transferred $5,000 into my PayPal account! You would need my email address to be able to do that," I said.

17

"Oh, I got your email address from your wife, Martha," Bubba quickly replied.

"From my wife, you say," I replied as I looked over at Martha who was busy staring at the television screen avoiding my eyes.

"Yes. She also told me about her inheriting a large sum of money and that you didn't need the money, but I kinda thought that if I gave you a retainer, you would be willing to help us out," Bubba said.

"I appreciate the fact you think I can help and have already given me some money, but let me think about it for a couple of days," I said.

"Oh, sure. No problem. My telephone number is 657-555-4567," Bubba said.

"Fine. I'll get back in touch with you in a couple of days with my decision."

We continued talking for a while discussing my golf, Bubba's bowling, and how things were down in Jonesborough and here in Rosecrest.

Hanging up the telephone, I turned to Martha, who still had her eyes glued to the television.

"Don't know a Gottfried Butz, huh?"

"He never said his name was Gottfried, only Bubba," she replied without taking her eyes off the television.

"And you gave him my PayPal user name so he could put some money into my account."

Martha now quit watching television, rose out of her chair, and walked over to me, sitting her tall, lanky frame in my lap, putting her arms around my neck and giving me a little kiss.

"Hey, cut that shit out!" I exclaimed trying to sound offended.

"Oh, Butch. After hearing Bubba's story, I just knew you should help find out what happened to Bertha's sister," she cooed into my ear.

"You could have told me about your conversation with Bubba when I got home. I would then have had time to think about helping him," I said.

"I know I should have," she mumbled as she nibbled on my ear and rubbed her hand under my shirt on my bare chest.

"You're not mad at me, are you?" she coyly asked.

"Nah, I ain't mad."

"But, if you don't quit what you're doing, I might get something else," I said.

"Would that be so bad?" she said just before kissing me again.

"I guess not," I mumbled as we continuing kissing.

# Chapter Three

As I was pulling into the parking lot of Maple Isle Golf Course on Thursday, May 5, my thoughts went back to the telephone call I had received last night. I didn't know Bubba and Bertha very well, but they seemed like nice people and they were asking for my help. What should I do?

As I approached the clubhouse, I saw the three guys I would be golfing with today, standing around their vehicles. Every Thursday, I golf with Daniel 'Babe' Parsons, David 'Donk' Trenton, and Doug 'Hogg' Evans.

I pulled along side of where the guys were standing and got out of my vehicle.

"Hi, boys," I said.

"Hey," said Hogg.

"About damn time you got here," said Donk.

"Did you and the misses have a quick roll in the hay this morning?" asked Babe.

"If I have a roll in the hay, it ain't gonna be quick," I quickly replied as I opened the rear door of the Escalade so I could remove my golfing equipment.

"I don't need to listen to your lies. Now get your shit and lets get golfing," Donk quickly retorted.

I put my Foot Joy Dry Joy golf shoes on as the other three grabbed their golf bags and started trudging down to the clubhouse. After getting my shoes on, I retrieved my golf bag from the back of the Escalade, along with my SkyCaddie, shut the rear door, and made my way to join the fellows. We all paid our green fees, said hi to Arnold the club pro, grabbed a golf cart key, and headed out of the clubhouse.

"Did you grab a score card?" Babe asked as we walked towards our golf bags.

"Of course. You guys never seem to remember to pick one up," I replied as I got to our golf cart and placed the score card on the holder located on the steering wheel.

After loading our golf bags on the golf carts and me attaching my SkyCaddie to the left upright supporting the roof of the golf cart, we headed to the first tee.

The first tee off went the same as usual, Babe being the first to get ready to tee off, with Donk telling him not to hit the ball to the right side of the fairway. Babe promptly hooked his drive left and almost ended up in the fairway sand trap.

"There, I didn't hit the ball to the right," Babe smugly replied to Donk.

Donk teed off next and did exactly what he had told Babe not to do, hit his drive into the right rough, leaving him no shot to the green. I managed to hit my drive down the center of the fairway, but only about two hundred yards.

"I'm playing the senior tees," Hogg said as he started walking to the gold tees, which were located about fifty yards in front of the white tees.

The first few holes were nothing spectacular, with only a couple of pars produced among us four. Everyone was fairly quiet until we got to the fourth tee box. This was the spot where Evans had found a woman's body several years ago. The three of them started talking about what that day was like. It seems as though every time we golf here, the woman's body is brought up in conversation.

We were getting ready to tee off on hole number five when Babe turned to me and said, "You're sure quite today. Anything wrong?"

"Nah. I'm just thinking about a telephone call I got last night," I said as I walked to the tee and teed off.

"What kind of call did you get?" Babe asked as we followed Hogg to the senior tees, which were fifty yards in front of the white tee.

"Oh, it was nothing bad."

"It was a request from a couple whom I had met several years ago when I was in Tennessee investigating a death on Southern Ridge Golf Course," I said.

"Oh, I remember that."

"You met the deceased's daughter and now you're married," Babe added.

"Yep, you're right. While I was down there investigating Martha's dads killing, I met Bubba and Bertha Butz," I said.

"She one of the Butts sisters?" Babe asked as he chuckled.

Ignoring Babe's reference to lines in a song of the fifties, I replied, "Bertha's kid sister has disappeared and they want me to come down and investigate her disappearance."

"So are you?"

"I don't really want to miss golfing with you guys that bad, but I feel I almost should because they're such nice folks," I said

"And they'll pay you money!"

"What the hell do I care about money. Martha's got more than we can ever spend," I said.

"That's providing she keeps your sorry ass around," replied Babe as he smiled at me and got out of the golf cart to hit his next shot.

"I'm so sweet and wonderful. I'm the love of her life," I quickly replied.

"Don't talk like that. You'll make me gag and screw up my next shot," Babe playfully replied.

We finished our round of golf with nobody getting hurt, nobody punching anybody out or losing any clubs.

"We going to the Sportsman?" Evans asked.

"Is it Thursday?" replied Donk.

After we finish our Thursday golf rounds, we always retire to a local watering hole to have a couple of drinks and continue to talk smart. After our two drinks, free popcorn and bullshit, we left the bar and got into our vehicles for the journey home.

As I drove home, I kept thinking about Bubba's request. What should I do? I want to help him if I can. I don't want to miss a lot of golf with the guys. I don't need the money. I don't want to be away from Martha for too long. I don't know Bubba that well. I should help Bubba and Bertha.

My mind was still spinning as I pulled into the driveway to my garage. I entered the house to see Martha standing in the kitchen even though I had expected her to be in the swimming pool.

"To cold to swim?" I asked.

"Oh, no. The pool is heated just right. I went swimming this afternoon," she replied.

"How was golf?"

"It was OK, but I kept thinking about Bubba's request," I said.

"And?"

"And what?"

"What did you decide?"

"I just don't know. I should try to help Bubba and Bertha, but I really don't want to be gone for too long," I said.

"You should be able to get some golfing in down in Tennessee."

"I know, but I just don't want to be away from you for to long," I replied.

"Oh, you're so sweet," Martha said as she walked over to me and gave me a kiss.

"I could go with you and assist."

"You told me as we were coming home from Holdenford that you never wanted to come with me on one of my investigations," I reminded her.

"I know, but if I went with you, I could see Kenny and his family," she said referring to her brother who still resided outside of Jonesborough, Tennessee.

"I know I have to decide one way or another," I said.

"I told Bubba I would give him a call today to give him my answer," I added.

We had a simple supper of brats and French fries cooked on the grill and retired to the family room. Martha was watching Wheel of Fortune and I was working on a crossword puzzle, when I made my decision.

I picked up the cordless phone from the lamp stand and dialed 657-555-4567. After several rings, I heard a male's voice.

"Hello,"

"Hi, Bubba. This is Butch."

"Hi, Butch. How's it going?"

"Great."

"Have you decided to help Bertha and me?" Bubba said with some trepidation in his voice.

"Yep, I decided to see what I could do for you folks. It's not about the money though. I just want to help if I can," I said.

"That's great!" Bubba excitedly said.

"When will you be able to come down?"

"Sometime in the next several days. I need to line up someone to tend to the lawn, feed the fish, etc," I said.

24

"Whenever you can make it will be fine with us," Bubba replied.

"I'll give you a call when I get to Jonesborough," I said.

"That's great! Bertha will be so happy you're coming to help us," Bubba excitedly said.

"I'm not guaranteeing anything. I'm just saying I'm willing to look into your sister-in-laws disappearance," I said.

"I know, but we're so happy somebody other than Dudley Dooright is willing to help us," Bubba said.

# Chapter Four

Martha and I left for Tennessee, Wednesday, May 11. As I drove along on I-90 towards Chicago, I wondered what I was getting myself into. Would I be able to find out anything to help Bubba and Bertha? If I found out anything, would they be happy with what I found out? Did Angel just run away or did something bad happen to her?

We pulled into Jonesborough, Tennessee around 5:00 p.m. on Friday, May 13.

"I'm gong to see if the place I stayed at when I was down here before is still open," I said to Martha.

"Sounds fine to me. I'm ready to stretch my legs and rest awhile," she quickly replied.

As I drove down Main Street, I saw the quaint place I was referring to. The sign still read, **Do Drop Inn**. I pulled into a driveway so I could turn around and park along the curb in front of the Inn.

"Why don't you park in the parking lot?" Martha asked.

"There is no parking lot."

"It is strictly curbside parking," I replied with a smile on my face as I stopped the Escalade.

We both got out of the vehicle and started walking up the sidewalk leading to the front door of the Do Drop Inn. I reached the front door before Martha, turned the doorknob, opened the door, and stopped so quickly, Martha almost knocked me over by running into me.

"What's the matter?" she asked as she untangled her body from mine.

"As Yogi Berra would say, 'It's Déjà vu all over again'," I replied as I entered the lobby of the Inn.

"What?"

"Nothing has changed since I stayed here several years ago," I replied as I looked around the lobby. The lobby was still immaculate. To the left were two over stuffed chairs, two foot stools and a small coffee table. To the right still sat a humongous fern plant and a parakeet cage. A hairball of a cat was still lounging on the windowsill.

I walked across the floor to the large solid walnut counter with a wood top that was so burnished it looked like glass. A small bud vase, containing a red rose, a ceramic coffee mug containing pens and a cordless telephone were the only items on the counter top. As Martha and I neared the counter, a small white haired lady emerged through a curtain that was hanging over a door behind the deck.

"May I help you?" the woman asked.

"Yes, we would like to rent a room, but we're not sure just how long we're going to be in town," I replied.

"You don't know how long you're staying?" the woman asked as her eyebrows arched over her blue eyes.

"What might be your business in town?"

"I'm a private investigator from Minnesota, and I came here to see if I could help a friend find his wife's sister," I answered.

"Private investigator you say."

"Yes. I was here several years ago and met your nephew, Bubba Butz, who recently asked me if I could help him," I replied hoping the mention of Bubba would allay the skepticism she showed.

"You're here to help Bubba and Bertha find Angel?" she asked.

"I told them I would see what I could do for them."

27

"Well, I hope you're of more help than the nitwit sheriff we have. He keeps saying Angel just ran away, but I know better," she replied with a slight huff in her voice.

"You know better?"

"Yes. She is just such a sweet child that I know she wouldn't run away. I say something bad has happened to her," she replied.

As with all good investigators, I continued the conversation with the woman in hopes she might say something of use.

"Something bad?"

"Yes. Angel has so much going for her, I know she wouldn't have just run off," replied the woman.

"So much going for her?" I asked.

"Yes, she had graduated from college last fall, had finally found a job in Johnson City which she was going to start next month and she was engaged to be married," the woman replied as she gave me a knowing look.

"Sounds like her life was really in order."

"Oh yes. That's why I say something bad has happened to her," she said.

"Oh my. You're here to get a room, not listen to me blab about Angel," she said as she reached under the counter top and removed a large leather bound book, which she gently sat on the counter top.

"I must have you sign in," she said to me.

"Please put both of your names down, if you don't mind," she said.

"Sure thing," I replied as I retrieved a pen from the ceramic cup.

"I'm Butch Brogen and this is my wife, Martha," I said as I nodded towards Martha and finally remembered to introduce ourselves. Remembering the chastising I had received the first

28

time I had stayed here, I remembered to put my name down as Larry Brogen, not Butch. Looking up from putting our names in the book, I was relieved to see a small smile on the woman's face. I had done alright!

"You're in room 1467," she said to me as she handed me a key, which was attached to a six by six piece of Plexiglas.

"I'll just keep the room available for as long as you're going to be here helping find poor Angel," she added.

"Thank you," I replied as I took the key and Plexiglas from her and turned to go out the door.

"Pleased to meet you Mrs. Brogen," the woman said to Martha as she turned to follow me.

After exiting the lobby and walking down the sidewalk to our car, Martha said, "Room 1467! It looks like there can't be more than six rooms here."

"Yep, that's right. I don't know where the numbering system comes from, but I stayed in room 1465 the first time I was here."

We retrieved our suitcases from the Escalade and made our way to room 1467, which was two doors down from room 1465! I unlocked the door without getting a broken wrist from the swinging Plexiglas, opened the door, and ushered Martha in. The room was exactly as I had remembered room 1465. The floor was carpeted with a dark purple carpet that had gold flowers and squares placed in various places. A double bed was situated in the middle of the room with a small nightstand located at the right side of the bed. It held a telephone. There was another nightstand at the left side of the bed that contained a lamp. Hanging from the ceiling next to the wall opposite the bed, was a nineteen-inch television. Two small stuffed chairs sat in opposite corners of the room.

A doorway to the left led to a small bathroom containing a claw foot bathtub, a small porcelain pedestal sink, and a toilet.

"Quite the quaint little place you have found us Mr. Brogen," Martha said as she gave me a kiss on the cheek.

"It may not be a Holiday Inn Express, but it's clean and the bed I had last time was fairly comfortable," I replied.

We placed our suitcases on the floor, out of the way and plopped down on the bed to relax.

"I should probably give Bubba a call and let him know that we are in town," I said.

"Go right ahead. I'm going to stretch out here for a while," replied Martha.

"Need any help stretching out?" I asked as I grabbed her around her waist.

"Just leave me alone and make your telephone call," she replied.

Because I do not have a Blackberry, Blueberry, or whatever, my cell phone was small enough to fit into the front pocket of my shorts. Removing the phone, I scrolled to 'Bubba' and pressed call.

After several rings a woman answered, "Hello."

"Hello, Bertha?"

"Yes."

"This is Butch Brogen."

"Oh, hello Butch."

"Martha and I are in town and wonder if we could meet with you and Bubba tomorrow," I said.

"You're here! Thank you so much for coming," she excitedly said.

"I'm not promising anything," I quickly interjected, because I had no idea what was going on and I didn't want to get Bertha's hopes too high.

"I realize that. It's just that we are not getting anyplace with the local authorities and any help you can give us finding Angel would be great," she replied.

"Bubba and I could meet with you tonight if you like. In fact, you can come out for supper. I have a big pot of pork spare ribs, sauerkraut, and potatoes that have been slow cooking all day. We have more than enough for you and your wife," Bertha said.

"Ah, well, we just kinda wanted to relax a little tonight, if you don't mind," I replied.

"I understand. It's just that I want you to get working on our case as soon as possible."

"I understand that. What time would be good to come visit you and Bubba tomorrow?" I asked as I was still thinking about the ribs, sauerkraut and potato meal that had been offered us.

"We are early risers, so just about anytime in the morning would be great," Bertha said.

"We don't sleep in ourselves, so by the time we have breakfast it would probably be around nine o'clock."

"You could just come for breakfast if you like," answered Bertha.

Wondering what they might be having for breakfast, I quickly replied, "You don't need to feed us. We'll eat here in town and then be out around nine, OK?

"Nine it is then," said Bertha as she hung up.

Putting down my cell phone, I turned to Martha and said, "I'm sorry that I might have screwed you out of a great meal tonight, but I turned down Bertha's request that we eat with them."

"That wasn't very friendly. She was nice enough to offer us a meal. You should have accepted," replied Martha as she rose up on one elbow in the bed.

"They are having pork spare ribs cooked with sauerkraut and potatoes," I replied.

"Oh yuck. You were such a sweetheart for turning her down," replied Martha as she scooted across the bed to throw her arms around my neck and give me a big kiss.

"Bubba's aunt Beulah has a great dinner featuring home cooking about six blocks up the street. Do you want to eat there?" I asked.

"Sounds good to me. I'm starved," Martha quickly replied.

"What's new!"

"What?"

"You're always hungry," I replied as I ducked her playful, swing at my head.

We walked the six blocks to where I remembered the diner to be, and was relieved to see Beulah's Diner still there.

We entered and I immediately noticed the place hadn't changed from the first time I was here. There were five long tables with four chairs aligned along each side. As the young hostess approached us, I noticed only four chairs available. Luckily, there were two side by side. I also noticed that the hostess didn't have a low cut dress and huge set of boobs as did the hostess who I had met before. As the hostess was leading us to the two chairs, I turned and said to Martha, "Be prepared for a great meal, but watch out for people passing things to you or past you left and right."

"I'm not sure I like this kind of dining."

"It takes a little getting used to, but the food will more than make up for the hassle," I quickly replied as we approached our chairs and sat down.

As before, the table was filled with dishes holding mashed potatoes, sweet potatoes, corn on the cob, two bowls of beans, three salads, a large bowl of peas, and five loaves of bread.

There were platters containing ham, pork, turkey, and other dark meat I had remembered Bubba telling me was woodchuck.

"I see they have your favorite veggie," I said to Martha as I pointed to the bowl of peas.

"Yuck. I'm not eating any of them. They're squishy," she replied as she wrinkled up her cute little nose.

The platters and bowls kept being passed and I kept taking something from them to eat until I couldn't hold anymore. The platter of woodchuck had never made it to Martha and I, and I never asked for it. I noticed Martha was taking something from almost all the dishes also. All except the peas! We finished our meal and even though some of the folks were still eating, we asked for our bill, paid it and left the diner. We started walking back to our room trying to breath in the fresh evenings air in hopes of relieving the stuffed feeling we both felt

"I can hardly move," I groused as I loosened the buckle on my belt while we walked.

"You shouldn't have been such a pig," Martha scolded.

"I didn't have to cook, so I'm pigging out."

We made it back to our room, I retrieved the killer key from the floor of the Escalade where I had placed it before our supper walk. It was hard enough opening the door with the thing, to say nothing of walking around carrying it, because it would never fit into your pocket. We watched television for a little while and then decided to turn in for the night.

# Chapter Five

Martha and I got up the following morning, showered, and went to Beulah's Diner for a wonderful breakfast. We then headed out of town to find Bubba's house. Bubba had given me his address, so I entered 14234 453$^{rd}$ Street into the GPS located in the dash of the Escalade and proceeded to follow the directions given to me by the woman's voice coming from the GPS speaker. It took Martha and me about twenty minutes to reach a mailbox with 14234 printed on it. Entering the gravel driveway, we saw a nice white ranch style home at the end. Off to the left of the house stood a large metal storage shed. I stopped the car in the concrete driveway leading to a three-car garage and we got out and started walking towards the front door of the house. Before we reached the small front porch of the house, the front door opened and both Bubba and Bertha emerged.

"Wow," said Martha.

"You were right. They are a couple of big people," she added.

I had explained that Bubba was six foot ten inches tall and Bertha must have been at least six foot six. Neither one was fat, but both were large framed.

"Howdy Butch," Bubba said as I approached him.

"Hi Bubba," I said as I extended my hand to him in greetings. My hand was instantly swallowed up in his huge meat hook as he returned my greeting.

"I'm so glad you're here Butch," Bertha said as she swung her arms around me, drawing my face into her large chest, and

34

giving me a squeeze that almost took my breath away. After several seconds, which seemed like minutes, Bertha released me and I caught my breath.

"Glad to be here Bertha."

"This is my wife Martha," I said turning toward where Martha was standing.

"Nice to meet you Martha," Bubba and Bertha each said.

"Come on inside," Bubba said as he placed his hand in the small of my back and almost pushed me forward.

The four of us entered through the front door into what looked like a living room. There was a large sofa, two large recliners, a coffee table, and two end tables sitting in the room.

"Have a seat," said Bubba as he gestured towards the sofa. I assumed the recliners were for Bertha and him.

Martha and I both sat down on the sofa, while Bubba and Bertha took seats in the recliners. We talked about what had gone on in our lives the past few years, with me explaining my meeting and eventually marrying Martha.

"So, what's this about your sister going missing?" I asked Bertha trying to get to the subject at hand.

"Angel had graduated from college last fall and finally found a job in Johnson City that was going to start June 1st. She moved back home with mom and dad while she was looking for a job. She was so excited about her first job. Then she just disappeared," Bertha said.

"Disappeared?"

"Yep. Just vanished," Bubba said.

"After her being gone several weeks, we contacted the sheriff and filed a missing person report," added Bubba.

"Yes and with no luck," Bertha quickly added.

"OK. Tell me a few things about Angel," I said as I pulled a notebook and pen out of the side pocket of my shorts.

"What, no recorder or electronic note pad to collect information on?" asked Bubba.

"I have a hard enough time getting him to carry a ten year old cell phone, to say nothing about any of the modern electronic things he could use in his job," said Martha as she smiled and looked at me.

"I don't need no damn Blueberry, Ipod, note pad or anything that fancy. I survived many years without a cell phone and using pencil and paper," I quickly responded.

"Yes, but you have every modern gadget ever invented for golfing," quickly replied Martha referring to the many electronic thing I used golfing, such as my electric golf bag kaddy cart and my SkyCaddie golf course GPS.

"They are a necessity," I said and quickly looked back to Bertha.

"What's your sister's full name?"

"Angel Rose McCoy," replied Bertha.

"Age?"

"Twenty three."

"Height?"

"Around five foot four."

"Weight?"

"One twenty."

"Hair color?"

"Dark brown and long."

"Eyes?"

"Hazel."

"Any distinguishing marks or scars?"

"Nope."

"Tattoos?"

"Heavens no."

"Do you have a recent picture of her that I could have?" I asked after I had finished writing the last bit of information Bertha had given me in my note book.

"I have one of her and me taken last Christmas. I'll let you take that one," she replied.

"Thanks," I said as Bertha got out of her chair and went to retrieve the picture.

Upon returning, Bertha handed me the picture of her and her sister, Angel. It showed a smiling Bertha and a smiling girl with long dark hair. She was a lot smaller than Bertha!

"We don't look like sisters," Bertha said as she noticed me staring at the two of them.

"Must have been the mailman," Bubba said as he chuckled.

"Shut up! It was no mailman."

"I know dear. It's just that the two of you are so different," Bubba quickly said as he tried to wiggle his way out of the current situation.

"Just because you and your two brothers are all big galoots, doesn't mean everyone has to look like their kin," Bertha said.

"So, I understand that Angel was also engaged," I quickly said trying to defuse the small spat going on between Bubba and Bertha.

I noticed Bubba and Bertha giving each other a quick glance before either said anything.

"Well, she was engaged," Bubba finally said.

"The engagement was broken off just before she disappeared," said Bertha.

"Broken off?"

"Yes. Her fiancée had found out that Angel had a small affair while she was away at college," Bertha said.

"A small affair?"

"Yes. It was just a couple of dates, but Frank was really mad after he found out," she said.

"How did he find out?"

"Angel told him. She was just so ashamed that she had strayed," Bubba said.

"What is her fiancée's name?"

"Frank Hatfield," Bubba quickly said.

"Wait a minute. You said Angel's last name was McCoy and now you tell me her former fiancée was a Hatfield. Is there any relation to the Hatfields and McCoys we have read so much about?" I asked.

"Yes. Both of our families are descendants of the feuding families you are referring to," Bertha said.

"I thought they lived in West Virginia and Kentucky, not Tennessee," I said.

"That's correct. The original McCoy's lived on the Kentucky side of the Tug Fork River and the Hatfield's lived on the West Virginia side," Bertha replied.

"They feuded from 1878 to 1891, with many lives taken on both sides. Even though the feud was over, my great-great-great-grandfather McCoy packed his family up and moved here to Tennessee to get away from the Hatfields. I assume that's how the Hatfields got here also," said Bertha.

"I remember reading about a McCoy woman named Roseanna, who had a relationship with a Johnse Hatfield and got pregnant by him. Because of the family squabble, they were not allowed to get together and Roseanna died of a broken heart," I said.

"That's the story we have been told also," said Bertha.

"In fact, Angel's middle name Rose comes from Rosanna McCoy," she added.

"Could the Hatfields from here still carry some grudge and not want young Hatfield and Angel to get together?" I asked.

"Nah. What few Hatfield's and McCoy's that are around here all get along," Bubba said.

"All except great grandpa Hatfield. His mind is failing and at times he flashes back to the feud he was told about by his father who was one of the last ones involved in the feud," Bertha said.

"He's become a recluse out on the old place and isn't very social even to his kin," Bertha said.

"So, what is gramps name?"

"Ephraim. He was named after one of the first Hatfields to settle in West Virginia in the seventeen hundreds," Bertha said.

"Very interesting story. I never though I'd meet a relative of the famous McCoys," I said to Bertha.

"Anything else that you think might have something to do with Angel's disappearance?" I asked.

"There is a religious sect that has a one hundred-twenty acre compound about ten miles from town. Nobody hardly ever sees anyone from there in town or anyplace else. Just the Reverend Jones and some of his henchmen," said Bubba.

"A religious compound, huh? Kind of like the Waco compound?" I asked.

"No one really knows for sure what goes on out there. The entire place is fenced in by a tall chain link fence and everyone is so secretive," said Bertha.

"There's a rumor that no one is joining the sect, so the Reverend is resorting to kidnapping to increase his flock to tend to the fields and whatever else they have in there," Bubba said.

"Do you think Angel could have gone there?"

"Not on her own," Bertha quickly said.

We continued talking for another couple of hours, with both Bubba and Bertha filling me in on anything they could think of in regards to Angels disappearance.

"Whew. I think I'm about to overload with all the info you two have given me," I said.

"I'll be talking to the people you've mentioned and see what they can tell me."

"Please don't talk to mom and dad," Bertha said.

"They are getting on in years and Angel's disappearance has really devastated them. I don't want to get them more worked up than they are, besides dad has a bad heart."

"No problem. I won't bother your folks," I replied as I noticed a look of relief come across Bertha's face.

"Just where is this religious compound you were telling me about? I think I'll go out there and talk to the Reverend Jones," I said.

"Go back into town and continue north on Main Street. About five miles out of town, you will see County Road 6 on your right. Take that road and go another ten miles or so. You will see a driveway on your left and a big white sign with blue lettering that says, Family of our Lord. Go down that driveway and you'll come to the fenced compound and a guard shack," Bubba said.

"I doubt that you will be able to talk to the Reverend though," Bertha said.

"He's pretty protective of his privacy and will only speak to a person if he initiates the conversation," Bertha added.

"Just the same, I think I'll give meeting with him a stab," I said.

"What you told me will give me many avenues to look down. I'm still not guaranteeing that I'll find out anything more than your sheriff," I said.

"Oh, I'm sure you will," Bertha said.

"You sure couldn't find anything less," Bubba quickly added.

"We should be getting back to town. I'm sure you're tired of listening to the three of us talk," I said as I turned to look at Martha who had patiently sat listening to the conversation that had gone on for the past few hours.

"Oh, no. I enjoyed the history lesson about the Hatfields and McCoys. I had read about them, of course, but had no idea I was sitting so close to some of the descendants," Martha said as she smiled.

"You're welcome to stay for lunch," Bubba said.

Thinking about the spare rib supper that had been previously offered, I quickly replied, "No thanks. I would like to start running down some of the ideas I have and Martha had told her brother she would come out and visit the family today."

"OK. We should get together at Aunt Beulah's one of these nights for supper," Bubba said.

"Sure thing," I said as I rose from the sofa.

"I'll keep in touch with you folks as to what I might be learning about Angel's disappearance," I said.

"If you don't mind, I would like to get rid of some of my morning coffee before we go," I added as I noticed a sigh of relief from Martha.

"Me too," she quickly said.

"Sorry I never showed you where the john was. Just go down that hall. First door on your right," Bubba said.

"You go first," I said to Martha as I noticed relief spread across her face.

After tending to our bathroom chores, we exited the house, got into the Escalade and backed off the garage apron, and headed down the driveway as we waved to Bubba and Bertha.

"Do you think you can help them?" Martha asked.

"I don't know, but I said I'd try."

"Would you mind coming with me to see the Reverend?" I asked Martha.

"I'm thinking if we go as a couple looking to join his little flock, he might be more receptive to meeting with me," I added.

"No, I don't mind going with you. Just don't get me killed," Martha replied as she chuckled.

## Chapter Six

I drove back into Jonesborough and headed north on Main Street as per Bubba's instructions. I found County Road 6, turned onto it and continued to drive until I saw the sign that read **Family of our Lord** at the entrance to the Reverend's compound. I entered the driveway and continued until I came to the guard shack situated in front of a chain link fence. The fence looked to be about eight feet tall with three strands of barbed wire placed at an angle at the top of the fence. I came to a stop at the gate and looked over to the guard shack to see if I could see anyone. Nothing was moving around at the moment, so we sat and waited for a little while.

"Bubba was right about this place being fenced in," I said to Martha while we sat.

"Yes, that fence sure looks menacing."

"Interesting," I said to myself aloud.

"What's interesting?"

"Oh, what? I was just talking to myself," I said to Martha.

"What's interesting about the fence?" she again asked.

"See the three strands of barbed wire on the top?"

"Yes, so what. There's three strands of barbed wire placed at an angle on top of the fence," Martha said.

"Look at the direction the barbed wire is sloped," I said as I looked towards the guardhouse and still saw no movement.

"It's sloped in towards the compound. So what?" Martha said.

"Right, but it should be sloped outward towards us if they are trying to keep someone from scaling the fence to get into the compound," I said.

"The way the barbed wire is sloped would allow someone from the outside to scale the chain link, place a jacket, blanket or something across the barbed wire, crawl over it and drop to the ground on the inside of the compound."

"With the barbed wire sloped inward like it is, a person on the inside could never scale the fence and get up and over the barbed wire. It looks as if the barbed wire was placed to keep people inside the compound, not people from getting inside the compound," I said as a person's head finally emerged at the window in the guardhouse and looked out at us.

The guard exited the guardhouse and approached the open drivers' side window of the Escalade.

"What do you want?" he gruffly asked as he rubbed his eyes. He looked as though we had wakened him up from a nap.

"We're here to see Reverend Jones," I replied.

"He don't see nobody unless he asks to see them and he hasn't asked to see you," the guard replied.

"How do you know he doesn't want to see us?" I asked.

"Cause he lets me know if I should be expecting anyone," the guard replied.

"Maybe he tried to contact you while you were taking a nap," I said as I smiled at him.

"I wasn't taking a nap," he snapped back at me.

"Well, my wife and I are interested in joining his flock," I lied.

"Nobody joins unless they're asked to join," the guard quickly snapped back.

"Could you just ask the Reverend if he would be willing to speak with a couple of prospective followers?" I asked.

"I suppose. Just wait a minute," the guard said as he turned and headed back towards the guardhouse.

"We want to join his flock, huh?" Martha said.

"I had to think of something so we can meet the Reverend and maybe get some answers about Angel," I replied.

Several minutes later, the guard emerged from the guardhouse and approached our car.

"Reverend Jones said he would see you. Just follow this road until you come to a big white building. Reverend Jones will meet you in front of that building," the guard said as he turned to go open the big gate that was across the entrance to the compound.

"Thank you, "I said to the guard as I started the Escalade and slowly made my way through the now open gateway. As I slowly drove inside the compound, I was looking around to see what I could see. All that was noticeable was many trees lining the roadway. Shortly we exited the tree line and came into a large opening and a large circle drive. Lined around the outside of the circle drive were several building, including a large white one.

"That must be where we're supposed to meet the Reverend," I said to Martha as I pointed to the large white building.

"Looks like it."

As we approached the front of the building, three men emerged through the open front door. The man in the middle was African American, about six foot four inches tall with a muscular build. He had a clean shaven face along with a shaved head. He was wearing a pair of beige dress slacks, a white long sleeve shirt, a beige vest that matched his dress pants, and a black necktie. Shiny black wing tipped loafers were on his feet and he was covered in more bling than a professional basketball player. Gold chains dangled from his neck, almost covering his necktie. Both of his ears held a large gold earring with diamond studs.

The other two men were the size of Bubba. Each must have been six foot ten inches tall and had huge muscular, tree trunk arms that made the arms of the their tee shirts stretch to the limit. Their necks were short and stocky, with bulging veins on each side. They looked straight ahead with an icy stare. They both wore blue jeans and tennis shoes.

I pulled up in front of the three, turned off the car, and started to get out.

"Welcome brother and sister," the well-dressed man said as he flashed a wide toothy smile that allowed his two gold-capped front teeth to glisten in the sunlight.

"As it says in Romans 12:13, 'When God's people are in need, be ready to help them. Always be eager to practice hospitality'," the Reverend said.

"I'm Reverend States Rights Jones," he said as he approached Martha and I with his right hand extended.

"And this is Brother Matthew and Brother Mark," he said as he gestured to the two men with him.

The two men that had been on either side of him, stayed put with their huge arms folded across their chest, still staring off into space.

Seeing the look on my face when he told me his name, he said, "By the look on your face, I can see you find my name a little strange."

"Uh, not strange, but a little different," I stammered.

"It's a family name."

"When Mr. Lincoln freed the slaves, my great-great-great grandmother was so thankful, she named her next son 'States Rights' as a symbol of being free. Ever since then, someone in

46

my family has named one of their boys 'States Rights'," the Reverend said.

"And, you will continue the tradition?" asked Martha.

"No. I'm not married and have no children, but one of my brothers has named his son 'States Rights'" said the Reverend.

"Of course in today's society, my nephew goes by SR. It's easier than putting up with the looks and guffaws associated with being called 'States Rights'," added Reverend Jones.

"I'm Butch Brogen and this is my wife, Martha," I said as I shook his hand and nodded towards Martha.

"Pleased to meet you maam," he said as he shook Martha's hand and flashed a gold toothy smile.

"What brings you two to our humble place?" asked the Reverend.

"We heard about your family and are looking at the possibility of joining," I once again lied.

"I see. You heard about the Family of our Lord all the way up in Minnesota," he stated as he looked at the license plates on the Escalade.

"No. We are down here visiting family and friends. That's how we became aware of your group," I quickly said.

"Very well. Since you're here I will be more than happy to show you around and explain our family."

"Let's take a short walk around our compound and I'll answer any questions you have," he said as he nodded at the two gorillas, which instantly came to the side of the Reverend.

"How big is your place?" I asked as we started to walk down the gravel circle drive following the Reverend and his two followers.

"We have one hundred twenty acres here," answered the Reverend.

"Wow, what do you do with the land?"

47

"We raise most of the food we consume. We also have some livestock and raise the grain for them to eat," he answered.

I had not seen one single sole since we arrived other than the Reverend and his side kicks, so I said, "It must take quite a few people to do all that work."

"Oh not really. As we are reminded in Psalm 133:1, 'How wonderful and pleasant it is when brothers live together in harmony!'" the Reverend answered.

"Our family consists of fifty two soles, of which thirteen are children," he added.

"So, do you accept new followers or is your family large enough?" I asked.

"New followers are always welcome," the Reverend said as he gave Matthew and Mark a quick glance.

"I haven't seen any other people since we arrived."

"That's because many are in the fields and others are attending their Bible lessons," answered the Reverend.

We continued walking around the compound while the Reverend explained small details to us. Whenever I would try to ask a pointed question, he would interrupt and cite some scripture passage without answering my question.

"How many people leave your family?" I finally asked.

"What makes you think anyone would ever leave us?" the Reverend quickly asked as his ever-present wide toothy grin disappeared.

"I noticed the fence you have surrounding your compound when we arrived. It looks to me like it is a fortress constructed to keep people in," I replied.

"This is not a fortress," snapped the Reverend.

"2 Samuel 22:2, says 'The Lord is my rock, my fortress and my savior'," he quickly added.

"That's enough for today. I think you and your wife should leave now. You don't seem like you two are interested in joining our family, but are only interested in asking non pertinent questions," the Reverend snapped as he once again nodded at Matthew and Mark, who instantly appeared at the side of Martha and me. We were quickly ushered back to the Escalade and instructed to get in and leave.

As we were driving back to the front gate, I looked into the rearview mirror and saw Reverend Jones talking to the two men standing next to him.

"Check with the sheriff and see what he can find out about those two. For some reason I don't trust or believe them. That Brogen seems like the type of fellow who could stir up trouble," the Reverend said to Matthew and Mark.

As we approached the gate, the guard appeared from the guardhouse and opened the gate, allowing us to leave the compound. As I drove back to town, I was wondering why the Reverend had got so uppity when I asked him about people leaving his family. I also wondered what he had been telling Matthew and Mark as we drove away.

"I wonder why Reverend Jones got so upset when you asked about people leaving his flock," Martha said.

"I was wondering the same thing."

"I think I'll do a little more research and see what I can find out about the good Reverend," I added.

As we neared Jonesborough, Martha asked, "What are you going to do tomorrow?"

"I thought we could get a round of golf in."

"Sounds great."

"How about Monday?" Martha asked.

I'm going to try to visit the county sheriff to see what he can tell me about Angel's disappearance," I replied and added.

"Why the questions about what I'm going to be doing?"

"You have something exciting planned that you want me to do?" I asked.

"What were you thinking of?"

"Sex on the beach."

"That's the name of a drink and besides there's no beaches around here," Martha promptly replied.

"There might be a lake close by."

"Forget it. I thought I would call Marcie and see if I can come out and visit Monday. Would you take me out there?" Martha asked.

"After sex?"

"Forget your sex. Now just answer my question," Martha said.

"Alright, I'll take you out to your brothers' place," I replied.

We got back to our room, freshened up and walked up to Beulah's Diner for supper. As usual, the meal was fantastic. As we were walking back to the Do Drop Inn, a silver Chevy S1500 pickup slowly drove down the street towards us. As they passed us, both Martha and I noticed the two people in the cab of the pickup.

"Those were the two guys with Reverend Jones today," Martha said before I had a chance to say anything.

"You're right," I said as I turned slightly and glanced behind us. The pickup had pulled over to the curb and looked like it was preparing to turn around.

"Looks like the boys might be turning around," I said.

"Why?" Martha asked as she turned and looked back down the street.

"You're right, they've turned around and are coming back towards us," she added.

50

"I can't imagine what they would want from us. Just keep walking," I said to her.

As we continued to walk, the pickup slowly passed us. I noticed both occupants looking towards Martha and me.

"Wonder what they're so interested in?" I asked.

"Do you think they want us for something?" Martha asked.

"I don't know why. We were just a couple who visited the Revered Jones. We didn't cause any trouble," I replied.

"Well, it just seems odd that they seemed to be interested in us," said Martha.

As we continued the walk towards our room, the pickup continued driving down the street, heading out of town.

"Looks like they're going home," I said to Martha as we got to the walk leading to our room at the Do Drop Inn.

I retrieved the room key from under the drivers' seat of the Escalade where I had placed it before our walk to the diner. The big chunk of Plexiglas attached to the key makes it impossible put the key in your pocket. It also makes impossible to carry the key around with you without having bruises on your body from being struck by the swinging Plexiglas. However, I'm sure Bubba's aunt never has a room key taken by a roomer.

We entered our room and I flopped down on the bed, once again being in anguish from over eating at Beulah's Diner.

Martha retrieved her cell phone from her purse, sat in one of the chairs, and called Marcie. Martha told Marcie that we were in Jonesborough and that she would like to come out and visit on Monday. Marcie was excited to hear from Martha and immediately said Monday would be fine. She told Martha the girls were still in school for another couple of weeks, but Monday was a teachers' workday so they would be home. After about twenty minutes, Martha finally hung up her cell phone and placed it back into her purse.

51

"I thought you were going out and visit Marcie tomorrow," I said as I slowly tried to prop myself up on one of the pillows on the bed.

"I am."

"Then why the six hour conversation tonight?" I asked as I still tried to get comfortable on the bed.

"We only talked for a few minutes, not six hours," Martha replied as she walked over to the bed, sat down, and smacked me on my overly protruding stomach!

"Shit! You want me to puke?" I exclaimed.

"No. I just want you to quit being such a creep," Martha said as she leaned over and gave me a kiss.

We watched some television and then retired for the evening. As I lay in bed before I fell asleep, I wondered just what the Reverend's two henchmen were doing in town. Why they seemed interested in Martha and me? Would they be causing any problems? I think I will suggest that Martha stays out at Kenny's for several days, just in case the boys are up to something sinister. I'll try to talk with the sheriff Monday morning. Maybe I can learn something. In the mean time, I'm looking forward to my meal settling and to a great round of golf tomorrow!

## Chapter Seven

Monday, May 16, we awoke to a bright sunny day. Martha
and I once again went to Beulah's Diner for breakfast. After
stuffing ourselves on every imaginable breakfast food you could
think of, we left the diner for our trip out to Kenny's house. I
left town, got on US 32, and headed towards our destination.
We reached the driveway to Kenny's place and I turned off the
highway. As I drove down the entrance, I was amazed at how
much of the wood and brush had been cleared out. The first time
I had been here, I didn't know if my car would fit through the
overgrowth. We reached the end of the driveway and
immediately saw a huge, modern new ranch style house.

"Whoa! Looks like Kenny spent some of his inheritance," I
said.

"I told you they had built a new house, Martha said as she
scowled at me.

"Musta forgot."

I drove onto the circle drive to the front of the house.
Remembering my previous trip here, I quickly looked around to
see if I saw any geese. I had been attacked by one of them when
I had visited before. I saw no geese but did see two large dogs
lounging on the front porch of the house. They looked like the
two that I had seen before. The two dilapidated buildings still
stood off in the distance. A new metal pole barn was located just
east of the two old buildings.

"I see Kenny didn't overdo himself. You would have
thought he could have taken those old buildings down," I said as
we got out of the Escalade.

"Kenny's busy, you know."

"Yea. Busy doing what." I replied and instantly knew by the look from Martha, I had better shut up.

Kenny has a habit of straying from time to time, but Martha says that it's none of our business and that he takes great care of Marcie and the two girls.

As we approached the porch, the two dogs raised their heads and gave us a quick glance before putting their heads back down. Just then, the front door flew open and two young girls looking to be around ten and twelve years old, came bounding out. Both of them were barefoot and wore shorts and tee shirts. I quickly glanced at the youngest to see if she had snot running into her mouth like she did the first time I saw her. Nope!

"Aunt Martha!" they screamed as they dashed over to Martha and gave her hugs.

"Hi girls," Martha said as she hugged them back.

"Say hi to Uncle Butch," Martha said to the two girls.

"Hi, Uncle Butch," they said in unison as Marcie came out the front door.

"Hi Martha and Butch. Come on in."

I noticed Marcie was dressed a lot nicer than when I had first met her, but her light blue tee shirt didn't hide the fact she was not wearing a bra. Just like her sister-in-law!!

"I can't stay. I have a meeting with the Washington County Sheriff," I said.

Giving Martha a hug, I said, "I'll give you a call to let you know when I'm finished and see when you want me to come and pick you up."

Martha and the girls walked towards the door where Marcie was waiting as I turned and walked back to the car.

I drove back to Jonesborough in hopes that I would be able to talk to the sheriff and see if he could give me any updated information on the disappearance of Angel.

I reached the sheriff's office at 112 West Jackson Boulevard and pulled into the parking lot signed *Visitor Parking*. I exited the car and walked towards the brick building where the sheriff's office was located. I entered the building and approached the front desk located about thirty feet from the front door. A dark haired woman of about thirty years old was seated in a chair behind the desk.

"May I help you?" she asked as she looked up at me.

"I hope so."

"My name is Butch Brogen. I'm a private investigator from Minnesota," I said as I retrieved my PI credential from my wallet and handed it to her.

"I'm in town investigating the disappearance of someone and I was hoping I would be able to talk to the sheriff about my case," I said.

"You're all the way down here from Minnesota on a case?" she asked as she handed back my PI credential.

"It's a long story. I visited here several years ago and became friends with a couple who live outside of town. They asked me to come here and see if I could help them," I said.

"Is the missing person from here, or did you follow someone here?" she asked.

Although it wasn't really any business of hers, I thought I had better be polite if I wanted to have any chance on meeting with the sheriff.

"The missing person is from here."

"The sheriff would be trying to find the person. I don't know why a private investigator would be necessary," she said.

"It's not my call. All I know is that the girl's sister and brother-in-law hired me to look into her disappearance," I said as I tried not to seem too annoyed.

"OK. I know the sheriff is in his office today. I'll check and see if he wants to talk with you. People usually make an appointment to meet with him," she said as she once again chastised me.

"I'm sorry I didn't make an appointment, but I just got into town yesterday and have been busy meeting with my clients. If he can't see me today, I'll make an appointment for another day," I replied.

"What did you say the name of the person is you are looking for?" she asked as she reached for the telephone sitting on the ledge behind the deck.

"I didn't, but her name is Angel McCoy."

"Oh."

"Anything wrong?"

"No. It's just that the sheriff has spent a lot of time investigating her disappearance and came to the conclusion she just ran away," she answered as she punched some numbers on the face of the telephone.

"Hello, Sheriff Hatfield. I have a private investigator standing here who's from Minnesota and says he's been hired to look into the disappearance of Angel McCoy," she said into the telephone.

"Although he doesn't have an appointment with you, he was wondering if you would meet with him now," she added.

"Oh, OK. I'll tell him. His name is Butch Brogen," she said.

"The sheriff said he would be happy to meet with you now," she said as she hung up the telephone.

"I must ask you to sign the ledger sitting on top of the desk. Here's a visitors badge for you to clip on you so the badge is visible at all times," she said as she stood up with a visitors badge in her hand.

Holy crap!! This is just like trying to get into the Rosecrest Police Department. Sign in, wear a badge, etc.

As I clipped the badge to the flap on the front pocket of my shorts, a gentleman appeared through a door directly behind the information desk. He appeared to be in his early fifties. He was dressed in a navy blue suit, a white shirt, and dark blue necktie. Black cowboy boots with gold tips, shown from under his suit pants.

He strode to where I was standing and said, "Mr. Brogen. I'm Sheriff Virgil Hatfield," as he extended his right hand towards me.

"Pleased to meet you sheriff. I'm sorry I didn't make an appointment, but sure am glad you're willing to talk to me," I said as I grasped his hand in a handshake.

"Let's go back to my office," he said as he started to turn towards the door he had emerged from.

"Libby tells me you are looking into the disappearance of Angel McCoy," he said as we reached a door, which he opened, and we walked through.

"That's right. Her sister and brother-in-law hired me to look into her disappearance," I said as I followed him into his office.

"We've spent a considerable amount of time investigating Angel's disappearance. I don't know what a PI from Minnesota can find that we didn't," he said as we entered the room.

"Come on in and have a chair. I'll tell you everything I know and try to answer any questions you might have," he said as we entered his office and he pointed to a chair sitting along one of the walls.

The office was about twenty feet by twenty feet. The walls were painted a light blue and the floor was covered in beige carpeting. A large oak desk sat in front of the wall to my left. Two large, oak, arm chairs sat in front of the desk. Against the opposite wall was a table with four chairs arranged around it. Several wildlife pictures hung on the walls as did a large clock.

The sheriff walked around behind his desk and sat down in a plush leather chair as I sat down in one of the chairs located in front of the desk.

"You want to ask questions or do you want me to tell you what we know?" the sheriff asked.

"You can fill me in on what you know, if you don't mind. If I have any questions, I'll ask them later," I replied.

"OK. Angel Rose McCoy is twenty-three years old. She graduated from Spartan College in Johnson City and had a job lined up in Johnson City. She came home after graduating while she waited for the start of her job. She lived with her mom and dad, Edward and Eunice McCoy outside of town," he said.

"Care for a cup of coffee?" he then asked as he reached for a ceramic coffee mug sitting on his desk.

"No thanks. I only drink coffee in the morning to get me going," I answered.

He reached for a small eight-cup coffee maker sitting on the far corner of his desk, filled his cup and continued, "Angel was engaged to be married to Frank Hatfield, but she had a fling while away at college and now Frank isn't sure he wants to marry her, so he called off the engagement."

"Frank acts like he still loves Angel, so I don't think he would harm her," he added.

So far, the sheriff hadn't told me anything I didn't know, but I sat quietly and just nodded my head as he continued.

"We have interviewed her sisters, brother, and parents and no one has any idea of why she would have gone missing or where she would have gone. Angel worked part time at the local Kum N Go while she was waiting for her new job to start. We interviewed her coworkers and they weren't much help either," he said and took a drink of his coffee.

"Although, one coworker remembered seeing Angel talking to a man near the candy counter five days before she disappeared. The man was a stranger to the coworker and when she asked Angel about him, Angel just kind of blew her off without giving a good answer," added the sheriff.

"The coworker said she saw Angel talking to the same guy in the parking lot three days before she disappeared."

"The last time anyone has seen Angel was the night of April 2nd, when her shift ended at 10:00 pm. Her coworker that evening said Angel seemed happy and in a good mood when she left. The two of them walked to their cars together, and the other worker remembered seeing Angel leave the parking lot and turn right, which is the direction towards her parent's home," he added.

"We contacted many of her friends that we know of and the answer was the same. They had no idea why she would have gone missing," he said.

"Did you talk with the fellow she had the affair with?" I asked.

"Yep, we tracked him down and interviewed him. His name is Rod Benson and he lives in your home state, Minnesota."

"Minnesota! What was he doing down here?"

"Going to Spartan College just like Angel."

"What did he have to say?" I asked.

"He told us that he had met Angel at a party and they ended up having sex that night."

"Did he see Angel after that?"

"Nope. She was so ashamed by what she had done; she called him the next day and told him that she never wanted to see him again."

"She had his phone number?"

"Guess so. You know how these young people share phone numbers, emails, etc." said the sheriff.

"Was he pissed that Angel didn't want to see him again?" I asked.

"No. He said having sex that night was great, but it was just a one night thing."

"He wasn't upset that Angel didn't want to see him again," the sheriff added.

"You believe him?"

"Sure, he seemed genuine in his answers and like he said, he has been told by other women that they didn't want to see him again and he's survived," answered Sheriff Hatfield.

"Have you found the stranger?" I asked.

"Nope. We put his description out to all other law enforcement offices in the area and have drawn a blank so far."

"This stranger has not been seen since Angel's coworker saw him," the sheriff added.

"Seems like he might be a good suspect," I said.

"My thoughts exactly, but we haven't found him yet."

"Are you still looking?"

"Of course. This is an open case and we are still doing whatever we can to find Angel," replied the sheriff with some agitation in his voice.

"Since no one has any idea why Angel would go missing, foul play seems like a logical assumption," I said.

"That's what we thought also, but we couldn't turn up anything that would indicate foul play. We checked on all the listed sexual predators that are in our data base, but they all seem to be clean," the sheriff said as he leaned back in his chair.

"I know a person just doesn't disappear from the face of the earth, but that seems to be what Angel has done," he added.

"Do you think she could be at Reverend Jones religious compound outside of town?" I asked.

"What?" the sheriff said with a startled look on his face.

"Reverend Jones's Family of our Lord compound ten miles out of town," I repeated.

"Why would you think Angel was out there?" the sheriff asked.

"I was just wondering if Angel was the type of religious person who might join a sect like the Reverend's," I said.

"I don't know about her religious beliefs," answered the sheriff, and continued, "But, I did go out and visit Reverend Jones to see if Angel might have decided to join his family."

"Reverend Jones assured me that Angel had never asked about joining his family or had joined it. In fact, he said he doesn't know any Angel McCoy," the sheriff said.

"How about if she had been forced to join the Family of our Lord?" I asked.

"Where did you come up with that idea?"

"It's just a thought I have. I have been out to the Reverend's compound and was puzzled by the fence around the entire place," I said.

"You have been out there? Why?"

"I wanted to talk to the Reverend and see if Angel had joined his group," I answered.

"I've already investigated that theory. She hasn't joined the Reverend's family," he replied.

"The reason the property is fenced is that the Reverend doesn't want people coming onto his property unless they are invited," the sheriff said.

"The way the top barbed wire strands are sloped, it looks to me like the good Reverend is trying to keep people in," I replied.

By now, the sheriff was leaning forward with his hands on his desk and a scowl on his face.

"The Reverend has no reason keeping people on the compound without their permission. Everyone of the family is devoted to God and the Reverend," the sheriff snapped at me.

"I've been out there many times visiting Reverend Jones and have seen no signs of anyone being forced to stay there," said the sheriff.

"Why do you go out there? Are you a member of the Family of our Lord?" I asked.

"No, I'm not a member of the Reverends group. I go out there to just visit the Reverend and to thank him," the sheriff said.

"Thank him?"

"Yes. He has been most generous in giving me support whenever I run for reelection."

"So, do you owe him favors?" I asked even though I could see that the sheriff was getting annoyed with my questions.

"I don't like your insinuations," snapped the sheriff.

"Now, I think you had better just leave," he said as he stood up.

I also got out of my chair and started for the door, before the sheriff decided to physically throw me out of his office. He followed me to the front desk without saying a word. As we approached the front desk, he said to the receptionist, "This gentleman is leaving right now!"

I handed my visitors badge to the receptionist and walked towards the front door. As I opened the door and exited the building, I glanced back and saw the sheriff still standing by the receptionist's desk, staring at me. So much for any friendly help from the sheriff, I thought to myself.

As I reached the Escalade, I grabbed my cell phone from the pocket of my shorts and called Martha to let her know I was finished talking with the sheriff. She told me that Marcie had invited us for supper, so I could come out anytime as long as I was there by 5:00 pm.

Knowing how much Martha likes to eat between 5:00 p.m. and 5:30 p.m., I assured her that I would be out to Kenny's by at least 5:00 p.m.

Seeing that it was only a little past 2:00 pm, I decided to see if Your Uncle's Place was still in business. Your Uncles Place was a bar that I had visited when I had been in Jonesborough before and bars are always good places to get some information. That is if you can convince the locals that you are an all right guy!

As I was driving away from the sheriff's office, the sheriff turned and quickly headed back to his office. He sat in the chair behind his desk and immediately picked up the telephone and dialed a number.

"Hello. Family of our Lord. Reverend States Rights Jones," came a voice over the telephone.

"SR, it's Virgil."

"Hello sheriff. Why the telephone call. It's not time to run for reelection is it?" asked the Reverend as he chuckled.

"Or have you decided to be a member of our little family?"

"No, SR, it's not election time and I don't want to be one of your flock. I just finished talking with a private dick from

63

Minnesota and he told me he had been out to see you," answered the sheriff.

"A private investigator, huh."

"What's his name?"

"Butch Brogen."

"I knew there was something fishy about the story he told me about he and his wife wanting to join our family," said the Reverend.

"He's here investigating the disappearance of Angel McCoy," said the sheriff.

"What did you tell him, Virg?"

"Only the facts as we know them. Angel has disappeared and we haven't been able to find her."

"Good. You didn't mention anything about the suspicions the townsfolk have about our little family here, did you?" asked the Reverend.

"No, I didn't mention that. You know I believe what you tell me."

"Good. I would appreciate it if you would keep an eye on the good Mr. Brogen for me," said the Reverend.

"I don't want him to throw a monkey wrench in our little endeavor."

"Sure thing, SR. I'll keep tabs on him and let you know what he uncovers."

"Thanks for the telephone call, Virg. We'll stay in touch," said the Reverend.

"Good bye, SR," said Sheriff Hatfield as he hung up the telephone and leaned back in his chair.

# Chapter Eight

As I slowly drove down the street to the building housing Your Uncles Place, I noticed that it looked like the bar was still in business. An illuminated neon beer sign hung in each of the two windows on the front of the building. I found a place to park next to the curb about two blocks away and pulled in. Thank god, I didn't have to parallel park I thought to myself. I exited the car and started the walk back to the bar.

Reaching the front door, I grabbed the handle and pulled. The door opened and just like the other times I had been in the bar, a cloud of smoke crashed into me as it made it's way out of the building. The pungent odor almost made my eyes water. I removed my sunglasses, propped them on my head and tried to focus my eyes in the darkened room. Not much had changed from before. There were several tables and chairs situated around the room. Two pool tables were located on the left side of the room near the back. Two dart machines and one pinball machine were located on the other side of the room. Next to the pinball machine sat a popcorn popper. Must furnish free popcorn, I thought to myself. A long bar, which looked like it could seat about a dozen patrons was located directly in front of me.

My eyes were now starting to focus through the dark and smoke. I saw two young guys seated at the far end of the bar to my right. They were dressed in the white clothes of a painter and they quickly cranked their heads around to get a good look at me.

A young woman stood behind the bar. She was about five foot four inches tall, with a small build and short strawberry blonde hair. As I made my way to a bar stool located directly in front of me, I noticed the woman's cute, small body. Her blue jeans looked like they were painted on which allowed her tight, small butt to be accentuated. The light green tee shirt she was wearing was stretched to the limits, showing off her quite ample chest. Babe, Donk and Hogg would have a good time in here, I thought to myself. I can just imagine the comments coming from them dirty old men.

"Hi," she said to me as I reached a bar stool and started to sit down on it.

"Hi," I replied as she placed a coaster on the bar in front of me.

"What'll it be?"

"Do you have Bud Light on tap?"

"Sure do. You want a mug or tall sixteen ouncer?" she asked.

"Give me the sixteen ouncer," I replied as I reached for the money clip in the left front pocket of my shorts.

The bartender retreated from me, walked a short distance behind the bar, and stopped at a small cooler located under the bar. She opened the cooler door, reached inside, removed a frosty sixteen-ounce glass, proceeded to the beer taps, and started drawing a beer. I couldn't help but look at her nice, petite figure even though Martha has a great body herself. Must just be a guy thing. No matter how good you think your wife looks, you are always checking out other women. I also checked out her front as she turned and started back to where I was sitting. Nice!

"Here ya go," she said as she sat the tall glass on the coaster she had previously placed on the bar.

"A buck fifty."

I handed her a ten and she walked over to a till to ring up the transaction. She returned with my change and laid it on the bar next to my beer.

"I haven't seen you in here before," she said as she smiled at me.

"I'm just visiting."

"Although, I was in here several years ago when I was in town," I added.

"Hey Kim! How about another," one of the guys at the end of the bar hollered.

"Sure thing Jerry," she replied as she turned and headed towards the two patrons.

After serving the two fellows at the end of the bar, she returned to where I was sitting.

"Who ya visiting?" she asked as she flashed me a cute smile showing off her slightly yellowed teeth caused by her smoking, I assumed.

"Bubba and Bertha Butz."

"Know them?" I then asked.

"Sure do. They come in here together fairly often and Bubba comes in every night after bowling."

After taking a couple swallows of beer, I asked, "Does Spike still own this place?"

I noticed a surprised look on her face and out of the corner of my eye, I saw the two drinkers at the end of the bar, turn their heads, and pay attention to what I was saying.

"Ah, no. He doesn't own it anymore," she replied as she reached down, grabbed a bar rag and started wiping the bar even though there was nothing on it.

"So he got smart and sold the place," I said.

She continued wiping the bar without giving me an answer. The two guys at the end of the bar were still staring in my direction. Wonder what I said wrong I thought. I finished off my glass of beer and sat it back on the bar.

"Think I'll have one for the road," I said to Kim as she still was wiping the bar.

"Sure thing," she replied as she took my glass and retreated to the beer taps again. I saw her say something to the two guys, but couldn't make out what was being said. She returned with my full beer and sat the glass on the coaster once again.

"Thanks," I said as I handed her two dollars. She went to the till and came back with my change, which she laid on the bar.

"Here you go."

I wondered what was going on with my question about Spike, so I spoke up.

"You said Spike sold the place, Huh?"

"I said he doesn't own it anymore."

"Well, if he doesn't own it he must have sold it."

"Or did he lose it to the bank?" I asked.

"Why the questions about Spike?"

"Nothing really. It's just I had a few conversations with Spike during my stay here before. He seemed like a pretty good guy and was just wondering about him," I said.

Just then, the door to the bar opened and two women entered. They immediately started walking to where the two men sat at the bar. Kim quickly left me and went down to where the women were sitting down. Kim waited on them, stood, and talked for a while before she made her way back to where I sat.

"Spike disappeared," she said.

"What?"

"Spike just disappeared one night after he closed up," she said.

"Nobody knows where he went or what happened?"

"Nope. The sheriff spent several months investigating his disappearance, but came up with nothing," the bartender said.

"Does the sheriff suspect foul play?"

"I don't really know what he suspects. All I know is that Spike left everything and went missing," she replied.

"So, who owns Your Uncles Place now?"

She hesitated slightly as she looked down to the four people at the end of the bar who were in deep conversation between themselves.

"Well, there's a Reverend of a religious sect located outside of town who bought the place," she said.

"Reverend States Rights Jones?"

"Yes," she answered with a surprised look on her face.

"You know him?" she asked.

"Nope. Bubba just told me about their religious compound," I lied.

"Seems kinda odd that a preacher would own a bar," I offered.

"I guess, but I don't care. I was hired as the manager here and I do everything from inventory, hiring, firing, wages, taxes, you name it. Reverend Jones has never been in the building that I know of," she said.

"He trusts you with everything, huh?"

"Yep. Once every two months he has a couple of his people come in and go over the books though," she said.

All the time this conversation was going on, I kept wondering if Spikes disappearance and Angel's disappearance had anything in common. I was finished with my beer, but I had a couple of other things I wanted to ask Kim, so I decided to have one more. I still would have time to get out to Kenny's for supper.

"I should be going, but I have time for one more," I said as I smiled at Kim and handed her my beer glass.

"I'll get you a cold glass," she said as she turned and walked away towards cooler and beer taps.

She returned with my full beer and kind of to my surprise, stayed standing in front of me. Does she want to tell me something else, I wondered. I didn't want to seem too curious, but I still wanted to get as much information from Kim as I could.

"It's sure too bad Spike disappeared," I said.

"You said he left everything," I added.

"Yep, the bar, his apartment, all his clothes, and his pick up truck," she said.

"Sounds like maybe he might have been kidnapped or something," I said.

"That was the talk going around town."

"Some folks were even talking about space aliens snatching him up," she added.

"Space aliens! You gotta be shittin me."

"Nope."

"Did people see space ships?"

"No. Nobody saw any space ships, but several other people have disappeared off the face of the earth in the past few months."

"Disappeared off the face of the earth?"

"Yep. One minute they're here, the next minute they're gone."

"Nobody saw them disappear?"

"Nope. All we know is that they are gone."

"I believe in UFOs, but not in little green men coming to earth," I said as I smiled and took a sip of my beer.

"I never said anything about little green me, just that several people have completely vanished, including Spike," Kim replied as she gave me a scowl.

"What does the sheriff think about the space alien theory?"

"He says it's all hogwash and he keeps saying he's sure Spike just left town and no aliens or foul play were involved," she answered.

"Seems strange to me that someone would leave their business and everything and just disappear."

"Me too."

"Unless he was trying to get away from some woman," I said as I smiled at Kim.

"I don't think that was the case. He wasn't married and was so busy with his bar, I don't even know if he had a girlfriend," she replied.

"Excuse me a minute. I have to wait on the others," she said as she once again smiled and left. She now seemed more receptive to answering my questions, so I thought I'd ask a couple more. I saw her talking with the others, who kept glancing in my direction. Must be talking about me, I thought.

After several minutes, Kim returned and I asked, "How long after Spikes disappearance before Reverend Jones bought this place?"

"It was about three weeks."

"Three weeks. Seems like an awfully short time passed before everyone was sure Spike wasn't coming back."

"I guess, but the local bank held the mortgage and the Reverend offered to pay cash, so the bank was more than willing to sell it," she said.

We continued talking for another fifteen minutes and I decided I had learned as much as I was going to and I knew I had better get out to Kenny's and not be late. Martha hates nothing

71

more than me being late for something because I was drinking. I placed three dollars on the bar as a tip and started to get off the barstool.

"Thanks for the conversation," I said as I smiled at Kim.

"No problem. I just don't know why you are so interested in Spikes disappearance seeing as you barely knew him."

"Guess I'm just the nosey type," I replied as I once again smiled at her. She returned my smile and started to walk towards the other customers while I headed for the door.

As I neared the front door of the bar, I glanced back and saw that all five people in the bar were staring at me. Kim must have told them what she and I were talking about.

Exiting the building, I took a big breath of fresh air and started toward my car. I got into the Escalade, found a driveway to turn around in, and headed out of town towards Kenny's place. As I drove along, I tried digesting everything Kim had told me. Spike disappeared, just like Angel. The sheriff didn't turn up any information on Spikes disappearance or Angel's disappearance either. Reverend States Rights Jones name came up in conversations I had about both disappearances. Could he have something to do with both disappearances? Where were Spike and Angel?

## Chapter Nine

It was about 4:45 p.m. when I pulled into the driveway to Kenny and Marcie's house. I drove onto the circular driveway leading to the house and stopped the car. I looked around, but still didn't see Kenny's pickup truck sitting anywhere. He must have parked it in the garage, I thought to myself as I exited the Escalade. I looked around the entire area, and didn't see any cats or geese, either. Walking towards the front porch, I spied the two old dogs laying in the sunlight, sleeping. These two mutts didn't make very good watchdogs. I walked past the sleeping dogs and knocked on the front door of the house.

"Hi, Uncle Butch," said the little girl who opened the door for me.

"Hi, Karla," I said as I patted her on the top of her head.

"I'm Kayla, Uncle Butch."

"I know that. I was just wondering if you knew that," I said as I walked into the house through the open door.

"Of course I know my name," she replied as she giggled and shut the door as I entered the house.

Martha and Marcie were seated in the living room watching some home decorating show on television.

"Hi gals," I said as I walked towards them.

"Hi Butch," Marcie replied.

"Hi Hon," Martha said as she got out of the recliner she was sitting in and walked towards me.

"Whew, you smell like a smokestack," she said as she neared me and gave me a kiss.

"Yuk and you taste like a brewery," she said as she pulled back.

"I thought you were going to visit the sheriff today," she said.

"I did."

"He serves cigarettes and beer," Martha said as she smiled at me.

"I wanted to see if I could find out some more information on Angel's disappearance, so I went to Your Uncles Place," I said.

"You went up to Johnson City and visited Uncle Claude?" Martha asked.

"What could he possibly tell you about Angel's disappearance? He doesn't even know her."

"No I didn't go to Johnson City to talk to your uncle Claude. Didn't you see the bar in town a few blocks from the Do Drop Inn as we walked to Beulah's Diner?" I asked.

"Nope, guess I didn't."

"It was a couple of blocks from the Do Drop Inn and on the opposite side of the street."

"You really don't pay much attention to things around you, do you?" I said.

"I most certainly do. I just don't go looking for bars. I don't need alcohol like you do," Martha huffed.

"Besides, I like to keep my eyes focused on the ground so I can see if there might be something I could trip on," she added.

"Doesn't help much, does it?" I asked as I remembered Martha tripping over a crack in the sidewalk and taking a tumble.

"The bar's name is Your Uncles Place and I thought I might get some information about Angel by stopping there," I replied quickly as I tried to defuse the discussion about my drinking and the fact that Martha seems to trip more than most people.

"Well, did you?" Martha asked as we walked towards the sofa in the living room and she gave me 'the look'.

"Yeah. I found out that the owner I had spoken to when I was down here before went missing," I said.

"Went missing?"

"Yup. The bar, manager said that Spike had just disappeared one night, just like Angel," I said.

"You think there's some connection?"

"Don't know, but it seems kinda weird."

"And on top of that, I found out that Reverend States Rights Jones bought the bar after Spike disappeared," I added.

"The Reverend State Rights Jones from the Family of our Lord?"

"Yep, the same," I replied as I sat down on the sofa.

"Supper will be ready in a little while," Marcie said to me as I sat down.

"We eating here?"

"Yes, we're eating here," Martha, said as she gave me a look that I couldn't figure out.

"Would you like a beer, Butch?" Marcie asked.

"Sure, that sounds good."

"Go get Uncle Butch a beer, will you Karla?" Marcie asked one of the girls who were sitting on the floor playing some game.

"OK, mama," Karla replied as she got up and went into the kitchen to retrieve a beer from the refrigerator.

"Here you are, Uncle Butch," she said to me as she handed me a cold bottle of MGD Light.

"So, where's Kenny?" I asked.

"Oh, he's still over in Springsburg doing some work," Marcie said.

"With all the money he has, why is he still working?" I asked.

"Because he wants to stay busy," Martha tartly replied as she gave me one of her famous 'shut up' looks.

"I had better check on supper. I don't want it to get over cooked and burn the onions," Marcie said as she got out of her chair and headed towards the kitchen.

Martha came over to me, leaned down and whispered, "Don't you say anything about tonight's supper."

"What?"

"Just be quiet and enjoy what we are eating," she said as she turned and walked towards the kitchen to join Marcie.

The two girls kept playing their game as I sipped on my beer. I picked up the morning newspaper off the coffee table and started searching for the daily crossword puzzle. I found the puzzle, a pencil lying on the coffee table and began to fill in the blanks of the crossword puzzle.

Marcie and Martha returned from the kitchen and Marcie announced, "Supper's ready."

I laid the newspaper and pencil down, grabbed my half-empty beer bottle, and joined the girls as we made our way to the dining table.

I bellied up to the table as everyone else sat down. The table contained several large bowls as well as our plates and utensils.

"Pass me your plates," Marcie said as she grabbed a big spoon and hovered over one of the large bowls,

"What are we having?" I finally asked and immediately drew a disgusted look from Martha.

"Bologna and onions," Marcie replied as she started scooping stuff out of the large bowl onto one of the girl's plates.

"Bologna and onions?"

"Yes. This is one of Kenny's favorite meals," Marcie said as she started to fill the other girl's plate.

"If this is Kenny's favorite meal, shouldn't he be here to enjoy it?" I asked.

"I told you he's working," Martha snapped at me as she glared.

"I love course bologna," I said as I tried to save myself from Martha's distain.

"You can't use course bologna in this dish. You need to use fine bologna. And you need to use the sweet Vidalia onions," Marcie said as she continued dishing the concoction onto another plate.

"You cut the bologna into quarter-inch-thick-pieces, about the size of silver dollars. You slice the onion into one-quarter inch slices. You then place the bologna and onion in a large skillet along with a glob of butter and sauté the onion until crispy done. You then turn the heat down to low and let it simmer, uncovered for about one-half hour," she said.

Don't these southern people know how to eat real food? I thought to myself. First Beulah serves woodchuck at her diner; Bubba has pork ribs cooked in sauerkraut and now this bologna dish!

"Do you put ketchup on this?" I asked as Marcie passed me a plate filled with the bologna and onion mixture.

"Oh no," Marcie replied as the two girls looked at each other and giggled.

"You eat it along with these sliced tomatoes," said Marcie as she handed me a large plate containing sliced tomatoes.

I took the plate from her, stabbed several tomatoes, and placed them on my plate along side the bologna and onions. I noticed the bologna-onion juice was running into the tomato slices I had just put on my plate.

I grabbed my fork and started pushing the tomatoes as far away from the juice as possible.

"No, no," Marcie said in a scolding tone.

"The bologna-onion juice running into the tomatoes just makes the taste that much better."

I shrugged my shoulders and looked back down at my plate, trying to figure out what to try to eat first. As I looked up, I saw all the women, even Martha digging into the concoction on their plates. If Martha is eating this stuff, it can't be all bad, I thought to myself.

After taking several sips of my beer and buttering a slice of bread, I finally had the nerve to take a bite of my meal. I had to admit it didn't taste as bad as it looked or sounded.

"This is pretty good," I said between mouthfuls of the bologna, onion, and tomato.

"I knew you'd like it," Marcie said.

"Tastes pretty good, doesn't it Hon?" I asked Martha while I watched her take several small bites and try not to make a face as to offend Marcie.

"I've never tasted anything like it," replied Martha as she gave me a quick 'don't say anything else' look.

I actually had a second helping of the stuff, while Martha finished hers, but deferred on seconds.

"Too bad Kenny missed out on this meal," I said.

"There's plenty leftover for him to have a meal tomorrow when he's supposed to get home," replied Marcie.

"Aren't you hungry, Martha?" Marcie asked because Martha hadn't taken a second helping like the rest of us.

"I'm stuffed. I shouldn't have had that pie as a snack this afternoon," Martha replied as politely as she could.

We finished the meal, the girls and I retired to the living room while the women cleaned up the kitchen. We were watching the evening news when Marcie and Martha joined us in the living room. All five of us watched television until 9:00 p.m. and the two girls got up and headed off to bed.

"Goodnight, Aunt Martha and Uncle Butch," they said as they went down the hallway towards their bathroom and bedrooms.

"I've been thinking about those two guys in the pickup that seemed interested in us," I blurted out to Martha.

"So."

"So, I'm thinking you should stay here with Marcie until we can figure out what's going on. I don't want you to be in any danger," I replied.

"I'm not afraid and if you think something bad might happen, maybe you should just stay here also," Martha replied.

"Oh yes. We have plenty of room. I would enjoy the company, also," Marcie said.

"I should stay in town. It will be easier for me to hear any local scuttlebutt about Angel's disappearance," I said.

"Well, I don't want to stay here without you," Martha said.

"It should be only a few days. Besides, it would give you, Marcie and the girls an opportunity to do girl things. You haven't seen them for a while," I said.

"That's right, Martha. Us girls could go shopping or whatever. Butch can come out here and eat. I enjoy cooking for more people," Marcie said as her eye sparkled at the idea of an adult being with her instead of just talking with the young girls.

"I don't know."

"I don't have any clothes, my makeup, or toiletries," Martha added.

"No problemo. I'll run back into town and retrieve your things," I replied.

"Kenny built this place so big, you can have your own bedroom and bathroom," Marcie interjected.

"Sounds good to me," I said as I gave Martha one of my 'please' looks.

"I suppose I could stay here," Martha sighed.

"It's settled then," Marcie said.

"What's settled, mama?" asked Karla as she came into the living room to get her goodnight kiss.

"Aunt Martha is going to stay with us for a few days," Marcie said.

"And Uncle Butch?" asked Kayla as she entered the room.

"No, not me. I've paid for the room we've rented in town, so I want to get my moneys worth," I answered with the hope my answerer would satisfy the girls enough so they wouldn't be asking too many questions.

The girls gave all of us a good night kiss and headed off to bed.

"I'll be back in a little bit," I said as I started to rise from the sofa.

"I'll bring your suitcase and all the junk you have all over the bathroom," I said.

"It's not junk. It's things I need," replied Martha as she got up and gave me a kiss on the cheek.

I left Marcie and Kenny's place for the journey back into town to retrieve Martha's things. As I neared the Do Drop Inn, I noticed the same Chevy pickup that had seemed interested in Martha and me, was parked across the street from the Inn. The curb in front of the Inn was empty as usual, so I pulled along side the curb, stopped the Escalade, retrieved the key attached to the Plexiglas from under the seat, got out and started walking towards the door of my room. I glanced over my shoulder towards the pickup and noticed the two men slightly hunch their shoulders and duck their heads as if they didn't want me to see their faces.

I reached the door to room 1467, inserted the key into the lock, unlocked the door, opened it, and started to walk in. Before entering, I once again glanced over my shoulder and saw that the pick up was slowly moving away from the curb. I retrieved Martha's items and walked towards the door. As I opened the door, I glanced out towards where the pickup was parked and saw that indeed, it had driven away. I went to the Escalade, got inside, and pulled away from the curb. I looked in the rear view mirror and didn't see the pickup. As I drove back out to Kenny's, I started thinking about the pickup and what I had learned today. Why did the sheriff seemed agitated when I asked him about Reverend Jones? Who was in the pickup? Why were they watching me? Were they involved in Angel's disappearance? Were they involved in Spike's disappearance? Is Martha and I in any danger? Where is Angel?

## Chapter Ten

I awoke Tuesday morning, May 17 around 6:00 a.m. from a wonderful sleep in my bed at the Do Drop Inn. Although I missed having Martha around, I didn't miss her loud snoring that keeps me awake half of the night. She always says that I snore more than she does, but I never hear myself!

Instead of lying in bed trying to grab a little more shuteye, I decided to get up and try to get a hold of Frank Hatfield before he left for work. I showered, brushed my teeth, shaved, and got dressed in a clean pair of shorts and tee shirt. I retrieved my wallet from the top of the nightstand and removed the piece of paper Bubba had given me with Frank Hatfield's telephone number and address. Although it was only 6:30 a.m., I thought Frank would be up and not left for work yet. I picked up my cell phone, sat on the edge of the bed, and dialed Frank's number. The telephone rang four times and was answered.

"Hello," came a voice through the earpiece of my cell phone.

"Hello. Is this Frank Hatfield?" I asked.

"Yep."

"I'm sorry for bothering you at such an early hour, but my name is Butch Brogen. I'm a private investigator from Minnesota whom Bubba and Bertha hired to try and find Angel McCoy," I quickly said.

"It's not that early. I was just going out the door to go to work," he replied.

"You say Bubba and Bertha hired you to find Angel," he quickly said.

"That's correct. Bubba told me that you were engaged to Angel and I thought you might shed some light on her disappearance," I said.

"You accusing me of having something to do with her disappearance," he snapped at me.

"No, no. I'm not suggesting anything of the sort. I just thought that if I could talk with you, you might have something to tell me that could be of importance in Angel's disappearance," I quickly said as I tried to soothe his ruffled feathers.

"I don't know any more than I've already told the sheriff," Frank replied.

"That may be true, but I might be able to figure out something the sheriff didn't," I said.

"Whatever. I gotta get going to work so I'm not late," he said.

"Ok, but is there some night I could visit with you after you get home from work?"

"I guess. I'm not doing anything tonight. If you want to stop out to my place around 5:00 p.m., I'll tell you exactly what I told the sheriff," he replied.

"Great. I'll see you around five. Thanks for agreeing to meet with me and have a good day at work," I said.

"Sure."

"Know how to find my place?" Frank asked.

"Bubba gave me your address, so I'll just put it into my Escalades GPS. Ms. Cadillac will get me to your house," I said.

"OK," said Frank as he hung up his telephone.

He doesn't seem to excited to talk with me, but at least he said yes. I looked at my wristwatch and saw that it was almost 6:45 a.m. Martha should be up, so I decided to give her a call before driving out to Kenny's place. I scrolled through the numbers on my cell phone until I came to Martha's cell number.

I pushed the send button and waited. After only two rings, she answered her phone.

"Good morning, handsome," she said in a bubbly voice.

"How did you know it was me, or do you answer all your phone calls like that?" I asked even though I knew my name and telephone number had come up on her cell phone.

"The name of whoever is calling me comes up on my phone. You know that," she replied.

"I know. I was just giving you some crap."

"Did you have a good night sleep?" I asked her.

"As good as it can be without you laying next to me," she said.

"How about you?" she then asked.

"I had a great nights sleep. No snoring zombie lying next to me keeping me awake."

"Well maybe you should just continue sleeping by yourself even after we get home," she said as she gave out a small chuckle.

"No, I really miss not having you by my side."

"That sounds better," she said as we both chuckled this time.

"What are you doing today?" she asked me.

"I don't know for sure. I'm meeting with Frank Hatfield at 5:00 p.m."

"Why don't you come out here for breakfast at least?" Martha asked.

I suppose I could do that. You're not having oat meal, are you?"

"No, we're not having oat meal. Marcie said she would cook up some fried eggs and hash brown potatoes before the girls head off to school," Martha replied.

Thinking of the previous evening's meal, I asked, "What kind of eggs is she frying?"

"They're not going to be quail, crow, or chicken hawk, are they?"

"Stop that. Just because the people down here eat some different things than you do, doesn't mean that all their food is weird," Martha replied.

"I know. It's just that I'm a little leery."

"We're having regular chicken eggs. Now quit your complaining and get your butt out here."

About twenty-five minutes later, I was pulling in front of Kenny's house. The sun was coming up over the grove of pines trees to the east of the house, casting various size shadows on the front porch of the house. The two dogs were nowhere to be seen and neither the geese or cats. As I walked up to the front door, it opened and Martha emerged. She was dressed in light tan shorts and a pink tee shirt. No bra, of course. Both items of clothing made her small, muscular body even more alluring.

"Hi, handsome," she said as she gave me a big kiss.

"Knock that crap out. Somebody might see us," I said.

"Who cares," she replied as she gave me another kiss.

"I don't care if anyone sees us kissing, it's what else is going to happen if you don't stop," I said as I playfully slapped her small butt as she turned and started to walk into the house.

"Hi, Butch," Marcie said as she looked up from the lounge chair she was sitting in.

"I'm glad you're going to have breakfast with us. I'll get it started as soon as the girls get up, which shouldn't be too long now, because they have to get off to school," she added.

"I swear that the closer to the end of the school year, the sleepier, and slower those two girls get," she said.

"No hurry. I'll just read the morning newspaper," I replied as I sat down on the sofa and unfolded the morning Tennessee Star, which I had purchased at the local Kum N Go before coming out. I remember a paper at the house, but I wanted to make sure I had some morning reading.

The girls got up; we had a great breakfast of chicken eggs, hashed brown potatoes, bacon, and toast.

"Do you always eat like this?" I asked Marcie as I was cleaning the last morsel of food from my plate.

"No, not all the time. I usually have a good breakfast whenever Kenny is home, otherwise the girls and I have cereal or toast," she replied.

We all got up from the table, the girls grabbing their backpacks, and heading out of the door for another day of school. I grabbed my coffee cup and headed into the living room to read the morning newspaper. The women starting cleaning up the breakfast dishes. In a little while, Marcie and Martha joined me in the living room where we all sipped on our coffee.

"So, did anything happen last night?" Martha asked.

"Nope, everything was quiet. Although I think that pickup truck which drove by us the other day, was parked along side the curb across from the Do Drop Inn. It took off as I looked at it," I replied.

"You think it has something to do with Angel's disappearance?"

"Don't know, but I'm more convinced now than ever you should stay here with Marcie," I said.

"I think you should also."

"Nope. There's no need for me to be bringing anybody around here that doesn't belong. Especially since Kenny is not home," I said.

"Kenny called and said he will be home today," Marcie said.

"That's great. It would be nice if he would keep an eye on all of you."

"So, what do you ladies have planned?" I asked as I changed the subject.

"We thought we would go to Johnson City, do some shopping and some visiting," Martha said.

"What else are you going to do other than meet with Frank Hatfield?" she asked.

"I don't know. I suppose I could get another eighteen holes of golf in."

"Another strenuous day for the private investigator," Martha said as she smiled at me.

"What can I say? I want to talk to Frank and he won't be home until 5:00 p.m., you women aren't going to be around for me to talk with, Kenny's not home yet, so in my mind there's only one thing to do. Golf."

"If you're going to meet with Frank at 5:00 p.m., you won't be here for supper will you?" asked Martha.

"No. Don't wait supper for me. I'll pick up something to eat either before I meet with Frank or afterwards," I answered.

"Do you have a tee time?" asked Martha.

"Nah, but I figured on a Tuesday it wouldn't be too hard to get on a course."

We sat around as I read the newspaper and talked with the women before they decided it was time to go shopping. They went to the bathroom, gathered their purse, and started towards the front door of the house.

"Have fun golfing," Martha said as she stopped, bent over the sofa I was sitting in and gave me a kiss.

"You didn't take your credit card, did you," I asked Martha.

"Of course and what's it to you. I think I have enough money to go shopping," she replied.

"I ain't worried about the money, it's just all the crap we'll have to haul back to Minnesota," I replied with a grin.

"I don't buy crap," Martha replied.

"Let's go," Marcie said as she tried to halt the minor bickering between Martha and me.

The women folk left, I finished reading the newspaper, and watched a little television. Around 11:00 a.m., I rummaged through the refrigerator and found some Braunschweiger. At least I have the same taste in sandwich meat that Kenny and Marcie does!

I made myself a Braunschweiger and mustard sandwich, which I ate along with some barbeque chips before I headed out to the Jones Valley Golf Course.

Jones Valley was a nice eighteen hole golf course with rolling fairways and a stream running through it. Very few trees were growing on the golf course.

I pulled into the gravel parking lot and noticed there weren't too many cars. Golf rounds must be down around here just like at home, I thought to myself as I parked the Escalade. I got out of the vehicle and walked towards the modest looking clubhouse. Although I didn't have a tee time, the clubhouse attendant assured me that the course was pretty much open, so I should be able to get a round in with no problem. I paid my green fees and cart rental, took the cart keys from the attendant and started towards the door.

"Hey, aren't you going to grab a score card?" the attendant asked me just before I reached the door.

"I don't need one. I enter my scores into my SkyCaddie GPS," I replied.

I had loaded twenty local courses into my SkyCaddie before we left home just in case I had some time to get some golf in. Jones Valley was a course that had been professionally mapped by the SkyCaddie company, so I could enter my score and upload it to their web site.

Just as the attendant had said, there weren't many people on the course and the ones that were there were moving along at a respectable pace. I wasn't supposed to meet Frank until around 5:00 p.m., so I took my time as I traveled around the course. My round wasn't anything spectacular, but I didn't lose a golf ball, so it counted as a good round. I finished my round at 4:30 p.m., which meant I had plenty of time to make it to Frank's place by 5:00 p.m. I took my clubs off the golf cart, parked the cart, returned the key to the clubhouse, and got in my car to make the trip to Frank's house. I took the paper Bubba had given me with Frank's address out of the cup holder, where I had placed it. I entered the address into the GPS located in the dash of the Escalade and started out of the golf course parking lot on my way to meet Frank.

# Chapter Eleven

Following the sweet sounding woman's voice coming from the Escalades GPS, I arrived at Frank's place at 4:55 p.m. I hoped that even though Frank told me to meet him around 5:00 p.m., he would be home now. As I pulled into the gravel driveway, I saw a small story and one-half house with a one car, attached garage. The house was painted an ecru color with dark brown trim on the fascia, around the windows and doors.

To the rear of the house sat a utility shed painted the same color combination. There was a Paper Birch tree in the front yard, but no other shrubs, trees or flowers. The lawn was a bright green, fairly weed free and well maintained.

As I parked near the apron of the garage, I saw some movement in the front window of the house. Frank must be home, I thought. I exited the Escalade and walked towards the front door of the house as I kept my eye out for any dogs, cats, or geese that might come to greet me. No critters approached me as I made my way to the front door, where I knocked sharply on the door.

The door opened in a couple of seconds and a ruddy looking man appeared. He looked to be in his early twenties. He was around five foot ten and one hundred fifty pounds. He had hazel eyes, mousy blond hair, and a blond moustache. He was dressed in a pair of denim sorts and an orange tee shirt that had *Get R Done* on the front.

"Hi, I'm Butch Brogen," I said as I extended my hand towards him.

"Frank Hatfield," he replied as he shook my hand.

"I hope I'm not too early."

"Nope. I've been home for awhile."

"Come on in, but I don't know what I can tell you that I haven't already told the sheriff," Frank said as he stepped aside to allow me to enter his house.

"Grab a seat," Frank said as he gestured towards a sofa and sat down in a recliner.

"I assume you've been asked all sorts of questions in regards to Angel's disappearance, but I would like you to tell me everything you can," I said.

"What do you want to know?" he asked.

"Everything in regards to you and Angel."

"I didn't have anything to do with her disappearance," he said.

"I know you told me that, but you might remember something that might be of importance," I said as I tried not to piss him off.

"Just start at the beginning of yours and Angel's life together," I said.

"We had gone together ever since we were sophomores in high school. Angel was the sweetest girl I had ever met," he offered.

"You two continued to date after she went off to college," I said.

"Yep. She went to college in Johnson City to get her degree and I went to work for Olerud's Construction Company as a cat skinner."

"You two stay close while she was away at college?" I asked.

"We sure did. We saw each other almost every weekend, until...."he said as his voice trialed off.

"Until she had an affair with some other guy?"

91

"That's right. I still can't believe she did that," Frank answered as he took a couple of deep breaths.

"I'm sorry that happened," I said as I tried to calm him down.

"I loved her so much, and then she did something like that!" he explained as he squirmed around in his chair.

"Everyone makes a mistake once in awhile."

"Not that big of a mistake! We were engaged to be married and then she goes off and does something like that," he said as he sighed.

"Do you know who she had the affair with?" I asked.

"No! I told her I didn't want to know anything about what had happened!"

"It might not be as bad as you think, Frank."

"Why's that?"

"The sheriff told me that Angel and the guy had only gone out one time," I replied and didn't mention that the sheriff had told me Angel and Rod had sex.

"That's what she told me too, but I don't know if I can believe her!"

I could see that he was getting upset, but I still wanted to find out what he might know about Angel's disappearance.

"I could say I know how you feel, but I don't. I've never had some one I love do that to me," I said as I hoped he would take some solace in my words.

"She shouldn't have done that!" he exclaimed.

"I sense that you still love her, even though you feel wronged."

"Yes, I still love her."

As calm as I could sound, I asked Frank, "Frank, you had nothing to do with Angel's disappearance, right?"

"That's right. I don't know why people think I did something to her," he said.

Changing the subject from Frank and Angel, I said, "Bubba told me that your great-grandpa, Ephraim Hatfield had a dislike for McCoys, even though the Hatfield-McCoy feud has been over for years."

"Oh yes, great-grandpa Ephraim totally dislikes McCoys."

"You're not thinking that he might have something to do with Angel's disappearance?" Frank asked.

"At this point, I don't think anything. I'm just trying to find out what facts I can in Angel's disappearance."

"I know Grandpa Ef, as we call him; is suffering from dementia and has spells where he thinks he's back in the days of the feud, but he couldn't have anything to do with Angel's disappearance," Frank said.

"Do you think I could meet with your great-grandfather and ask him some questions?"

"Sure, we could meet with him, but I don't know what you could learn. He's not himself sometimes."

"Even with his dementia, he lives alone by himself?" I asked.

"Yes. We tried to talk him into going to an assisted living place, but he said he'd kill himself before he went to an old folk's home," Frank answered.

"Do you think we could go and see your great-grandfather now?"

"Sure. I wasn't planning to have supper for a while and I know Grandpa is at home. He never gets out unless one of us takes him."

"He lives about ten miles on the other side of Jonesborough, so it won't take long to get there," Frank added.

"I'll drive, if you want to ride with me," I said.

"Sure thing. I haven't ever ridden in one of those fancy Escalades," he said with a smile.

"In fact, I couldn't afford the insurance and license for one," he added.

"My wife has money," I said as I smiled and didn't bother telling him just how many millions Martha had.

We exited Frank's house and started towards my vehicle.

"I just have one rule, you have to wear your seatbelt," I said to Frank as we climbed into the Escalade.

"No problem. I always wear mine," he answered as he gave out a soft whistle.

"Whoa, this baby looks loaded," he exclaimed.

"Yeah, it's got everything that Cadillac offered on this version," I replied as I backed out of his driveway and started driving back towards Jonesborough.

"You gotta give me directions."

"Sure. Just keep going back into town. We'll hang a right at our famous diner."

"Beulah's Diner?"

"Yep. You eaten there?"

"Several times," I answered as I patted my ample stomach.

"Yep, you ate there," Frank, said as he smiled.

We continued to chat about everything except Angel as we drove into Jonesborough. I drove into town and turned right at Beulah's Diner, just as Frank had instructed. He gave me directions as we exited town and drove on several gravel roads.

I'm going to have to wash my vehicle tomorrow, I thought to myself as we drove on dusty gravel roads for several miles.

"Take a right at the next mailbox," Frank said.

I saw a mailbox at the end of a long gravel/dirt driveway and asked, "This one?"

"Yep. This is Grandpa Ef's driveway."

I drove down a driveway that I considered more of a lane or cattle trail, for almost one-half of a mile. Finally, a small white house appeared in our vision. As I slowly drove up to the house, I noticed that it was quite small, well kept, and early nineteen hundreds vintage. The house had a small porch attached to the front, on which was a rocking chair, just as you see in the movies. In the rocking chair sat an elderly gentleman, who was slowly rocking and pulling on a briar pipe that was in his mouth.

"Let me talk to Grandpa, first," Frank said as I stopped near the porch.

"Hi Grandpa," Frank said as he exited my vehicle and started walking towards the elderly gentleman.

"Hey, boy. Who's fancy falutin vehicle?" Ephraim asked Frank as Frank started walking up the steps to the porch with me closely behind.

"This is my friend, Butch Brogen. It's his SUV," Frank said.

"Got pretty rich friends, there boy."

"Ah, he ain't so rich. His wife's got all the money," Frank replied as he glanced over his shoulder, gave me a smile and a wink.

"Pleased to meet you. Butch was it?" Ephraim asked as I stopped in front of him and extended my hand.

"Pleased to meet you, Mr. Hatfield," I replied as I grasped his gnarly, leathery, weathered hand.

"Yes, I'm Butch."

"No Mr. Just call me Ef," he said as he shook my hand and continued his slow rocking.

"So, why you boys come to see me?" he asked Frank who was standing along the railing on the porch.

"Um, well, ah, Butch is kinda looking into Angel's disappearance," Frank finally answered.

The old man's eyes narrowed to only slits and he stopped rocking.

"Why'd you bring up that name?" he demanded of Frank.

"Now, grandpa. You know I love Angel and we were going to get married."

"You ain't ever marrying no damn McCoy," Ephraim shouted.

"Grandpa, the feud is over. We all get along now," Frank replied as he gave me a look that said, see what I was talking about.

"You young pups may get along, but a real Hatfield never forgets what was done to us by them McCoys," Ephraim spat.

"Grandpa, we're not feuding anymore. There's no need to get all upset," Frank said as he tried to calm down his great-grandfather.

"You ain't no damn McCoy lover are you?" he asked as he turned his steely gaze towards me.

"No sir. I'm not even from around here. I grew up in Minnesota," I replied.

"Don't care where you come from. Damn McCoys infested the entire country as far as I can tell," he said to me.

"I promise I'm no McCoy. My grandparents came from Denmark and Bohemia," I said.

"Damned foreigner."

Realizing no matter what was said, the old guy was going to be upset talking about a McCoy, so I just continued talking.

"I was just wondering if you might have any ideas of where Angel might be," I said.

"In hell for all I care."

"Why did you have to come out here and upset your old Grandpa?" he asked Frank.

"We didn't come out here to upset you Grandpa. Mr. Brogen is just trying to find out what happened to Angel," Frank replied.

"What do I care? One less McCoy is great as far as I care," Ephraim answered.

"When was the last time you saw Angel?" I asked.

"The one and only time this young pipsqueak brought her out here. I promptly threw them both off my property. Ain't no damn McCoy gonna be setting foot in my house," the old man snapped at me.

He had still not started rocking yet, so I figured he was still upset and I wouldn't be getting much more information out of him, but I had to ask.

"Did you have anything to do with Angels' disappearance?" I asked.

Although Ephraim was in his early nineties, he sprang from his rocking chair with the speed of a cougar and lunged towards me.

"You get outta my place, right now," he screamed at me as Frank grabbed a hold of his shoulders and steadied him so he didn't topple over.

"I'm sorry I upset you, Mr. Hatfield," I said as I backed away from the two of them.

"Just git," he yelled as he waved his right fist in the air.

"The only good McCoy is a dead McCoy, and don't you forget that, sonny," he spat.

"Calm down Grandpa," Frank said as he tried ushering Ephraim back into his rocking chair. Frank gave me the look that said I should go back to my vehicle and he would join me as soon as he got his Grandpa calmed down.

I retreated to my Escalade, got inside, and waited for Frank to join me. I watched as Frank ushered his Grandfather back into the rocking chair and stood talking to the gentleman for a while. Even though I couldn't hear what was being said, I know the old guy was still pissed at me because he kept glancing my way as he and Frank talked. Several minutes passed and then Frank turned away from the old man and walked off the porch towards me. As Frank got into my vehicle, I apologized for upsetting his Grandfather.

"I'm sorry I got your great-grandfather so upset," I said to Frank as I started driving down the driveway to take Frank home.

"Don't worry about it. Grandpa always gets upset whenever the McCoys are brought up."

"You didn't really think Grandpa had anything to do with Angel's disappearance?" Frank asked.

"I don't know what to think. I'm just trying to cover all the bases and see if anyone who knew her, had any ideas about what happened," I said.

"Yeah, I guess you need to ask, Grandpa may still carry a grudge for the McCoys, but he would never hurt anybody," Frank replied.

"He sure got pissed and came after me."

"That he did," Frank replied with a chuckle.

"I never saw him move so fast," he added.

"With a temper like that and his dislike for the McCoys makes him someone of interest to me," I said.

"So be it, but Grandpa had nothing to do with Angel's disappearance. Just like I have nothing to do with her disappearance," he said to me with strong conviction in his voice.

We chatted as I drove back to Frank's place, but not about Angel. I almost believe both of them, but I still have to do some more sleuthing before I'm totally convinced.

We reached Frank's place, I stopped, and he got out of the Escalade.

"I hope you learned whatever you were searching for," Frank said as he started closing the car door.

"I hope so too," I replied as he shut the door.

It was past 7:00 p.m., I thought I'd just go to Beulah's Diner for supper and retire to my room. I figured I had better call Martha and let her know what I was going to do. I explained to her that because of the hour, I would just eat in town and come out to Kenny's tomorrow morning for breakfast. I didn't exactly know what I was going to do, but I had some ideas.

I stuffed myself as usual every time I eat at Beulah's and went back to my room to relax and watch some television. As I laid on the bed watching NCIS, my thoughts went to today's events.

Did Frank have anything to do with Angel's disappearance? Although he had broken off the engagement, he still seems to carry a flame for her. Did Great-grandpa Hatfield have anything to do with Angel's disappearance? He had a temper and a terrible dislike for McCoys. Would the thought of Frank marrying a McCoy drive the old guy to do someone bodily harm?

As Gibbs was once again solving a murder, I still had no clue as to the disappearance of Angel!

# Chapter Twelve

I woke up at my usual time, 6:30 a.m., on Wednesday, May 18. After showering, brushing my teeth, shaving, and getting dressed, I gave Martha a call.

"Good morning, handsome," came her voice over my cell phone.

"Hi, beautiful."

"So, did you enjoy another night without me?" she asked.

Although I did enjoy a night without having to listen to her snoring, I used common sense and replied, "No I didn't. I miss having you lying next to me in bed."

"I know you're lying, because you are always complaining about my snoring."

"How could I complain about such a wonderful person as you."

"Cut the BS, and get your butt out here for breakfast," she replied.

As usual, I obeyed, hanging up the phone and getting ready to drive out to Kenny's place.

I left the Do Drop Inn and got into my Escalade that was parked at the curb. As I drove out to Kenny's, I was thinking about what I was going to do today. I had to come up with something in regards to Angel's disappearance. Maybe I would drive to Johnson City and visit Spartan College. Although it was near the end of the semester, some students should still be around and the office personal would still be around. I might be able to get some information on Angel's' life at college.

I arrived at Kenny's, parked the car, and walked up to the front door. The two hounds were once again laying on the porch and as usual, neither one even raised their heads as I approached them. I knocked on the front door and the door was opened almost immediately by one of the girls.

"Hi Kayla," I said as I patted her on the head and walked into the house.

"Hi, Uncle Butch," she replied, indicating that I had gotten her name right.

As I entered the living room, I saw Kenny sitting in a recliner, reading a sportsman magazine. Martha and Marcie came into the room, both of them looking quite attractive.

"Hi Hon," I said as Martha approached me and gave me a kiss.

"Yuk," one of the girls said.

"Don't yuk me. One of these days, you'll be sucking face with a boy," I replied as I looked at both girls.

"No way," they both replied in unison.

"Boys have germs!"

"They have more than germs, honey," Martha said as she smiled at me and pinched my butt.

"Hi Kenny," I finally said as I acknowledged Martha's brother.

"Hey, Butch."

"I've heard that you've been real busy," I said and quickly noticed a discerning glance from Martha.

"Yep. Although we don't need the money, I still like to keep busy," he said.

Keeping busy doing what? I thought to myself.

I sat down on the sofa while the women went into the kitchen to cook breakfast. One good thing about being here is that I haven't had to do the cooking, I thought to myself.

After several minutes, Martha hollered from the kitchen, "Breakfast is ready."

Kenny, the girls and I trouped into the kitchen where a feast of scrabbled eggs, hash brown potatoes and sausages were sitting on the table.

"Set down and dig in," Marcie said as she brought a pot of coffee out and sat on the table.

We all sat down and started to dig in.

"So, what are you going to do today?" I asked Kenny between mouthfuls of eggs and potatoes.

"I don't have any projects right now, but I'm working on a job that might start in three, four days," he replied.

Yeah, right, a job, I thought.

"What are you going to be doing, Hon?" Martha asked me.

"I thought that I might go over to Spartan College and see if I could come up with anything that might help me figure out what happened to Angel," I replied.

"Are you going to be back in time for supper?"

I didn't want to ask what was on the menu, so I just replied, "Sure."

"Another great meal, ladies," I said as I finished my breakfast, stood up from the table, grabbed my coffee cup and headed back into the living room.

Kenny followed me and we chatted as we both drank our coffee. Martha and Marcie soon joined us with their coffees. We sat around for a while; chatting and then I decided that I should get going.

"Well, I think I'll get going to Johnson City," I said.

"I hope you find out something that will help you solve Angel's disappearance," Martha said.

"I'll be sure to be back in time for supper, if you don't mind feeding me again," I said as I stood up from the sofa.

102

"No problem, we have plenty of food," Marcie said.

What is it going to be? I thought to myself.

"I'll see you later," Martha said as she walked over and gave me a kiss.

"Yuk," came the response from one of the girls again.

"Quick your yuking, grab your back packs and get your butts out of the door down to the bus stop," Marcie said as she ushered the girls out of the door on their way to school.

I exited the house just after the girls, got into the Escalade, started it, put it in gear, and began driving down the driveway towards the road. As I drove towards Johnson City, I began wondering what, if anything I might learn. It might be a total waste of time, but I might learn something in regards to Angel's disappearance. It was a nice sunny day and not too hot yet, so I turned the air conditioner in the car off and cracked the drivers window a little bit, letting the fresh air in. I had to turn up the SiriusXM radio a little, so I could continue to listen to the fifties music which was blaring from the Bose speakers.

As I neared the half way point in my journey, my thoughts turned to the Reverend States Rights Jones and his enclave. What was going on inside the compound? Why the high fence that looked like it was designed to keep people in? Were the rumors of him kidnapping people to become one of his followers really true?

The longer I drove, the more I was convinced that I needed to get into that compound and see what or whom I could find. Getting in wouldn't be a problem, I thought. There had to be a secluded area where I could scale the fence. Getting back out was another story, though. I kept running thoughts through my mind as I continued driving. Before I knew it, the GPS in my vehicle started talking to me, giving me directions to Spartan College. I followed the sweet woman's voice coming from the

GPS and as she directed me to the address, I had entered into the GPS before I left Kenny's house, the administration building. Shortly, I found my self in front of the administration building, where I turned into a parking lot that contained six vehicles.

Could be an employee parking lot, I thought to myself as I stopped my vehicle. I hope I don't get into too much trouble for parking here.

I parked, got out of the Escalade, locked it, and started walking towards what looked like the front doors of the building. I walked up the sidewalk to the door, grabbed the handle, and opened it. Looking around inside, I saw no one, but was amazed how the décor looked about the same as when I went to school many years ago. I started walking down the large entry way, looking for some signs directing people to the proper place they were looking for, when a door to the right of me opened, and a woman stepped out. She was of medium height, a small build, and short red hair.

"May I help you?" she asked as she stopped right next to me.

"Uh, I guess I'm looking for the Administration Office," I stammered.

"Something specific you are trying to find out?" she asked as she gave me the once over.

"My name is Butch Brogen. I'm a private investigator looking into the disappearance of one of the former students here," I replied.

"And you think some one here can help you?" she asked as if she didn't believe me.

"I was hoping some one in the office could give me some specifics about the student's life here. Like classes they took, whom their friends were, where they lived. Stuff like that," I said.

"A lot of the clerical staff has already left for the summer, but I think Sally, the Dean's secretary might be able to help you," the woman said as she finally smiled at me and extended her hand towards me.

"My name is Dorothy. Just call me Dot, though," she replied.

"Hi Dot."

"Follow me and I'll take you to the office of the Dean," she said as she started walking down the hall.

"I'm between classes right now," she offered as we walked down the hallway.

"What do you teach?"

"Right now, I'm teaching a class involving the study of dinosaurs."

"Many kids take a dinosaur class?"

"The ones who need a good grade without doing very much homework," she said as she smiled at me again.

"Oh, so your class isn't too tough."

"Nope. It's basically for students who need to improve their grade point average. It also gives me a class I can teach without doing too much myself," she said.

"I show a lot of movies and the students are allowed to access You Tube to see any other movies which might be out there."

Very honest teacher, I thought to myself as she stopped in front of a door with a frosted glass window in it.

"Here's the Dean's office," she said as she stopped in front of a door and reached for the door handle.

She entered the room with me following right behind. A young woman of no more than twenty three years of age, sat behind a desk typing on a computer key board.

"Hi Sally," Dot said as she got near the desk.

"Hi Dot," Sally replied as she looked up from her typing.

"This gentleman is a private investigator, who's looking into the disappearance of one of our former students. He was hoping your records might reveal something about the person," Dot said as she more than explained the reason why I was there.

"Some one's disappeared, huh? I'll do whatever I can to help you as long as it's within the law. Some of our information is confidential," Sally said as she looked at me, blinking her bright blue eyes.

"I understand," I replied.

"I should be getting back to my class room and prepare for my next class, so I'll leave you two alone," Dot said as she started towards the door.

"Are you sure you can find your way to the front door?" she asked me with a twinkle in her eye as she paused at the open door.

"I think I remember."

"If not, I think Sally could be of assistance," I added.

"OK, I'll see you then," Dot said as she exited the room.

"Dot didn't tell you, but my name is Butch Brogen," I said as I stood in front of Sally's desk.

"Pleased to meet you, Mr. Brogen. Now I assume you are here asking about Angel McCoy," she said.

With a startled look on my face, I asked, "How did you know I was inquiring about Angel?"

"Sheriff Hatfield was here asking questions when Angel first disappeared," she replied with a smile on her face.

Of course, dummy, I thought to myself. The sheriff said he had done a very complete investigation into Angel's disappearance.

"Why don't you ask him for the information that we gave him?" she asked.

106

"Ah, well. We're not on the best of speaking terms," I replied as I smiled at her.

"I see. The sheriff is a little put out about a private investigator nosing around in a case which he feels has been completely investigated," she answered as she smiled back at me.

"Yep. You hit the nail on the head. He's not very happy that Angel's sister and brother-in-law hired me to see if I could find out something that the sheriff couldn't," I replied.

"I'll get Angel's file and let you see the items which I can legally show you," she said as she started typing on the computer keyboard.

Within a couple of minute the printer sitting on the counter behind Sally, began to hum as it started printing out the information Sally had requested. When the printer stopped, she rose from her chair, made her way to the printer, retrieved the papers, and walked back over to where I was standing.

"Here's everything about Angel that I can let you see," she said to me as she handed me about a dozen pieces of paper.

"Thanks," I said as I took the papers from her.

"I could save you a little reading time by telling you that two of the girls who Angel roomed with are still living on campus finishing up classes of their junior year. The other two girls who lived with Angel graduated when she did, so they are gone."

"Thanks. I most certainly would like to talk to some of her room mates."

"Angel and the girls lived in Burton House. It's about seven blocks from here. I can give you a map showing how to get there," Sally said.

"That would be great."

"They might remember something that they didn't tell the sheriff when he talked to them," I said.

Sally pressed several keys on the computer key board and the printer once again began to hum. She walked over to the printer, retrieved a single sheet of paper, and returned to me.

"Here's a map of the campus," she said as she handed me the piece of paper.

"Burton House is right here," she said as she poked her finger on a spot on the map.

"It's not hard to find. Just follow the streets as shown on the map."

"Thanks, again," I said as I placed the campus map on top of the pile of papers which Sally had already given me.

"I don't know if anyone will be around, but you can check if you want," she said.

"Sure will. As long as I'm here, I might as well cover all the bases I can," I replied as I turned towards the door.

"Can you find your way out, or do you need my help?" she asked as she smiled at me.

"I think I remember the way, but why don't you give me your telephone number in case I get lost and have to call you to rescue me," I said as I stopped and walked back to where Sally was seated.

"That's the most unusual way I've ever had anybody try get my telephone number from me," Sally said as she smiled.

"Most guys nowadays just come out and ask for a woman's telephone number as they are hitting on them," she said.

"Don't worry. I'll only use it if I get lost."

"Although I might also want to call you if there is something else about Angel I would want you to look up," I added.

"Oh, I was hoping you were trying to pick me up," Sally said as she smiled at me.

"I don't think my wife would think that is too wise of me," I said as I laughed.

"Also, I'm old enough to be your father."

"I kinda like older men, but tell your wife not to worry, I have a boyfriend who I am more than happy to continue to see," she said as she also laughed.

Sally continued smiling, wrote her telephone number on a post-it note, handed it to me, and said, "Good luck. I didn't know Angel, but her disappearance is just terrible. I hope you find out what happened."

"Thanks. I hope so too," I replied as I walked back to the office door, opened the door and stepped out into the hallway.

I found my way to the front door with no problem, got into the Escalade and proceeded to put the address of Burton House into the GPS. I'm not very good with maps and the sweet talking GPS lady will get me to where I want to go.

Following the GPS directions, I shortly pulled along side of the curb in front of Burton House. It was a quaint small two-story house located amid other two-story houses of the same era. They were typical houses in an older section of town that universities buy and convert into student housing.

I got out of my vehicle and started walking up the side walk leading to the front door of the house. Looking around, I didn't notice a soul sitting on any of the house porches or lawns of the adjoining properties. Nobody was walking on any of the sidewalks either. Everybody must be in class or already done with classes for the year, I thought.

Upon reaching the door, I sharply knocked on the door several times. No one opened the door, so I knocked again, just a little harder. Still no response. Damn, I thought, nobody home, and I wanted to talk to these girls. I stood near the door a little longer and once again rapped on it. Still nothing, so I turned and walked back to the Escalade and got in.

I sat there for several minutes scanning the papers Sally had given me, when out of the blue, it hit me! I know how I'm going to get in and out of Reverend Jones compound! All I need to do now is find a Menards or whatever store which sells the items I need.

## Chapter Thirteen

I reached toward the GPS located on the dash of my
Escalade, and pressed, *Where to*, then *Points of interest*, then
*Shopping*, then *Home improvement*. The next screen showed
several stores in the Johnson City area, with one of them being a
Farm and Fleet. I figured I could get the necessary supplies
there, so I touched *Farm and Fleet*. Instantly driving directions
started appearing on the GPS.

As I straightened up from touching the screen of the GPS, I
glanced back towards the house. I was sure there was a person
looking out at me from behind the curtain covering the front
window!

Should I go back up to the house door I thought? but
dismissed the idea. If someone were in the house, they would
have known I was knocking on the door, and didn't want to
answer the door, so why would they answer the door if I
knocked again.

I started my vehicle and proceeded to pull away from the
curb. I followed the sweet woman's voice coming from the GPS
for only about ten miles and found myself at the entrance to the
Farm and Fleet parking lot. I entered the parking lot, parked in
the first vacant parking stall I found, exited the vehicle, and
walked towards the front door of the store.

As I entered the store, I grabbed one of the orange shopping
carts that sat near the entrance. I walked a little ways and then
started looking at the large overhead signs showing where
specific merchandise was located. As I was looking upward,

trying to figure out which direction, I should start going, I was startled by a man's voice.

"Can I help you, sir?" the gentlemen asked.

Looking down, I saw a middle-aged man with an orange apron covering his torso.

"You sure can. I'm looking for tarps."

"Tarps are in aisle thirty-seven. Just go straight ahead for three aisles and then turn right. You'll find the tarps about half way down that aisle."

"Thanks," I replied as I started walking the direction he had told me, while I pushed my shopping cart.

I don't know how these people seem to know exactly where everything is located in this huge store, I thought to myself as I turned down the aisle I had been instructed to take. I found the area containing tarps and was looking for a heavy-duty canvas tarp, when once again I was startled by a man's voice.

"Can I help you?" he asked.

This time the speaker was a guy who looked to be in his mid twenties.

"I'm looking for a heavy duty canvas tarp."

"The canvas tarps are down this way," he replied as he started walking farther down the aisle.

"Here they are," he said as he stopped in front a huge selection of just what I was looking for.

"Thanks," I replied as he walked away and I started searching for the size of tarp I wanted. I finally found a tarp with the size eight feet by ten feet printed on the cardboard wrapper. I grabbed the tarp and placed it in my shopping cart.

Now to find the flashlights. Not just any flashlight, but a brilliantly shining one like I had back home. As I craned my neck, looking at the signs stating what was in the aisles I walked down; I once again heard a voice.

"Can I help you find something?" the male's voice asked.

Turning around, I saw an elderly gentleman, decked out in his orange apron.

"I'm looking for a heavy duty, bright flashlight."

"Come on. I'll show you where they're at," he replied as he turned and started walking down the aisle.

I followed him as we made our way through aisle after aisle. I was kind of feeling like a rat in a maze. He finally stopped in front of a large selection of flashlights.

"I'm looking for a flashlight that has a very bright beam," I said as I started scanning the array of flashlights stacked on the shelves.

"Here's a beauty," he said as he reached for a flashlight that looked to be about eighteen inches long.

"This baby has five hundred thousand candle power. You can see a gnat's ass at fifty feet with this one," he said as he proudly handed the flashlight to me.

"It looks almost like the one I have at home, although mine is one million candle power," I said as I looked the flashlight over.

"Whew. You could see a hair on a gnat's ass with that one," he replied as he chuckled.

"Seeing as I'm not going to be looking for hairs on a gnat's ass, I'll take this one," I said as I smiled and placed the flashlight in my shopping cart along with the tarp.

"Need anything else?"

"I have to get a couple of two by fours."

"The lumber is way in the back of the store. Want me to help you find your sticks?" he asked.

"No you don't need to. I think I can find them."

"Thanks a lot for your help," I added.

"No problem. I enjoy doing this and it gets me away from the misses a couple of days a week," he said as he smiled and started walking away.

"Don't forget the batteries for that bad boy. You can find them at the front of the store near the checkout," he said.

"You'll need six D size," he added as he neared the end of he aisle.

"Thanks," I replied as I turned my shopping cart around and started walking back down the aisle towards the lumber section of the store.

I found the lumber section and started looking for the two by fours. I found the two by fours and went to the stack that had a sign above it proclaiming, *two by four- twelve feet*. I started looking through them trying to find two that were fairly straight, when once again I was startled by a voice.

"Can I help you?" a soft woman's voice asked.

Turning around, I saw a petite young lady who stood no more than five foot two inches tall. She had short blonde hair, soft blue eyes, and a huge smile. She wore the same orange apron my other helpers had wore.

"I'm trying to find two, nice straight, twelve footers," I replied.

"Here, let me help you," she said as she grabbed a stick and started pulling it out of the pile.

"Nope, this one could make a ski jump," she said as she laid it aside.

Between the two of us, we finally found two twelve foot two by fours that I figured would serve my purpose.

"I'll take these two," I said as I tried to place one of them on top of my shopping cart.

"Stop that. I'll get a flat bed cart and help you get them to the checkout," she said as she walked away.

114

She shortly returned with a flat bed cart and put the two sticks on it.

"You need anything else?"

"Nope, got everything I need," I replied as she looked into my shopping cart. She must have wondered how a tarp, flashlight, and two by fours went together, but she didn't say anything as she started walking towards the checkout.

As we neared the checkout stations, I spied the rack of batteries I had been informed of.

"Just a sec. I need to get some batteries," I said to the girl who was pushing the cart with my two by fours on it.

"Sure."

I stopped in front of the rack of batteries and searched for D size batteries. I grabbed a package containing eight and dropped them in my shopping cart.

"Got em. Let's go," I said.

We arrived at an open checkout, which I found amazing, and she pushed the flat bed cart containing my wood through as she said, "Two twelve foot two by fours, Marie."

"Have a great day," she said to me as she stopped the flat bed cart next to a wall, turned around and walked passed me back to help some other customer.

I paid for my items, placed the tarp, the bag containing the flashlight and batteries on the flat bed cart, and headed out of the store to my Escalade. By laying down the back seats, and keeping the back hatch door open, I could get the two boards into the vehicle with only about four feet sticking outside. I used a couple of bungee cords I always carry in my vehicle to strap them in place. I found a red flag at the lumber loading area and attached it to the boards. No sense in getting a ticket as I drove back to Kenny's.

I started driving back to Jonesborough with the wood protruding from my vehicle. They seemed to be riding pretty good, so I decided to take a trip around the Family of our Lord compound with the hope I would find just what I was looking for before I went back to Kenny's.

As I drove on the gravel roads surrounding the compound, I was delighted in finding just what I was looking for. In the back corner of the property, the high chain link fence was close to the road. A small grove of oak trees was located about one hundred feet inside the fence. There were no buildings in sight. Perfect! I had my plan, now I just needed some time to pull it off. I completed my surveillance of the property and drove back to Kenny's

As I approached Kenny's house, I saw Martha, Marcie and the girls out front sitting in some lawn chairs. I didn't notice Kenny, though.

I parked in front of the house; Martha waved and started walking over towards me.

"I thought you were going to Spartan College to see if you could find out anything about Angel," she said as she eyed the two by fours sticking out of the back of the Escalade.

"I did," I replied as I walked over and gave her a kiss.

"So, what's with the wood?"

"I'll explain," I replied as I started to undo the bungee cords holding the two by fours and remove them from the Escalade.

"Kenny around?" I asked as I lay the two boards on the ground next to my vehicle.

"He just ran into town to get some things Marcie needed for supper," Martha replied.

"Supper three days from now?"

"Stop that. Kenny was around all day, so Marcie asked him to get some things for her," Martha said in a sharp voice.

"My brother doesn't always act out. He's very nice to Marcie and the girls," she added.

I figured I should keep my mouth shut, so I grabbed the boards and started walking down towards the new pole shed that contained Kenny's workshop, where I deposited them on the ground near the door.

I returned to where the ladies were sitting and grabbed an empty lawn chair.

"Got any Tangueray and tonic?" I asked Marcie.

"Kenny is going to get some while he's in town," she replied.

"I do remember Martha telling me that a Tangueray was your favorite summer drink," she added.

"You're going to be staying for supper, right?" Marcie asked.

"I guess I can. Although Beulah's Diner serves a mighty good spread, I really don't need all that food," I replied as I noticed Kenny's pick up coming up the driveway towards the house. He pulled in front on one of the four garage doors, stopped his truck, and got out.

"Hey, Butch. Got you some Tangueray. I have my hands full with the groceries, so do you want to grab the Tangueray and tonic?"

"You betcha," I replied as I jumped from my chair and started walking towards Kenny.

"I haven't seen you move that fast since you caught your pants leg on fire," Martha said to me as she chuckled.

I heard Marcie ask, "Caught his pants leg on fire?"

"It's a long story. You'll have to have Butch tell you some time," I heard Martha reply.

I reached Kenny's truck, grabbed the liquor store sack from the rear seat, and proceeded to follow Kenny into the house.

"Glasses are in that cupboard, ice is in the frig," Kenny said as he sat his grocery bags on the kitchen counter and pointed to one of the kitchen cupboards.

"Need a shot glass to measure with?"

"Nope," I replied as I reached for the cupboard door, which contained the glasses.

"I've got this measuring down pat," I proudly said as I opened the cupboard door and grabbed a glass.

"Thought so," Kenny replied as he walked over to the refrigerator, opened the door, and grabbed a cold long neck.

I mixed my drink and we both headed back outside to join the ladies.

"Did you put the groceries away?" asked Marcie.

"Don't know where they go," Kenny replied with a grin.

"If you did some of the cooking, you might know where things are," Marcie replied as she rose from her chair and started towards the house door.

"I'll help you," Martha said as she also got up and followed Marcie.

The girls followed along, leaving Kenny and I alone.

"I need your help with some woodworking," I said to Kenny as I looked around to make sure Martha was in the house.

"What kind of woodworking?"

"I need some help in making a pair of stilts," I replied and took a drink out of my glass.

"Stilts! You planning on joining the circus?" Kenny said with a quizzical look on his face.

"No. I ain't joining the circus."

Looking around to make sure the ladies were still in the house, I explained to Kenny what I was planning to do.

"You're flippin crazy!" he exclaimed as I finished my story.

"You're either going to kill yourself or get killed."

"Just don't say anything to Marcie or Martha for a while. I want to make sure my idea will work before they find out," I cautioned.

"No problem. I know my sister would kill you herself if she knew what you had in mind," he said and smiled.

"That's why I don't want her to know just yet."

Kenny and I sat in the chairs long enough to finish our drinks, so we decided to go into the house and grab a couple more.

"Supper's almost ready. Why don't you guys clean up and stay in here," Marcie said as I was making another drink and Kenny was uncapping another beer.

Kenny and I adjourned to the living room while the women put the final touches on supper.

"Time to eat," said Martha as she walked into the living room.

We had a great meal consisting of Swiss steak smothered in a mushroom cream sauce, mashed potatoes, and whole kernel corn.

"I'm almost as stuffed as when I eat at Beulah's Diner," I said as I pushed myself away from the table.

"Thanks," said Marcie as she got up and started picking up the dishes.

"And, I didn't have to cook," I added as I looked at Martha.

"You like to cook and you know I'd cook if you would let me," she said.

"I know. Just giving you crap," I replied as I rose from my chair and followed Kenny back into the living room.

The ladies finally joined us and the two girls went off to their separate bedrooms where they could watch whichever television shows they wanted.

"Why don't you spend the night, here?" Martha asked.

"Why don't you just come on out here and stay all the time, like Martha?" Marcie quickly added.

"The reason Martha is here, is because we saw a couple of guys who seemed to be watching us a few nights back. I didn't want her to be in any danger," I replied.

"If I stay here, they might follow me here."

"Are you sure they could cause harm to Martha or you?" asked Marcie.

"No I'm not. I have no idea who they are, but they were watching me a couple of nights ago as I went back to my room," I said.

"You didn't tell me that," Martha said.

"You didn't ask," I replied with a smirk on my face.

"Yeah, what the heck. We have plenty of room and it makes no sense for you to pay to stay some place. I have enough firepower here that we can protect ourselves with," Kenny quickly added.

"That's why I don't want to put you folks in any danger. Just in case there might be some gun play," I protested.

"We won't be in any danger," Marcie said.

Knowing how I dislike staying with people in their homes, and my reason for not wanting to stay here was not what I was telling Marcie and Kenny, Martha quickly jumped back into the conversation.

"I think it would be a good idea if you stayed here. I miss sleeping next to you," she said as she tried to make it a little more difficult to say no.

"I didn't come here to put you folks out," I protested.

"You're not putting anyone out," Marcie said.

"We hardly ever see you two and now that you're down here, you should at least be kind enough to stay with us," she added.

Sensing that the two women had been planning this maneuver for some time, I decided I might as well quit fighting and accept the invitation to stay there. In fact, it would give Kenny and me some time to start my plan for visiting the Family of our Lord in motion.

"OK. I'll stay tonight and go check out of the Do Drop Inn tomorrow," I said.

"That's great," both Marcie and Martha said in unison.

"As long as you're staying, you might as well have another Tangueray," Kenny said as he got out of his chair.

"I'm having another beer," he added.

"I'm suddenly not sure if Butch staying here is a good idea. He doesn't need any encouragement to drink," Martha said.

"Leave him alone Sis," Kenny said as he headed towards the kitchen with me right in his back pocket. We returned to join the women and started watching some television.

At a commercial break, Martha asked me, "What are those two by fours you had sticking out of the Escalade for?"

"It's just a little project I have in mind," I replied as I shot Kenny a glance.

"You're down here to find out what happened to Angel, not screw around making things," Martha said.

"I'm still working on Angel's disappearance," I said just as the show began again.

"I'll tell you about my little project in due time."

"Whatever," Martha huffed as she went back to watching television. She knew I wasn't going to tell her what was going on right now.

After the 10:00 p.m. news got over, we all retired to our rooms for the night. I figured Martha would continue to grill me about what I was up to, but she didn't say a thing. As Martha drifted off to sleep, I lie there thinking about what I was

121

planning. Could I make it work? What would I find in the Family of our Lord compound if I did pull off my plan? Would Spike be there? Would Angel be there? I still had no answers as I also drifted off to sleep.

# Chapter Fourteen

The following morning, Thursday May 19th, I awoke later than I usually do, 7:00 a.m. Martha was already awake.

"Good morning, beautiful," I said as I patted her on her butt.

"Good morning," she replied as she leaned over in bed and gave me a kiss.

"Alright!"

"Forget it bud. We're not having sex in my brother's house," she replied as she gave me another kiss.

"I thought you wanted me to stay here with you," I replied as I returned her kiss.

"I do, but it's just because I want your company," she replied as she returned my kiss.

"You know we left home eight days ago," I stated as I reached over and started to slide my hand under her sheer nightgown.

"Stop that!" Martha snapped as she slapped my hand.

"Get up and go take a cold shower."

I reluctantly did what I was told to do. I got up, had a warm shower, got dressed, and headed out to the kitchen as Martha was showering. The scene was just like I had dreaded, Marcie, Kenny and the two girls were already sitting around the kitchen table, eating. The girls were babbling the way young girls do, Kenny was reading a newspaper, and Marcie was watching the morning news on the television in the kitchen.

"Good morning, Butch," Marcie said as she took her eyes off the television.

"Morning," Kenny said as he lowered his newspaper slightly and looked over the top.

"Good morning, Uncle Butch," the girls chimed in between mouths full of cereal.

"What can I get you for breakfast?" Marcie asked as a commercial came on the television.

"Nothing. I'll just grab a bowl of cereal and some coffee," I replied as I walked towards the kitchen cupboards.

"Bowls are to your left, cups in the cupboard right in front of you and the silverware in the drawer just to the right of the sink," Marcie said.

I got everything I needed for my breakfast and sat down to eat as Martha entered the kitchen.

"Morning, everybody," she said as she walked over to the cupboard to retrieve a coffee cup and some coffee.

She sat down next to me and inquired, "So, what are you planning for today?"

"I'm going to go into town and check out of the Do Drop Inn, then Kenny and I are going to work on that little wood project I told you about," I replied.

"I just wish you would just tell me what you are going to be making," she said.

"When we're finished, I'll let you know," I replied and began eating my bowl of cereal.

After finishing breakfast, I got up from the kitchen table and started towards the front door of the house so I could go into town, retrieve my things from the Do Drop Inn, and get started on my project.

"I'm going into town and retrieve my things. Do you want to give me a hand with my project when I get back?" I asked Kenny, who was still reading the newspaper.

"Ah, what? Oh sure. I'll give you a hand," Kenny replied from behind the newspaper.

I left the house, drove into town, and parked along side the curb in front of the Do Drop Inn. I grabbed the Plexiglas attached key from under the front seat of the Escalade and made my way to my room. I retrieved all of my belongings, placed them in my vehicle, and started towards the front door of the inn. When I opened the door, the little bell tinkled as usual. I spied the fur ball cat lounging on the window sill and proceeded to the counter. Bubba's aunt emerged from the curtained doorway behind the counter.

"Can I help you, Mr. Brogen?" she asked.

"I would like to check out."

"You've found Angel?" she asked excitedly.

"No, I haven't maam. But, I've been coerced into staying at my brother-in-laws house for the rest of the time I'm here," I replied as I rolled my eyes.

"That's good. A person should stay with family whenever they can. You never know when your maker is going to call. Too many people just ignore relatives," she said as she retrieved a receipt book from under the counter.

"I hope you've enjoyed your stay here."

"I sure have. I'll stay here the next time I'm in town. That's if I don't have to stay with the in-laws."

"Let's see. You had the room for six days. At twenty-seven dollars a day, that would be one-hundred-sixty-two dollars," she said as she was writing in the receipt book.

"You wouldn't possibly have the correct change?" she asked as she tore a page out of the receipt book and handed it to me.

"I think I might," I replied as I reached for my money clip.

I took five twenty-dollar bills and two fifty-dollar bills out of my clip and handed them to her.

"Here's two-hundred dollars. Give the maid a tip."

"Thank you so much Mr. Brogen," she replied as she gave me a smile.

"And the maid thanks you too," she added knowing that I knew she was the maid.

"I hope you find that poor girl before you leave us."

"So do I maam," I replied as I walked towards the front door keeping an eye on the mangy fur ball that had jumped off the windowsill and started walking towards me. I managed to make it out of the door without the hairy fur ball rubbing up against my leg, so I felt good. Now to get back to Kenny's and get started on my project.

I drove back to Kenny's house, ready to get started. I happened to see Kenny come around the corner of one of the sheds as I got out of my vehicle, and started walking towards him.

"Hi, Kenny. You ready to give me a hand?" I asked as I neared him.

"Sure thing, although I think you're going to kill yourself or get killed," he replied.

"I've heard that before. Now let's get started," I said as I started walking towards the two by fours I placed in front of Kenny's shop.

As we were carrying the boards into his shop, I asked, "Do you have any two by four stubs we could make foot holds out of? I only bought these two sticks."

"Sure. I got plenty of scrap lumber that we can use," he replied.

We then proceeded to cut and taper several pieces of wood that could be placed on my two by fours, creating foot holds. We placed the footholds eight feet up on the two by fours.

"Whoa. Those foot holds look mighty high. How in the hell are you going to get up on them?" Kenny asked after we had finished attaching the footholds with three-inch deck screws, which he had in his shop.

"I've got an idea," I replied as I started wondering if my idea was a good one or not.

"Now, lets take these babies out to the big elm tree behind your shop," I said.

"Why the tree?"

"Just wait and see. I think my idea is going to work," I replied.

"You sure these thing are going to get you into the Family of our Lord's compound?" Kenny asked.

"If they work, getting in won't be much of a problem, but getting out could be dicey," I replied as we each carried a two by four out of the shop and down to the big elm tree.

"This is something I gotta see in comfort. I'm going to get a lawn chair so I can sit and watch you break your fool neck," Kenny said as we reached the elm tree.

While Kenny went to find a lawn chair, I walked over to the elm tree with a stilt in each hand. I backed up to the tree, pressing my back firmly against it. Taking the right silt, I placed it out in front of me, jabbing it firmly into the ground. I did the same with the left stilt. I then carefully put my right foot on the foot hold of the right stilt, straightened my leg slightly as I kept pressured on my back against the tree. I then slowly did the same with my left leg. I was now wedged between the tree and the stilts that stuck out eight feet in front of me, wedged firmly in the ground.

As I stayed in my wedged position, Kenny returned.

"What the hell are you doing?" he asked as he placed his lawn chair on the ground and sat down.

127

"I'm getting on my stilts," I replied as I stayed wedged against the tree.

"How are you going to get standing up?"

"I figure that if I keep my back wedged against the tree and the stilts stuck into the dirt, I can slowly scoot myself up the tree until I get high enough to stand up."

"Ain't gonna work, bro," said Kenny as he took a sip of the beer he had brought along with the lawn chair.

"It has to. I need to get up on these suckers," I replied as I slowly moved my right stilt a little closer to me and inched my back up the tree.

Just then, Kayla and Karla appeared from around the corner of the shed.

"What are you doing Uncle Butch?" Kayla asked.

"Killing himself," Kenny responded and took another drink of beer.

"I'm trying to stand up on these stilts," I replied.

"Why?" Karla asked.

"I've always wanted to do this, so I thought today would be a good time."

"Whatever," she replied as both girls started walking away.

"Why aren't you girls in school?" I asked.

"Tomorrow is our last day, so we were let out early today," Kayla replied as the girls continued walking away.

By now I was getting tired wedged in my position, so I slowly started inching my way up the tree again. I had slowly progressed up the tree about three feet, with the stilts still on my feet, when the right stilt gave way and I slid down the tree, scrapping my back as I went.

"Son of a bitch!" I exclaimed as I hit the ground at the base of the tree.

"You OK, Butch?' Kenny asked as he jumped out of his lawn chair and came over to me.

"I think I scrapped the shit out of my back," I replied as I reached around to try to touch my back, which was already starting to burn.

"No shit, bro. You got some major scrapes there," Kenny offered as he lifted my tee shirt and looked at my back.

"Want me to get something to put on those scrapes?"

"No. I don't want Martha to know what I'm up to just yet," I replied as I grimaced, and backed up to the tree again.

I tried several more times to get erect on the stilts, but the results were always the same. I slid down the damn tree!!

By now my back was hurting so much it felt like raw hamburger!

"Why don't you put small footholds every foot on the inside of each stilt. You could just walk up them," Kenny said.

"Why in the hell didn't you come up with this idea before I scrapped the shit out of my back?" I asked as I sat dejectedly on the ground in front of the tree.

"You didn't ask," Kenny replied as he smiled and took another drink of beer.

"Let's go put those steps on and let me try them while I can still move," I said.

"Sure thing."

We went into Kenny's shop and attached two by four stubs on the inside of my stilts every foot until we reached the footholds. We grabbed the stilts and headed back down to the big elm tree.

"OK, now you're going to have to back up against the tree, hold the stilts upright and with your back pressed against the tree, gently place each foot on one of the small steps, and make your way to the top of the stilts," Kenny said.

"My back hurts too shitten much to place it against the tree anymore," I whined.

"You're the fool who wanted to do this, so just try it," Kenny said.

Just then, the two girls appeared once again.

"Still trying to get on your stilts, Uncle Butch?" Karla asked.

"Yep, still trying and I think I'm going to get it this time," I replied as I once again backed up to the tree.

The girls left, probably because they didn't want to see me break my neck.

As I pressed my body against the tree, I slowly started placing my right foot on the first step. I then place my left foot on the first step of the other stilt. I was now standing on each stilt with my back pressed up against the tree. I gingerly placed my right foot on the next step, and then the left foot on the next step.

I was now two feet off the ground with my back still pressed against the tree. My back hurt like shit from all the scrapes, but I was going to master these stilts!

"Where's your dad and Uncle Butch?" Martha asked the girls as they came into the house.

"Uncle Butch is trying to get up on some stilts and daddy is watching him," Kayla replied.

"He's what!"

"He's trying to walk on stilts," Karla said.

"Where's he at?" He's an idiot!" Martha exclaimed as she bolted towards the front door of the house.

I had slowly made my way up to the seven foot mark on the stilts using the steps Kenny had suggested when I heard a familiar voice screaming at me.

"Butch Brogen, what the hell are you trying to do?" Martha screamed.

As I turned toward the sound of her voice, my arm let go of the top of my left stilt and I started to fall.

Now, the fall from seven feet isn't that bad, but the landing can suck. Gathering all the police training I could remember, I tried to hit the ground with both feet and tuck and roll. After landing, tucking and rolling, I lay in a prone position on my back and slowly moved my appendages to see if any of them were broken. After verifying that all my parts moved, I collected myself and sat up, feeling fortunate that the twelve-foot stilts hadn't hit me on the head when I fell.

I quickly glanced over to where Kenny sat; hoping one of the two by fours hadn't hit him either. He was standing along side of his lawn chair, beer in hand and a smile on his face. One of the boards lay about three feet from the chair, so it must have come close to him.

"What the hell are you doing?" Martha once again screamed

Knowing that Martha very seldom swears, I figured out that I might be in deep shit.

Since I had known Martha, I had only heard her swear twice, and both times, it was at me. Both times, I was in deep shit!

"Trying to walk on stilts, dear," I said as I stood up, brushed my shorts off, and felt relieved nothing seemed broken.

"Yeah, he's gonna join the circus," Kenny said as he reveled in the fact I was getting my butt chewed.

"Do you realize that you swore at me?" I asked Martha.

"You're lucky that's all I did. Now put those damn stilts away and come into the house. Supper is just about ready," she huffed as she turned and walked away.

"Sucks to be you," Kenny said as I gathered my two stilts and started walking toward Kenny's workshop

131

I placed my stilts on the floor of Kenny's workshop and joined him for the walk to the house.

"I had them almost nailed. I would have too, if Martha hadn't scared me," I said to Kenny as we walked along.

"Yep, you were almost there. But, I enjoyed watching you take a digger more than I would have if you had made it to the top step," Kenny said.

"Thanks for the sympathy."

We reached the house and went in, with me looking around to see if I could see Martha.

"You guys might as well get washed up for supper, then come and eat," Marcie said from the kitchen as she heard us walk into the house.

I started walking towards one of the bathrooms, when Kenny stopped me.

"Whoa. You had better go get a clean tee shirt on before Martha sees you. You've got quite a bit of blood showing through the back your shirt."

"Thanks," I replied as I headed towards the bedroom, which contained my suitcase full of clothes.

Martha would discover the bloodstained shirt soon enough, so I didn't need to make a scene about it right now. I reached the bedroom and gingerly tried pulling the tee shirt up over my head. My back felt like it was on fire from all the scrapes, but I managed to get my shirt off and a new one on. I went to the bathroom, washed the dirt off my face, hands, and arms, and returned to the kitchen.

We all sat down around the table and began to eat. I had to lean forward in my chair a little, so as not to put too much pressure on my back, which was still burning like a son of a gun.

Martha kept giving me little glances the entire time we were eating. I didn't know if she could tell I was sitting tenderly or if she had noticed the clean tee shirt I was wearing. Could be she was just pissed at me!

We finished eating and Kenny and I headed into the living room. Kenny turned on the television and we started watching the evening news.

"You know Martha's going to see your scrapped back tonight when you guys go to bed," Kenny said.

"What scrapped back?" asked Martha as her and Marcie appeared in the doorway.

Giving Kenny a 'you dumb shit' look, I said, "I must have scrapped my back a little when I fell."

"You're lucky you didn't break your neck," Martha said as she walked over to me.

"Let me see your back."

"It's nothing. Just a little scrap," I replied, as I stayed seated on the sofa.

"You've already made me mad once today, so don't go trying for two," she said as she stopped in front of me with her hands on her hips.

I glanced at Kenny, who grinned and shrugged as if to say 'What did I tell you.'

Knowing that I had no other choice, I stood up and slowly started lifting my tee shirt up as I turned my back towards Martha.

"My god! Your back looks like it was whipped with barbed wire," Martha exclaimed when she saw my back.

"What on earth did you do?" she demanded as Marcie walked over and also took a look at my back.

"Ouch," was all she said.

"Do you have some hydrogen peroxide, cotton balls, and salve?" Martha asked Marcie as she continued to stare at my back.

133

"You haven't answered me," she demanded as she grabbed my shoulder and turned me around, facing her.

"You haven't given me time. You've been too busy chewing my butt."

Knowing that I was going to have to tell Martha about my plan to visit the Family of our Lord compound, I quickly added, "As soon as you get done with my back, I'll tell you what I plan on doing."

Marcie returned with the items Martha had asked for and I was instructed to take my tee shirt off and sit on one of the footstools.

I quickly obeyed, even though I knew what was about to transpire was going to hurt like heck. I was right! Martha swabbed my back with the peroxide as I tried not to yell out in pain. I knew that if I said anything, she would just get madder at me. After several minutes, which seemed liked several hours, Martha finished swabbing down the scrapes on my back and applied the salve, which felt soothing.

"Now put your shirt on and tell me what's going on," Martha said as she sat her items of torture on the coffee table.

I noticed that Kenny's grin had gotten a lot wider as I started to explain my plan. I explained that I was going to go into the Reverend Jones's compound and see what I could find. I explained how I was going to get into and out of the compound and what I was hoping to find. When I had finished, I looked over to Martha, who said, "You're an idiot. You are either going to kill yourself or get killed."

"That's exactly the words I used," Kenny chimed in with.

"Stay out of this, Kenny," I snapped.

"We're both right, you know," Martha said.

"I've got everything covered. I'm extremely careful when I go out searching for clues. Nothing will happen."

"Just like nothing happened when you went to meet a deranged killer on a golf course," she said as she was thinking back to a case that I had been involved with several years ago.

"Mister, I have everything under control, got his head smashed with a garden shovel and darned near died," Martha said to Kenny and Marcie.

"I survived, that's all that matters; besides I told Bubba and Bertha that I would do my best in trying to find Angel. And my best means that I have to check out the Rev's compound," I firmly stated.

"If you have to get into the compound, why don't you just use a couple of Kenny's ladders?" Martha asked.

"Because I don't want to leave anything leaning against the fence while I'm in the compound. Someone might see it," I replied.

"You wouldn't have to leave the ladder leaning on the fence," Martha said.

"How's that?"

"Once you're on top of the fence, just lift the ladder up and over the fence. Lean it against the fence on the inside so you could just walk down it. You could then lay the ladder in the grass along side of the fence," she said.

"Even if I used an aluminum ladder, the weight of it and my weight might be enough to put enough pressure on the tarp so the barbed wire could poke up through the tarp. Thus, poking the shit out of me," I replied as I was getting a little annoyed having to explain everything to Martha.

"Now, let's forget about this for now, enjoy the evening and we'll see what happens tomorrow," I said as I tried to stop the discussion of my plan.

"Sounds good to me," Kenny replied as he started to get out of his chair.

"I'm getting a beer. Want a Tangueray, Butch?"

"As sore as my back is, I might have three or four," I replied as I also got up and gingerly followed Kenny to the kitchen.

We all watched television until it was time to hit the sack. I was dreading the tongue-lashing I was probably going to get once Martha and I reached the bedroom. As Martha was in the bathroom, I got out of my clothes and slowly lay down in bed on my stomach.

"Back hurts too much to lie on?" Martha asked as she came out of the bathroom.

"Yep," I replied as I slowly lifted my head and saw Martha standing almost naked, wearing only her pink panties. No nightgown! Her tall slim body showing a slight golden glow from the early summer sunshine she had been soaking up while swimming nude in her swimming pool at home. She was holding the jar of salve in her right hand.

This might turn out better than I thought, I thought to myself.

"Are we going to have some fun?" I asked as I slowly rolled over on my back.

"Get back on your stomach," Martha commanded.

Lying on my back hurt so much that I was more than happy to oblige her on this occasion.

"Let me put some more salve on your back for you. That might make it feel better," she said as she crawled onto the bed, straddled her legs on either side of my butt, and sat down.

"Whoa. Is this how Clara Barton took care of her patients?"

"Shut up and just relax."

As Martha slowly rubbed more salve on my back, she would lean forward and gently swing her boobs so they caressed my back.

"Oh, that feels good," I moaned.

"The salve or my boobs?" she asked.

"Both."

"Well don't get any ideas. As I told you before, we are not having sex in my brother's house," she replied and she continued to apply salve and massage my back with her boobs.

"There, that should do it," Martha said as she got off me, crawled onto her side of the bed, wiped her hands on a towel she had brought from the bathroom and put the salve on the night stand.

"I know something else that would make my back feel even better," I pleaded.

"Forget get it," she replied as she pulled the covers over her almost naked body, leaving me outside of the covers with my back exposed to the cool air.

Well, I hope tomorrow goes this smooth, I thought to myself as I tried to forget about what I was missing, get comfortable and fall asleep.

## Chapter Fifteen

I woke up the following morning, lying on my back and it didn't hurt as much as I had feared. It's going to be a good day, I thought. Martha was still asleep, so I quietly climbed out of bed and headed towards the bathroom. The morning shower water was not the most pleasant feeling I had ever experienced as it hit my very tender back. After showering and getting dressed, I went into the kitchen where Kenny and Marcie sat around the kitchen table, drinking coffee.

"You don't look like you're too sore," Kenny said as I walked into the kitchen, grabbed a coffee cup out of the cupboard, and walked over to the coffee pot.

"I don't hurt as much as I thought I would, although the hot shower water didn't feel so great," I replied as I filled my coffee cup and walked over to the table to join them.

"So is Martha still pissed?" Kenny asked.

"She's still sleeping, but she had mellowed by the time we got into bed last night," I replied as I took a sip of my coffee.

I didn't mention anything about how she had applied salve to my sore back!

"Are you still going to try to walk on those stilts?" Kenny asked.

"You bet. In order for me to get in and out of the compound, I need to master those babies," I replied.

"Master what babies?" asked Martha as she entered the kitchen looking as perky as usual.

Kenny glanced at me with a smile on his face as Martha stopped next to my chair.

"Do you want me to get you some coffee?" I asked Martha.

"Yes, I'm going to have coffee, but first you're going to tell me what you're going to master," she replied as she sat down in the chair next to Marcie.

"It's not those stupid stilts is it?" she quickly asked.

"I'll just get your coffee and we'll talk about my plan."

"Gonna get your ass chewed again," Kenny whispered to me as I walked over to the coffee pot.

I filled Martha's coffee cup and walked over to the table where she was sitting next to Marcie. I sat the coffee cup down in front of here and returned to my chair.

"Thanks," she said.

"I know what you told me yesterday, but you're not really going to use those stupid stilts and try to get into the Family of our Lord's compound, are you?" she asked.

"Yep. I believe that's the only way I can get in and out without being seen," I replied.

"So you get in. What happens if there's a pack of dogs patrolling the compound?" Kenny asked.

"I never saw any dogs the day Martha and I were there," I replied.

"Doesn't mean there aren't any."

"Kenny's right, you know. What are you going to do if you're attacked by a pit bull or something?" Martha asked.

"You're sure a lot of help," I said as I gave Kenny a dirty look.

"I'm going to have my 9mm Glock with me. It will stop any dog that might want to get too close," I replied with a small smirk on my face.

"Yeah, and wake up every one of the disciples," Kenny said.

"How about getting some of that dog repellant, spray mace?" he asked.

"I never thought of that. That would be better than making a lot of noise."

"You don't have to be helping him so much," Martha snapped at Kenny.

"He's going in, whether I help him or not," Kenny quickly said.

"I'm just trying to come up with some ideas so that he will be able to make it out," he added.

Just then, the two girls appeared and we changed the conversation. We all either had cereal or toast with peanut butter for breakfast and then I got away from the table and started walking towards the front door.

"Where are you going?" Martha asked.

"To practice," I replied and continued walking as Kenny quickly fell in behind me.

"I gotta see this," he said as we reached the front door.

Martha must have decided that I was going to do what I was going to do and never said another word as Kenny and I left the house. We went down to Kenny's shop and retrieved the stilts from where I had placed them and once again headed over to the big elm tree.

The next four mornings found me practicing getting on and off my stilts and golfing in the afternoons. Every morning, Kenny was sitting in his lawn chair watching and giving encouragement. When I came home from golfing, he was still around the place, doing some yard work or something else. He must either be enjoying watching my try to kill myself, or none of his dollies were available. Martha was becoming more acclimated to the idea of me checking out Reverend Jones, although I knew she wasn't too happy with my plan.

I returned from golfing, Monday afternoon, May 23 to see Kenny once again at home. He was sitting in a lawn chair in front of the house, sipping on a beer. I parked the Escalade, got out, and walked over to Kenny.

"It's Tangueray time," he said as he hoisted his beer bottle sky ward.

"You darn right it is," I replied as I walked towards the front door of the house. I entered and walked to the kitchen. Marcie and Martha were doing a jigsaw puzzle on the kitchen table.

"Hi, Hon," Martha said as she looked up at me.

"Hi," I said as I bent down and gave her a kiss.

"Hi, Marcie," I then said.

"Hi, Butch. How was golf?"

"Oh, I can tell you don't know 'mister who gets upset with his golf game'," Martha quickly said.

"You never want to ask him how his game went. It will be less stressful for you, if you let him eventually tell you about his round," she added.

"I'm not that bad," I quickly responded.

"Whatever," replied Martha as I mixed myself a drink, and started towards the front door.

I walked over to where Kenny sat, grabbed an empty lawn chair, and sat down.

"I went into town today and bought you some of that dog repellant," Kenny said.

"You didn't need to. I could have got some."

"What do I owe you?"

"Nothing. It's not like I don't have a few bucks to spend," he replied as he smiled at me.

"Well, it looks like I have everything that I need for my excursion, then. I have a backpack I bought in town, loaded with my flashlight, a lock picking kit, which I always have in the

Escalade, and a pair of leather gloves. I'll just add the dog repellant you got me and I'm good to go," I said.

"I think I'm as good as I'm going to get on those stilts, so I think I will venture into the Reverend's compound tonight," I said as I took a sip of my drink.

"You taking your gun?" Kenny asked even though he already knew the answer.

"Yep. I have my 9mm Glock in the holster locked in the glove box of the Escaladed.

"You tell Martha yet?"

"Nope. I thought I would wait as long as possible before I told her I was going. Less time for a family blowup," I said.

"Just what are you looking for?"

"I don't know. Just anything which might lead me closer to figuring out why Angel disappeared and where she disappeared to," I said.

"You really think Reverend Jones had something to do with her disappearance?" he asked.

"At this point, I don't know what I think. I just need to check out his compound to satisfy my curiosity if nothing else," I replied.

"Need another drink?" he asked as he rose from his chair.

"I had better not. Tonight's going to be tough enough without the influence of alcohol," I replied.

Kenny went into the house as I sat and thought about what I was going to finally do. I've gotten fairly good walking on the stilts. Would it be good enough to pull my stunt off? Would there be dogs around? Would there be hostile family members?

I was broken from my thoughts when Kenny reappeared.

"The ladies said we're having home made pizza tonight and it would be ready in about one half hour," he said as he sat back down in his lawn chair.

"You sure you want to go through with this?" he asked as he sipped on his beer.

"I have to. I told Bubba and Bertha I would do my best to try to find Angel. If I don't get into that compound, I won't be doing my best," I replied.

"I figured as much. If you want me to do anything to help, just let me know," he said.

"Thanks, but I have to do this on my own."

We sat there in silence until we were called for supper, and then went into the house. The pizza was great, although I just drank water instead of the beer I usually drink whenever I have pizza. I saw Martha looking at me several times, but she didn't say anything. I'm sure she must know that I'm going tonight. Why else would I forgo a good beer with my pizza?

Everyone ate their fill, Kenny and I adjourned to the living room while the ladies cleaned up the mess.

"Need help loading your stuff?" Kenny asked as we sat down in the living room.

"I have everything but the stilts in my vehicle already, but if you want to help with them, that's OK," I replied.

"Let's do it then before the women come in," he said.

I'm sure he knew what his sisters' reaction would be once she realized that I was going to actually carry out my plan.

We went outside and down to his workshop where my stilts were laying against the outside wall, picked them up and carried them back to the Escalade. I opened the back door, we placed the stilts inside, and I tied them down with bungee cords just as I had done to carry the two by fours home. Kenny went to his pick up, retrieved the dog repellant, and gave it to me.

"Hope you don't have to use this," he said as he handed it to me.

"Me too. I'm not too fond of some vicious dog trying to grab my ass," I replied as I placed the can of repellant in my backpack.

Just then, the front door of the house opened and Marcie and Martha stepped out.

"What's going on?" Martha asked as she walked closer to where Kenny and I stood next to the Escalade.

"Just loading some things," I replied as I noticed her looking at the stilts sticking out of the back of the Escalade.

"You're going there tonight," she said as she walked over to me and laid her head on my chest.

"Yep. Tonight is a waxing moon, giving me a little more darkness to maneuver in," I replied as I stoked her hair.

"Any chance you would reconsider?" she asked as she lifted her head off my chest and looked me in the eyes.

I detected small tears forming in her eyes, but tried not to be influenced by them.

"I need to get into that compound. I could find something that would help us find Angel," I replied.

"Besides, Bubba paid me money to find his sister-in-law," I said as I lifted her head and gave her a kiss.

"I should never have given him your PayPal account user name," she said as she sighed.

"Ah heck, I probably would have told him that I would have helped him, even if you hadn't done that," I said as I wiped a tear off her cheek.

"Now, lets go inside for awhile. I want it to get a little darker before I start my journey."

The four of us walked into the house and went to the living room where the girls were watching television.

"Time for bed girls," Marcie said as we walked into the room.

"Only ten minutes left in the show, mama. Let us finish watching it out here on the big screen in stead of the little screens in our bedroom," Kayla whined.

"Little screen. The televisions in your bedrooms are thirty-six. Most kids wouldn't consider that small," Kenny said as he sat down.

"Please," pleaded Karla.

"OK, just till the end of this show," Marcie said.

The television show ended, the girls got up, gave all of us a goodnight kiss, and headed off to their bedrooms.

The four of us sat and watched the next television show. Nobody spoke and I doubt if any of us really knew what was going on in the show. At 10:00 p.m., I got up and walked into the bedroom, put on a pair of blue jeans, a black tee shirt, and my tennis shoes. Although the tennis shoes were white, they were quite dirty so I figured that they wouldn't stand out. I walked back into the living room, over to the front door, opened it, and looked out into the night. It was fairly dark. Time for me to go. I walked back into the living room and glanced at everyone. Without saying a word, they knew I was about to leave.

"Good luck, Bro," Kenny said.

"Be careful Butch," added Marcie.

Martha got up from the couch, walked over to me and gave me a big hug.

"You be careful," she said as she gave me a kiss. I once again noticed tears in her eyes.

"I will," I replied as I gave her a kiss, pulled away from her and started towards the front door. Standing there would only make things worse. I opened the door and stepped out into the slightly muggy, warm May evening. I could hear the cicadas and katydids chirping in the distance darkness. I walked to the

Escalade, got in without turning around to look back at the house where I knew Martha was standing in the doorway. I started the engine, put my vehicle in gear, and started to drive down the driveway. It was now time!

I hoped my idea of how to get into and out of the compound would work. I hoped my practice on the stilts would pay off enough to make this work. I hoped I didn't run into any dogs. I hoped I didn't meet up with any of the occupants of the compound. I hoped I would find something that might lead me to find out where Angel was.

# Chapter Sixteen

I drove down Kenny's driveway and turned left onto the county road leading to the Family of our Lord's compound. I drove past the entrance to the compound at a normal rate of speed, so as not to arouse any suspicion and continued to the first gravel road on my left. I turned down the gravel road, knowing it would take me to the back of the compound. I drove to the next gravel road on my left and turned onto it. I now started driving slowly, as not to miss the spot I had previously determined to be my entrance point. Shortly, I saw the grove of trees I had figured would be where I wanted to enter the compound.

I stopped my vehicle, left the engine running, got out and slowly looked around. I saw nothing, and only heard the sharp sounds of the Katydids filtering through the still night air. I went to the rear of my vehicle and removed the stilts. I carried them across the road and lay them next to the eight-foot tall chain link fence. I then returned to my vehicle, picked up the tarp, which I had previously rolled into a bedroll. When unrolled the tarp would be a four by four square, several layers thick. I carried it over to where the stilts were, and laid it down. I once again returned to my vehicle and then slowly drove down the road for about one-quarter mile, where I saw the field entrance off to my right that I had found on my previous visit. I cut the headlights of the Escalade and pulled into the entrance. Shutting off the engine, I opened the driver's door and listened. No sounds, but the insects of the night.

I unlocked the glove box of the Escalade and removed my holstered Glock. Sure hope I don't have to use this, I thought as I stood outside the vehicle, checked to make sure it was loaded and strapped the holster over my shoulder. I then went to the back, left door of the vehicle, opened the door and removed my backpack. I unzipped the backpack and looked inside just to make sure that I had everything. My five-hundred thousand-candle power flashlight was there along with a smaller flashlight, which I thought I might need. My lock picking kit, the dog repellant, my leather gloves, and a small coil of one-quarter inch sisal rope, which I had purchased at the local hardware store in Jonesborough. I put the backpack over my shoulders; made sure the car was locked and started walking back down the road to where I had left my stilts and tarp.

As I neared the area of my stilts, I once again looked around and was relieved to see nothing. The waxing moon was a dim glow in the sky, not even giving me much light to see things with. I took the backpack off, opened it up, and removed the small flashlight. That would give me enough light to see well enough to get my stilts positioned without using the big light.

Holding the small flashlight in my mouth, I removed the coil of rope from the backpack and tied one end around the rolled tarp. Still holding the flashlight in my mouth, I propped the stilted against the chain link fence. I turned the flashlight off and placed it back into my backpack. I removed my cell phone from the right front pocket of my pants and turned it to the vibrate mode. I had instructed Martha not to call me, but you never know when you might get a wrong number. I didn't need *Waltzing Matilda* screaming out into the darkness. I placed my cell phone back into my pocket, removed the leather gloves from the backpack, and put them on. I put the backpack on, placed the rolled tarp at the bottom of my stilts, uncoiled some rope off the coil of rope I was holding, and looped it over my neck. Not the smartest move, considered that if I would fall, I could be chocked to death even if the fall didn't hurt me.

I slowly backed up to the fence, grabbed a hold of each stilt, and slowly started stepping up the cleats Kenny and I had put on the stilts. After what seemed like an eternity, I reached the footholds at the eight-foot mark of my stilts. I was still standing!

My body was now teetering above the chain link fence and the barbed wire located on top. I slowly started pulling up the rope attached to the tarp. I was slightly weaving back and forth, as I pulled the tarp nearer to me. I finally had the tarp at arms length and took a hold of it. I slowly turned my body without moving the stilts and laid the tarp bedroll on top of the barbed wire, which protruded towards the inside of the compound. I then gently grabbed each stilt and slowly moved them in a clockwise rotation until I was facing forward towards the compound. I let go of the stilts, slowly removed the rope from around my neck, and then untied it from the tarp. I coiled the rope up as well as I could and laid it on the barbed wire. I then slowly unrolled the tarp and placed it on top of the barbed wire. So far so good!

Placing my hands on the tarp, which covered the barbed wire, I slowly lifted myself to where I was kneeling on the tarp. Thank goodness, the stilts had stayed rested against the fence when I got off them. I now reached around behind me, grabbed the right stilt and lifted it up until I could place it on the other side of the compound, resting it on the edge of the barbed wire. I repeated the same actions with the left stilt. I now had both stilts resting against the barbed wire section on top of the fence that sloped inward toward the compound. I slowly crawled the three feet to the edge of the barbed wire, hoping the tarp would keep the barbs from poking into me.

Upon reaching the edge of the barbed wire, I made a decision that might turn out to be painful. I brought my legs up under me and sat down on the barbed wire, with my legs hanging over the edge. I was relieved the barbed wire didn't poke through the tarp into my butt! I took hold of the stilts, slowly put my feet on the eight-foot footholds, and eased myself onto them. I was now standing inside of the compound, eight feet in the air on a pair of stilts. I hadn't thought about it much before, but this might not be the best idea I've ever had. Leaving the tarp in place, so I could use it as I exited the compound, I slowly started walking the one-hundred feet to one of the big trees in the grove that I had located earlier.

I reached the tree without falling, dropped my backpack to the ground, and slowly turned around, pressing my back against the tree. Using the technique I had developed practicing at Kenny's, I inched my way down the stilts. When my feet touched the ground, I breathed out a small sigh of relief. I was now in Reverend Jones' Family of our Lord compound! I hadn't broken my neck or anything.

I laid the stilts down as the base of the tree, picked up my backpack and began my journey towards the buildings on the compound. Because the night was fairly dark, I had to bring out my big flashlight to illuminate the way as I made my way forward. I didn't want too much light shining in the darkness, but I had to find my way. As I exited the small wood plot, I approached a cornfield. If this would be in July or August, the corn would be tall enough for me to walk through hidden. Because this was May, the corn was only ankle high, leaving me totally exposed as I made my way towards the warehouse sized buildings I could see in the distance.

I finally made it to the buildings located inside the compound. I looked around and once again was relieved I saw no one.

I walked over to the first white painted building. It was a wood structure, which seemed to be about thirty feet by sixty feet. I stopped, listened, and looked around. Nothing seemed to be moving. I walked around the building until I found a door. It was locked with a hasp and padlock. Sweet! I could pick most padlocks in several seconds. I now turned off my big flashlight, removed my backpack and unzipped it. I took off my gloves, placed them and my big flashlight into the backpack, while I removed the little flashlight and my lock pick kit. Once again, I held the flashlight in my mouth while removing the picking tool I would need. In several seconds, I heard a distinct click. The padlock was open! I removed the padlock from the hasp, slowly pushed the door open, and stepped inside.

I removed the big flashlight from my backpack, put the small flashlight, and lock pick kit into the backpack. I switched on the big flashlight with the hope that there weren't many windows on the building that would let the ray of my light out. I stood still and panned the room. Large bundles of something wrapped in shrink-wrap sat on pallets all over the floor of the building. I walked over to the first bundle, shined the light on it, and took a close look. The shrink-wrap blurred whatever was wrapped up, so I decided to make a small slit in the shrink wrap to see if I could tell what was inside.

I laid the flashlight on top of the bundle, removed my small penknife from my pants pocket, walked around to the back of the bundle and made a two-foot slit in the shrink-wrap. I put the knife back into my pocket, grabbed a hold of the wrap on either side of the slit, and pried the wrap apart giving me a glimpse of what was inside. Cigarettes! Cartons and cartons of cigarettes.

I walked over to one of the other bundles and cut it open, just as I had done the first one. More cigarettes! Looking closely at one of the cartons I could clearly see, I tried to find a tax stamp. I couldn't see any!

There must have been over one hundred of these bundles sitting around this warehouse. Therefore, the good Reverend must be dealing in bootleg cigarettes!

I decided to check out one of the other buildings, so I walked to the door, opened it, and peered out. Everything was still quiet, so I turned off the flashlight and stepped outside. I closed the padlock on the hasp and looked around for another building to check out. There was another building of about the same size as this one, located a couple of hundred feet to my right. I could make out the outline of a door, so I headed towards it. Upon reaching the door, I saw it was also padlocked just like the building I had left. I laid my big flashlight on the ground, grabbed the little one and my lock pick kit out of the backpack, and once again went to work. Just as with the first padlock, this one popped open in several seconds. I placed the little flashlight and pick kit in my backpack, picked up my big flashlight, removed the padlock from the hasp and slowly opened the door. I stepped inside, closed the door behind me, and switched on my flashlight.

There were no big bundles in this building, but there were stacks of wooden crates sitting on pallets throughout the building. I walked over to where one pile of crates sat and saw that the crates had no printing or markings on them. The crates were stacked four feet high on the pallets. I grabbed what looked like a lid on the top crate and lifted. It didn't give an inch! The lid felt like it was fastened securely. I had to see what was inside one of these crates, but how do I get the lid off? I wasn't prepared for this development. If I had only brought some sort of a pry bar, but who knew I would want to look inside a wooden crate with the top securely fastened. I panned the flashlight around the building. The light revealed many more crates stacked on pallets, but nothing I could use to open a crate.

As I panned the light around the room, my eyes caught what I thought was a glint of metal. I quickly moved the light beam back to where I thought I had saw something. I was right! Leaning against one of the building walls was a crow bar! How lucky can a guy get? The Reverend Jones has supplied me with a way to get into one of the crates.

I went over to the crowbar, picked it up and walked to the nearest crate. I looked the top of the crate over and discovered that it looked like it was just nailed on, not screwed. I laid my flashlight on the lid and slowly started prying on it with the newly found crowbar. I slowly inched my way around the crate, prying on the lid every few inches. After what seemed like an hour of prying, I finally had the lid loose enough to lift off. I took the flashlight off the lid, laid it on the floor, and lifted on the lid. It came loose; I took it off and leaned it against the end of the stack of crates. As I picked up my flashlight from the floor, excitement flooded my body. What was in the crate?

I shined the light inside the crate and was once again amazed at what I saw. It wasn't cartons of cigarettes, but neatly packed bottles. I gently lifted one of the bottles out of the crate. It was a bottle of Tennessee whiskey! I wonder if this booze is untaxed just like the cigarettes? So, it looks like Reverend States Rights Jones has a good little business going other than his saving of souls. I wonder whom he is selling the cigarettes and whiskey to?

I placed the lid back on the crate and pressed it down as well as I could. I didn't want to hammer the nails back in and create noise that someone in the compound might hear. I decided not to open any more. I'm sure they all contain the same items.

I walked to the door of the building, opened the door, and looked out. Still perfectly quiet, so I exited the building, snapped the padlock back on the hasp, and pointed my flashlight at the ground so as to not give off much light.

Just then, I saw two light beams coming in my direction. I quickly shut off my flashlight, went to the back corner of the warehouse, and ducked around the corner. I peered out around the corner of the building, as the lights grew nearer. I could now make out the forms of two men, who were walking towards the building I was hiding behind. They were almost at the door of the warehouse now and I could hear them talking.

"I don't know why we have to check theses damn buildings every night," said one guy.

"Because the Reverend tells us to."

"I know, but there's no way anybody can get into this compound without going through the front gate. So what can happen?" said the first guy.

They now had reached the door, unlocked it, and went inside. Shortly, they emerged from the building.

"See, I told you nothing would be out of place," the first guy said.

"Yeah, you're right. Now let's get on with the rest of our round. I want to hit the sack," replied the second guy.

"We only have two more buildings to check, then the barracks and we're done for the night," said the first guy.

They started walking away and I wondered what am I going to do now? I didn't find anything that would lead me to Angel, or Spike for that matter. I have discovered that Reverend Jones seems to be running a good market of selling bootleg cigarettes and Tennessee whiskey. That doesn't mean he had anything to do with Angel's disappearance. However, it doesn't mean he didn't either. Maybe she heard some conversations she shouldn't have at the Kum N Go where she worked. There's the report of her talking to a stranger some time before she disappeared. Could the stranger have been one of Reverend Jones' disciples? Could the stranger have abducted Angel? I wonder what else Reverend Jones is involved in other than his cigarette and whiskey trade?

I decided I wouldn't do anymore sleuthing, but get out of the Family of our Lord's compound before I was discovered. I did wonder why the two guys had to check the barracks. Are the people kept locked so no one can get out at night? Grabbing my big flashlight, I tried to follow the path that I had taken when I came into the compound. I found the cornfield, walked through it and came out in the grove of trees I had left my stilts. I wasn't at the exact location I had left my stilts, so I started looking around. I glanced over my shoulder to see if there was any activity coming from behind me. I was close to getting out of the compound and didn't want anything to go south now.

I finally found the tree where I had laid my stilts. I put my big flashlight into my backpack, removed my leather gloves from my backpack, and put them on. I put the backpack on so it was hanging in front of me. I needed to be able to rest my back on the tree in order to scale the stilts. I propped the stilts up against the large tree, stood between them with my back to the tree, and slowly started to walk up the cleats on the stilts. I finally made it to the eight-foot footholds, breathed a sigh of relief, adjusted my backpack, and slowly started walking away from the tree towards the fence located in front of me.

As I slowly neared the fence, I saw my tarp was still in place. I came to the barbed wire top of the fence that leaned into the compound, and slowly turned around so my back was facing the fence. I inched my way to the fence and sat down on the tarp. So far so good! The tarp has kept the barbs of the fence from poking into my butt. I then lifted the right stilt up and without turning around, slid it down the outside of the fence. I repeated the same maneuver with the left stilt. Both stilts were now leaning against the top of the fence on the outside of the compound. I slowly lifted my legs up as I braced my gloved hands on the tarp, trying to take some pressure off my butt. I managed to turn around without being skewered and inched my way forward along the tarp. Reaching the other edge of the barbed wire, I swung my legs over the edge and grabbed a hold of my stilts. You're so close, don't screw up now, and fall, I thought to myself. I removed my backpack and dropped it to the ground on the outside of the fence. I then placed my feet onto the footholds and stood up.

I turned myself around; facing the fence, as I jitter bugged my stilts in the proper position. I grabbed the tarp, pried it off the barbs of the barbed wire, and threw it to the ground. I slowly inched my way down the stilts, using the cleats and pressing my hands against the fence in order to keep my balance. My feet hit ground! I sighed and stood there for several seconds. The stilts were now leaning against the fence, so I took them down and laid them on the ground at the base of the fence.

I removed my leather gloves and placed them in my backpack. Picking up my backpack and tarp, I headed to where my Escalade was parked. I reached my vehicle, put my things inside, and drove back to where I had left my stilts. I loaded the stilts, got back into my vehicle.

I looked at my watch as I drove along and saw that it was 12:45 a.m. I thought about calling Martha. She should be sleeping at this hour, but then again she might not be. I finally decided I would call her. I selected her from my contact list on my cell phone and pressed send. One ring later, I heard, "Hello,"

"Hi honey. I didn't know if you would be awake or not," I said.

"Are you all right?" Martha quickly asked.

"Yep."

"You're not in the emergency room? You're not lying out in some field with a broken neck?" she excitedly asked.

"No. I'm fine. No broken bones, dog bites, or bullet wounds."

"Thank god!" she exclaimed.

"He might have had something to do with it," I replied as I smiled to myself.

"Where are you?"

"About eight miles from Kenny's place."

"What happened?"

"I'll tell you all about it when I get to Kenny's."

"I'm so glad you're safe. Hurry home and tell me all about what went on," she said.

"Will do. See you in a little while," I said as I turned off the township road onto the county road leading to Kenny's place.

I arrived at Kenny's, parked the Escalade leaving the stilts protruding out of the back, and went up to the house. The door had been left unlocked, so I walked in. I didn't have my flashlight, so I had to turn on some of the house lights so I could make my way to the bedroom. I stopped at the bathroom, brushed my teeth, washed up and headed towards the bedroom where I knew Martha would be waiting to find out what had happened tonight.

I entered the bedroom to find Martha snoring comfortably in the bed. 'So much for her caring about what happened tonight,' I thought as I quietly crawled into bed next to her.

Although I was tired, I lay next to Martha, listening to her gentle snoring as I tried to sort out the night's activities. I survived my stilt stunt! I found what looked like bootleg cigarettes in one of the buildings on the compound. I found crates of Tennessee whiskey in another building. I didn't find anything that helped me in locating Angel. Was the Reverend Jones at all responsible for Angel's disappearance? Was I going to ever figure out what was going on?

## Chapter Seventeen

I awoke the following morning, Tuesday, May 24, to find Martha's head resting on my chest. I gently stroked her hair and she woke up.

"Morning," I said.

"Good morning," she replied as she lifted her head and gave me a kiss.

"I'm so glad that you are safe and well," she added as she gave me another kiss.

"From the sound of your snoring last night, I gather that you were very concerned with my health," I replied.

"I was. You called and said you were almost home, so I relaxed. I guess I must have fallen asleep," she said as she raised herself up on one elbow to look at me.

"I guess you did, but I'm glad I made it home too," I said as I gave her a kiss.

I got up, showered, was dressed, and headed towards the kitchen. As I got to the kitchen, I saw Kenny and Marcie already sitting at the kitchen table, drinking some coffee.

"Good morning, folks," I said as I approached them.

"Morning," Kenny replied.

"Good morning Butch," Marcie said.

"I don't see any dog bites or bullet wounds," Kenny said.

"I also surmise by the fact you are walking, you didn't break your neck either," he added as he chuckled.

"Nope, I'm in good shape," I replied as I got myself a cup of coffee.

I grabbed a chair next to the kitchen table and sat down.

"So, did you find Angel?" Kenny asked.

"Nope, but I did find out something interesting," I said as I picked up my coffee mug and took a sip.

"What was that?" asked Marcie.

"I went into two of the buildings on the compound and was surprised at what I saw," I said.

"What was that?" asked Martha as she entered the kitchen, grabbed a coffee cup and poured herself a cup.

"One of the buildings contained multiple bundles of cigarettes that didn't have any tax stamp on them," I replied.

"So," said Marcie.

"That means the Reverend Jones must be selling bootleg cigarettes," Kenny said.

"That's correct."

"What else did you find?" asked Martha.

"The other building I went into contained crates of Tennessee whiskey."

"Any labels on the bottles?" asked Kenny.

"Only one big one stating what it was," I said as I took a sip of my coffee.

"No mention of a distillery?" asked Kenny.

"Nope."

"Whoa. So, the Reverend Jones is dealing in bootleg cigarettes and booze," Kenny said.

"Looks like it."

"Shouldn't you report that to the sheriff?" Martha asked.

"Yeah, but that won't do anything in helping me find Angel," I replied.

Just then, my cell phone rang. I took it out of my shorts pocket and flipped it open. Bubba's phone number shown on the screen of my cell phone.

"Hello."

"Hello, Butch. It's Bubba."

"Hi Bubba. What's up?"

"Bertha and I don't want to bother you, but we were just wondering if you had found out anything about Angel's disappearance," Bubba said.

"I've been running down some leads, but I haven't found her yet. I just need to keep up my investigating for a little while longer and I'm sure that I will come up with something."

"How would you and Martha like to come out for supper tonight? You could fill us in on what you have found out," Bubba said.

I thought about the meal Bubba had offered earlier and wasn't too sure I really wanted to eat at his house, but how could I say no again without offending him?

"That would work. I'm sure Kenny and Marcie are getting tired of us eating here," I replied.

"Oh, you're staying at Kenny's."

"Yeah. It gives Martha time to spend with her family," I replied.

"We get home from work at 5:00 p.m. and I'll get the ribs starting to grill right away so we should be eating around 6:30 p.m. You guys can come out anytime before that," Bubba said.

Grilled ribs. Sounds better than ribs and sauerkraut, I thought.

"Sounds good. We'll see you sometime around 5:30 p.m.," I said.

"Great. See you tonight," Bubba said as he hung up.

"What was that about?" Martha asked.

"Bubba invited us out for supper tonight so I could fill them in on what I've found out so far," I said.

"Supper?" Martha said as she gave me one of her looks.

"Yep. He said he was having barbequed alligator," I quickly replied.

"Oh, gross. Why did you say yes? There is no way I can eat alligator," Martha tartly said.

"Have you ever eaten it?" asked Kenny as he looked at me and grinned.

"It tastes a lot like salty chicken," he added.

"Yeah, I understand that the part closest to the anus is the most tender," I replied as I kept my hoax going.

"Just stop. I'm not eating any alligator," Martha said as her voice rose several octaves.

"We need to go. I want to tell Bubba and Bertha what I have discovered," I said as I enjoyed Martha's discomfort.

"I don't care. I'm not going. Now you call him right back, Butch Brogen and tell him we have other plans," Martha said as she placed her hands firmly on the table and stared at me.

"That wouldn't be very polite," Kenny said as he grinned. He was enjoying this as much as I was. I finally thought it was time to tell Martha the truth about tonight's supper.

"I'm just kidding about the alligator. Bubba said he was grilling some ribs," I said as I laughed with Kenny joining in.

"You jerk. Why do you have to keep getting me upset?" Martha asked as she sat back into her chair.

"Because it's fun, sister," Kenny replied before I had a chance to answer.

"You two quit teasing Martha," Marcie said.

"We're going to Bubba's at 5:30 p.m. and have a great meal," I said as I thought, I hope he grills the ribs in a normal fashion.

We sat around the kitchen table, talking and drinking coffee as the girls ate breakfast. Since school was out for the year, and they were happy, they did more giggling than eating.

"What are you going to do today?" Martha asked as she had finally gotten over her snit.

"I should call the sheriff and somehow tell him what I saw at the Family of our Lord's without letting him know I was in the compound last night," I said.

"Then, I think I'm going to drive over to where Angel lived at Spartan College. I have a feeling I could get some information if I could get someone to answer the door."

"What about you guys?" I asked.

"I have a job in Pratt," Kenny said.

"More than one day?" I asked as I looked at Martha.

"Yeah, might take me two days," he replied.

"Marcie and I are going to freeze some asparagus," Martha said as she gave her 'don't say anything' look.

After finishing breakfast, I went and got the stilts out of the Escalade and carried them down to Kenny's shop where I placed them on the ground outside of the door. I don't know if I'll use them again, I thought.

I retrieved the Sheriff's business card from my money clip, where I had placed it, when I visited him. I took my cell phone from the front pocket of my shorts, entered the Sheriff's phone number, and pushed the send button.

"Hello, Washington County sheriff's Office," came a voice from the phone earpiece.

"Hello, this is Butch Brogen. I'm the private investigator who visited the sheriff in regards to Angel McCoy's disappearance. I was wondering if I could talk to the sheriff," I said.

"Just a minute. I'll see if the sheriff is busy," the receptionist replied.

Several seconds passed and she came back on the line.

"The sheriff said he would talk with you, Mr. Brogan," she said.

"I'll connect you to him."

There was a click followed by several seconds of silence, and then, "Hello, this is Sheriff Hatfield."

"Hello, sheriff, Butch Brogen here."

"So, you're still around," he said with tartness to his voice.

"Yep, I'm still here."

"Have you found Angel McCoy yet?" he asked in a cold voice.

"No I haven't."

"I told you we had done a complete investigation and didn't find out what happened to her," he replied curtly.

"I don't know what makes you think you can uncover something my department didn't," he quickly added.

"That's not why I called."

"It isn't. Then why the phone call?"

Trying to be careful and not let the sheriff know that I had been inside the Family of our Lord compound, I said, "In my investigation of Angel's disappearance, I was told by someone that the Reverend Jones might not be just a religious guru."

"How so?"

"Well, I was told that there are bootleg cigarettes and whiskey stored in buildings on the compound," I said.

"What! You are telling me that Reverend Jones has stockpiles of cigarettes and booze," the sheriff said in a raised voice.

"That's what this person told me."

"Just who is this person?"

"I promised them I wouldn't revel their name as a matter of safety," I lied to the sheriff.

164

"I can't believe what you're telling me is true, but if it is, you're going to have to give me the informant's name," he sternly said.

"If the time comes where the persons name is relevant, I'll be more than glad to tell you," I replied as I detected uneasiness in the sheriff's voice.

"I usually don't go off half cocked on some purported information, but I'll have my men check out this so called information you have," he said.

"Thanks sheriff, that's all I can ask."

"Thanks for taking my call and listening to me. I'll give you another call if I hear anything else," I added.

"Sounds good," he said as he hung up the phone.

I hung up my cell phone and put it back into the front pocket of my shorts. I hope the sheriff wasn't wise to the fact that I had personally seen the items I had told him about and I wonder how much he will investigate it, I thought to myself as I started walking back up to the house.

Sheriff Hatfield quickly picked up the telephone again and pushed '3'.

"Hello, Family of our Lord, Reverend States Rights Jones speaking."

"SR, Sheriff Hatfield here."

"Well, hello Virg. What blesses me with your phone call?" the Reverend asked.

"I just got done talking to that damn nosy PI, Butch Brogen, and he was telling me a story from someone he had talked to," replied the sheriff.

"So what did he have to say?"

"He told me about the bootleg cigarettes and whiskey you have stored at the compound," the sheriff quickly answered.

"Son of a bitch!"

165

"Now SR, a man of the cloth shouldn't be using that type of language."

"Shut up, Virgil! If this clown actually knows about our stored supplies, we could be in trouble," snapped the Reverend.

"He was just telling me about some hearsay. He hasn't actually seen the stuff himself," the sheriff said as he tried to calm down Revered Jones.

"I don't give a shit! I don't want anyone to know about our venture here," the Reverend snapped.

"Who was it that supplied him with the information?" asked the Reverend.

"Don't know. Brogen wouldn't give me a name," replied the sheriff.

"I don't know how anybody could get into our compound. I have people walking the perimeter all the time," said Reverend Jones.

"Maybe it was someone from inside your compound," replied Sheriff Hatfield.

"No way! Brogen never talked to anyone the one time he was inside our compound and there's no way anyone could get out of here without me knowing."

"They would have to go through the front gate or over the fence. The way the barbed wire is slanted inward, they would need a ladder to get over the top and then they would have to crawl on three feet of barbed wire. We have never seen a ladder leaning on the fence or noticed any of my flock with barbed wire scratches," added Reverend Jones.

"Could someone have sneaked a ride in one of your trucks when they make deliveries or go into town?" asked the sheriff.

"I doubt it. The men who drive my trucks are very loyal to me. They check every load as I have instructed them to," answered the Reverend.

166

"Well, Brogen knows what is stored in two of your buildings, so he must have gotten inside your compound," said Sheriff Hatfield.

"Impossible. Even if he scaled the outside of the fence and somehow got on the ground inside the compound, he never could have gotten back out. Trust me," said Reverend Jones with conviction in his voice.

"All I know is that he knows what's in those buildings," said the sheriff.

"I don't care what he knows! You are going to make sure he doesn't find out anything else!" said the Reverend as his voice rose.

"You hear me, Sheriff Hatfield?" Reverend Jones added excitedly.

"Just calm down, SR. I told Brogen I would check out what he told me. I already know that I won't find anything," the sheriff said.

"I know you won't find anything, because you won't be looking."

"That's right, SR. I won't be looking. If Brogen contacts me again, I'll make up some cock and bull story about what I didn't find," replied the sheriff.

"You're damn right you'll give him a story to get him away from us. We have too much invested in this little venture, Virg," said Reverend Jones.

"I know SR. Nothing is going to happen. I'll satisfy Brogen and you can continue on with your endeavor," said the sheriff.

"Our venture, Virgil. You have to remember that if I go down, you'll be dropping right along side of me," said the Reverend.

"That sounds like a threat, SR."

"Ain't no threat, Virg. Just the truth. Now, get that damn PI off my back," growled the Reverend.

"No problem, SR. I'll see to it that he doesn't find out anything else," said the sheriff.

"You had better. Now I have to get back to my flock. You have a good day and keep me informed on what you have found out about who told Brogen about our goods," said the Reverend as he hung up his phone.

"Will do, SR," replied the sheriff as he heard the click of a phone being hung up.

Damn. I wonder how Brogen found out about the cigarettes and whiskey. The compound is completely surround by a chain link fence and the Reverend has men walking around the compound all the time, the sheriff thought to himself as he rubbed his chin and leaned back in his chair.

## Chapter Eighteen

As I neared the house, I saw Kenny opening the garage door to the stall were his truck was parked. He saw me and waved.

"See ya in a couple of days," he said.

"See ya. Be good," I replied as I waved back to him.

"I'm always good," he said with a smile as he walked into the garage.

I entered the house and went to the kitchen where Martha and Marcie were getting things ready for their chore of the day.

"I'm going to Johnson City and see if I can find anyone home at the house where Angel lived," I said as I neared Martha and gave her a kiss.

"I hope you find out something this time," Martha replied as she returned my kiss.

"When will you be home?" she asked.

"I don't know. If I get back soon enough, I might get in a quick round of golf before we go to Bubbas for supper," I answered.

"Don't remind me of our supper date. I'm still not all that keen on eating something Bubba cooks," Martha said.

"Don't worry. Everything will be just fine," I replied as I turned to walk out of the kitchen.

I left the house, got into the Escalade, and entered the address for Burton House into the GPS.

As I drove to Johnson City, I wracked my brain with thoughts of what happened to Angel. Did she meet up with foul play? Did she disappear on her own for some reason? Did

Reverend Jones have anything to do with her disappearance? Had Angel found out about the Reverend's bootleg trade and he had her kidnapped to keep her from telling anyone? Did Sheriff Hatfield know more than he was telling me? What about Frank Hatfield? Was he involved in her disappearance? Did Ephraim Hatfield harm her? He surely hates McCoys. What am I going to tell Bubba and Bertha? All I know for certain is that I don't know shit about Angel's disappearance!

Following the sweet talking voice on the GPS, I arrived at Burton House once again and parked curbside in front of the house. Sure hope someone's home, I thought to myself as I got out of my vehicle. I walked up the sidewalk leading to the door of the house. When I reached the door, I knocked loudly on it and waited. Nothing! I knocked once again and this time I heard some rustling coming from inside the house. A couple of seconds passed and the inside front door started to open.

"Hello," said a young woman of about nineteen. Even though I was looking through the screen door, I could see that she was around five foot six inches tall with a small build. She had short blonde hair, bright blue eyes, and a good tan. She was wearing blue Capri's and a snug yellow tee shirt, which revealed her ample chest.

"Hi. My name is Butch Brogen. I'm a private investigator who has been hired to find out what happened to Angel McCoy," I said as I introduced myself.

"Oh," she replied.

"I understand that she lived here while she was going to college."

"Yes, she lived here," the woman answered as she stood holding the door open while leaving the screen door closed.

"I was wondering if I could ask you a few questions?" I asked.

"Who's there Olivia?" asked a voice in the background.

"A guy who says he's a private investigator looking into Angel's disappearance," the woman replied to the voice.

"We don't know any more than we have told law enforcement when they questioned us about Angel," said a woman who appeared along side Olivia.

Just then, I caught some movement behind the front window, which had the drapes pulled. Is someone else in the house?

"I know you have talked to the sheriff's people and told them what you know, but I would like you to tell me also. Sometimes a person remembers something after their initial conversation," I said to the woman who had appeared.

She was about the same height as Olivia, but she had long, flowing black hair. Dark brown eyes and an olive complexion. She was wearing a pair of short denim shorts and a halter-top.

"I don't think we can tell you anything that we haven't told the sheriff," she replied.

Just the same, could you give me a couple of minutes and tell me what you know," I pleaded.

Once again, I heard some movement inside the house, but no other person appeared at the door.

"How do we know you're a private investigator?" asked the black haired woman.

"Here's my Minnesota credentials," I said as I reached into the left front pocket of my shorts and removed my money clip, which contained my PI identification.

The dark haired woman slowly opened the screen door, reached her right hand outside, and took my ID from me. She pulled her hand back inside the house and looked my ID over.

"OK, looks like he is who he says," said the dark haired woman.

"Then let's just talk to him, Ahron," Olivia said addressing the woman who had joined her at the door.

"OK," said Ahron as she opened the screen door and walked out onto the porch, followed by Olivia.

"We can talk out here," Ahron said as she handed me my ID back, walked across the porch and leaned against a post supporting the roof of the porch.

Olivia quickly glanced inside the house, shut the front door and joined Ahron and I.

"Thanks for talking to me ladies."

"As I told you, I'm trying to find out what has happened to Angel," I said.

"I don't know what I can tell you. We weren't real close," Ahron said.

"She lived here while she went to school, didn't she?" I asked.

"Yes. She lived here the past two years," Olivia said.

"I would think you'd know quite a bit about someone if you'd lived with them for two years," I said.

"We all had different schedules and some of us worked part time, so we didn't see a whole lot of each other," Ahron replied.

"Yeah, we didn't talk with each other that much," added Olivia.

"Are you the only two ladies living here?"

"There were five of us during the school year, but now Olivia and I are the only two people living here," Ahron replied.

"You're the only people living here?"

"Yep, just us two," Olivia quickly replied.

"Did Angel ever tell you ladies about any fears she had?" I asked.

"Like what?" asked Olivia.

"That someone might be harassing her or stalking her," I replied.

"No, she never mentioned any of those things. She always seemed pretty happy when she was around us," replied Ahron.

Just then, I caught some movement out of the corner of my eye and quickly looked towards the front window where I thought I had seen movement. I could swear that I saw a pair of eyes peering from an opening along the drapes as if someone was in the house, pulling back the drape and looking out.

"You said that you are the only two people inside the house today," I said to the girls.

"Yes, we're the only two," Olivia quickly replied.

"Yep, only us two," added Ahron.

"I thought I saw someone looking out from behind the front window drape at us," I said.

"You couldn't have. There's no one in the house," Ahron said.

"Has Angel contacted either of you since she went missing?" I asked.

"Why would she? I said we weren't very close," said Ahron.

"I just thought that if she was in trouble, she might contact the people whom she had lived with the past two years," I said.

"Nope, we haven't heard anything from her since she moved out after graduation," Olivia said.

"OK, thanks for talking to me," I said as I realized I wasn't going to get any information from the two girls.

"No problem. I just wish we could have been more help to you and the sheriff's department," Ahron said as she started walking towards the house door.

"If you find out anything about Angel, let us know," Olivia said as she started to follow Ahron.

"I sure will," I replied as I quickly glanced towards the front window before I started to walk away.

The drape on the window was in place and I didn't detect any more movement behind it. I walked to the Escalade and as I started to get in, I once again looked towards the window of the house. The drape had moved and it looked like someone was looking out the window at me.

Was Angel inside the house? I thought as I pulled away from the curb. I'm sure the sheriff's department looked around inside when they talked to the girls, so they would know if there were more than the two girls living there.

I looked at the clock on the dash of the Escalade and saw that I had time to get in at least nine holes of golf before I needed to pick up Martha and go over to Bubba's.

I decided to rent a golf cart for my round and the course wasn't busy, so I got eighteen holes in before I headed back to Kenny's place.

I arrived at the house at 5:00 p.m., Martha and Marcie were sitting outside, reading and the girls were running around chasing butterflies.

I pulled up in front of the house, got out and walked towards Martha and Marcie.

"Hi ladies. Did you get your asparagus put up?" I asked as I got near them.

"Sure did," said Martha.

"Did you find out anything today?" she asked.

"I didn't find out anything about Angel, but I did find out my golf game still sucks."

"Golf. I thought you were working on a case," Martha said as she smiled at me.

"Have to take some time off and let the grey cells regenerate," I said as I sat down on the front steps.

"I did talk to two girls who were still living in the house that Angel had lived in and they both told me the same thing. Neither one knew anything about Angel's disappearance," I said.

"That's too bad," Martha said.

"Although, I'm sure that there was someone else inside the house," I said.

"Why do you think that?" asked Marcie.

"Two things. The two girls came outside to talk to me instead of inviting me in and I'm sure I saw someone looking at us from behind the front window drapes," I said.

"They probably didn't invite you in because they felt safer talking to a stranger outside," Martha said.

"Could be, but I still believe I saw movement inside the house even though the girls claimed they were the only two there," I said.

"We should be getting out to Bubba's," I said as I glanced at my watch.

"I can't wait to get some of his alligator ribs," I said as I smile at the two women.

"You said we weren't having alligator," Martha said.

"Bubba actually didn't tell me what kind of ribs we were having," I said as I kept needling Martha.

"We don't have alligators around here, so I'm sure he's cooking beef or pork ribs," Marcie said as she tried to reassure Martha.

"It had better be beef or pork ribs," said Martha as she got up from her lawn chair and joined me as we walked to the Escaladed.

"Have a good supper," Marcie said as she waved us goodbye.

"Why do you always have to kid me?" Martha asked as I drove down the driveway.

"Because you're so gullible."

"And beautiful," I quickly added.

"You had better say that," Martha replied as she hit me on the shoulder.

# Chapter Nineteen

As we drove to Bubba's house, I told Martha more about my meeting with the girls who used to live with Angel.

"Do you really think someone else was inside the house?" she asked me.

"Yep, pretty sure."

"You think it might have been Angel?"

"I don't know. Why would she try to disappear?"

"You're the detective. You're supposed to figure those things out," Martha replied as she smiled at me.

"You discovered who killed my father, although you were a little off on the poor girl you found dead at Maple Isle Golf Course," she added.

"Hogg found her, not me I keep telling you and I had my ideas about her death, I just didn't get enough time to prove them," I replied as I tried to defend myself.

"That's OK. I still love you," she replied as I made a left hand turn into Bubba's driveway.

I could see smoke rising in the air from behind the house, so I figured Bubba had the ribs on or else his house was on fire. I pulled onto the concrete apron of the garage, turned off the Escalade and Martha and I got out. My nostrils were immediately filled by the tantalizing aroma of wood smoke and barbeque sauce.

"Boy, smell those gator ribs Bubba is cooking," I said as I sniffed the air and looked at Martha.

"Stop it!"

"I'm not eating alligator ribs," Martha said as she wrinkled her nose and we started walking towards the house.

We had only taken a couple of steps, when the front door opened and Bertha came out.

"Hi Butch," she said as she grabbed my hand in a vise like grip.

"Hi Martha," she said as she let go of me and gave Martha a hug that I could tell was a strong one.

"Bubba is out on the patio grilling the best beef ribs you are ever going to taste," Bertha said as she turned to lead us around the side of the house to the patio located in the back.

"Beef ribs," I mouthed to Martha as we followed behind Bertha. I could tell by the look on Martha's face that she was relieved she wasn't eating alligator ribs. Now I just hoped the ribs were not devil spit hot. We rounded the house and found Bubba sitting in a chaise lounge. There was a large red Igloo cooler sitting next to his chair. A beer bottle nestled inside a huggy, sat on a little stand beside his chair. Bubba was watching the smoke coming out of his grill.

"Hi Butch and Martha," he said as he saw us.

"Come on over, grab a chair and a cold beer," he offered as he extended his hand towards me without getting up from his chair. I accepted his hand, although I knew his grip would be twice as strong as Bertha's.

After the handshake, I walked over to the Igloo cooler sitting only a few feet away from Bubba, opened the lid, reached into the ice to retrieve a cold beer. The ice felt soothing on my throbbing hand that Bubba had just gripped. Martha said she would prefer a glass of ice water, so she and Bertha went into the house while I uncapped my beer and sat down in a chair next to Bubba.

"There's another huggy laying on the ground along side the cooler," Bubba said.

"These are going to be the best ribs you've ever eaten," Bubba proclaimed as he dragged his large frame out of the chair and made his way to the grill to check the cooking ribs. As he opened the top of the grill, the aroma of barbequed ribs wafted through the air. The smell was awesome. I hoped they tasted as good as they smelled. Bubba applied more barbecue sauce to the ribs, closed the lid of the grill, walked back over to his chair, and sat down.

I had retrieved the huggy, placed the cold beer bottle inside it, and sat down in one of the vacant chaise lounges on the patio.

"The barbecue sauce is a passed down family recipe. You'll never taste any better sauce in the state of Tennessee," Bubba proudly proclaimed.

"So, what have you got for us?" he immediately asked.

I took a swallow of my beer and said, "I wish that I could tell you I had found Angel, but I can't."

Just then, Bertha and Martha reappeared on the patio.

"Butch was just going to tell us what he's found out about Angel," Bubba said to Bertha as she and Martha each sat down.

"That's great," Bertha said.

"Not really. I was just about to tell Bubba that I've been running down all the leads I could find, but I still haven't found Angel," I said.

"Oh, you think she's dead?" asked Bertha.

"I didn't say that. At this time I just can't figure out what is going on," I replied.

"Neither the sheriff or I have found her car or discovered any of her belongings in some place they didn't belong," I said as I tried to calm Bertha.

"Because her car hasn't been found means she's alive, then," Bertha said.

"We don't know that, but usually, if a missing person's car isn't found, it means they are still using it," I said.

"None of her belongings, such as purse, credit cards and such have been found either. Another indication the person might not have disappeared because of foul play," I said.

"But, there has been no activity on her credit or debit cards, which could indicate she might have met with foul play," I added.

"You said you didn't think she was dead," Bertha said excitedly.

"That's right. I'm just telling you the facts as I know them."

I continued to tell Bubba and Bertha everything I had discovered, which wasn't a whole lot, as Bubba continued to grill the ribs.

"The ribs are getting close to being done," Bubba said.

"Would you go and get the sweet corn?" he asked Bertha.

"There's no better way to cook sweet corn than to grill it," Bubba said to Martha and me.

Bertha returned with the sweet corn still in the husks and Bubba placed them on the grill next to the rack of ribs.

I then told Bubba and Bertha what I had discovered at the Family of our Lord compound.

"No shit. You found cigarettes and whiskey in the compound!" Bubba said.

"Yep."

"Too bad it wasn't Tangueray. You could have helped yourself to a few bottles," Bubba said as he laughed.

"How in the world did you get in and out of there without being seen?" asked Bertha.

"You will never figure out what mister genius did to get in and out," Martha said.

"Most people would just use a ladder to scale the fence, but not Butch. He used stilts," she added.

"He used stilts?" asked Bubba.

"Yep, I used stilts."

I then explained to Bubba and Bertha why I used the stilts and how I got them to work.

Bubba got up, checked the grill again and proclaimed, "Everything is done. You can finish your story while we eat."

With that, we all got up and I grabbed the tray Bubba had placed the sweet corn on. Bubba then placed the ribs on a platter, grabbed it and we followed the women into the house.

The ribs and sweet corn were absolutely delicious. I even knew Martha would like the ribs, because they were not spicy, but had a golden honey flavor.

We ate and talked about different things, but not Angel.

"These are the best ribs I've ever eaten," I finally said as I leaned back in my chair and loosen the waistband of my shorts.

"I told you they would be," Bubba replied as he gave me a grin and started to wipe the barbeque sauce off his face.

"I've never had grilled sweet corn," Martha said.

"Good, isn't it?" asked Bertha.

"It's very good."

"You need to soak the corn in water for a little while before you put it on the grill. Otherwise, it will dry out too much and the husks might burn," Bubba said.

"You're going to have to cook it this way," Martha said as she looked at me.

"No problem."

"What I really want is for Bubba to teach me how to make the sauce and cook these ribs," I replied as I wiped the sauce from my face.

"Like I said, the sauce is a family secret, but I don't think Grandpa Butz would mind me telling you how to make it and cook the ribs," Bubba replied.

After the table was cleared and dishes put in the dishwasher, we retired to the patio once again. Although I was stuffed, I accepted another beer Bubba offered.

"I'm sorry I don't have anything solid I can tell you about Angel's disappearance," I said.

"I should just probably call it quits, return your money and head for home," I said.

"You can quit if you want to, but you are not returning our money," Bubba said.

"I didn't say I was going to quit, I just meant that I've come up blank at every turn," I replied.

"You discovered that Reverend Jones has illegal cigarettes and whiskey in his compound," Bertha said.

"I know that, but that doesn't mean I've figured out what has happened to Angel," I replied.

"That is the reason I came here. I wanted to find Angel and figure out what or who was behind her disappearance," I said.

"I think you're doing the best you can. Why don't you stay for a little while longer and see if you can discover anything else," Bertha asked.

I could tell by the tone of her voice that she was disappointed that I hadn't found her sister, but she was more disappointed that I was going to call it quits.

"I just know something bad has happened to her," Bertha said.

"Not necessarily."

"Her car has not been found. That could mean she drove out of the area on her own," I added.

"She had no reason to disappear on her own. She had just graduated from college and had a job lined up. The last time I talked with her, she was just beaming with excitement," Bertha said.

"You have a point there, Bertha. Why would a happy person just go off without telling someone," I replied.

"What about her problems with Frank?" I asked.

"I'm sure they were going to work that out. They have gone with each other for so long and seemed so in love," Bertha said.

"Frank seems pretty broken up," I admitted.

"I know and so did Angel. I just know that Frank didn't have anything to do with Angel's disappearance," Bertha said.

"We'll stay around for a few more days and I'll look into a couple of ideas I have," I finally said.

"You've got an idea what happened to Angel?" Bertha asked with excitement in her voice.

"I didn't say that. I don't have anymore concrete evidence than when I started looking for her, but I have a couple of things I want to check out," I replied.

"If I find out anything you will be the first to know," I added.

"That's great," Bubba said.

"Now, let's have another beer before you two leave," he said as he reached towards the ice packed cooler sitting next to his chair.

"I'm so stuffed, I don't think I could get another beer down," I protested.

"A person always has room for another beer," Bubba said as he uncapped a beer and handed it to me.

"Besides, you have a designated driver in Martha."

"It's a good thing I do," I said as I took the beer from Bubba and slowly tried to get it down.

I finally finished my beer while Bubba had three more.

"We need to get going," I said as I rose out of the chair, half expecting to topple over. My legs worked fine, but I could tell I had put away more alcohol than I was used to. Even with all the food to soak it up, the beer was getting to me.

"I had better use the john before we go," I said as Martha got out of her chair.

"Yes you had better. I'm not stopping along side of the road so you can pee," Martha said as she smiled at Bertha.

"Oh, don't worry Martha. I've had to stop for Bubba before," Bertha said.

I returned from the house, gave Martha the keys to the Escalade, thanked Bubba and Bertha and followed Martha as she walked to our vehicle.

"I sure hope you find Angel," Bertha said just before we rounded the corner of the house.

"Me too," I replied.

"Oh, I feel miserable," I complained as I got into the Escalade.

"You shouldn't have drank so much," Martha replied as she started the vehicle.

"I don't think it's just the beer. I think I ate way too much also," I replied in half defense and half-truth.

We talked about the evening as Martha drove back to Kenny's house.

"You have an idea what happened to Angel?" Martha asked, as we got closer to Kenny's.

"I have a couple of ideas."

"What are they?"

184

"I'm not saying anything right now. I might be way off base and don't want to cause any problems," I said.

"Problems for who?"

"Just people. If my thoughts are correct, you'll know soon enough," I said.

"You know we aren't supposed to keep secrets from each other," Martha said.

"That secret keeping has to do with our lives. It has nothing to do with one of my cases," I quickly replied.

"Whatever."

We rode the rest of the way to Kenny's place in silence.

# Chapter Twenty

I woke up Wednesday, May 25. Martha was already out of bed, so I got up, showered, brushed my teeth, got dressed, and went to the kitchen. As I entered the room, the aroma of freshly brewed coffee wafted through the air. Marcie and Martha were seated at the table, drinking coffee and chatting. The two girls were still sleeping and Kenny wasn't home yet.

"Good morning," I said as I grabbed a coffee cup from the cupboard.

"Good morning, sleepy head," Martha replied.

"It isn't that late and I had to sleep off Bubba's ribs," I said as I poured myself a cup of hot java.

I joined the ladies at the kitchen table.

"What's on the agenda for today?" I asked.

"Cousin Betty invited us to go shopping and to a movie," Martha answered.

"She hasn't seen me for quite some time, so she asked if we would stay over night and get caught up on some girl chatting."

"Her husband works construction and is gone all week, so she has plenty of room for the both of us," Marcie added.

Fearing the job of babysitting the two girls was going to be left to me, I quickly asked, "Who's going to watch the girls?"

"Kenny's coming home this afternoon. He will be here to cook the girl's supper and watch them," Marcie said.

"You don't have to worry about watching them," Martha added as she gave me one of her disapproving looks.

"Oh, it's not that I would mind. It's just I have several things I wanted to do today, so I wouldn't be around here to watch the girls," I replied as I felt a wave of relief come over me.

"Like a longer than usual golf game?" asked Martha as she scowled at me.

"What are you going to do today?" Marcie asked me, unaware of my dislike for watching kids.

"I'm going to try to get into the Family of our Lord compound and talk with Reverend Jones," I said.

"Not on those stupid stilts," Martha quickly said as her voice raised a couple of octaves.

"No, not on the stilts. I'm going to drive to the front gate and see if I can get admittance," I said with a chuckle.

"If that doesn't work out, I can always go golfing."

"How is golfing going to help you find Angel?" asked Martha.

"I get some of my best ideas when I'm on the golf course," I said.

"Yeah, right."

"I decided that I liked you while I was golfing," I said with a smile.

"OK, you made your point," replied Martha.

"So, you're going to stay over night?" I asked.

"We thought we might," said Marcie.

"Is that all right?" asked Martha.

"It's alright by me. I can fend for myself."

"You're sure Kenny is going to be home to watch the girls?" I asked Marcie knowing just how dependable Kenny was.

"Yes. He called before you got up and said he would finish his job this morning and be home this afternoon," Marcie replied to me as Martha gave me another one of her looks.

"We will wait for him to get home before we go visit cousin Betty," Marcie added.

"You girls go have fun. I just might have found Angel by the time you get home tomorrow," I said.

"I sure hope you do," said Martha.

We continued to chat for a while, and then I got up and went into the living room, picked up the morning newspaper, sat down in one of the recliners and got caught up on the national news and sports. It didn't take too long to find out all I wanted to about either one.

Around ten o'clock, I decided to drive into town, put some gas in the Escalade, and then drive out to the Family of our Lord compound.

Before I left, I walked back into the kitchen where the two women still sat, but now they were accompanied by the two girls.

"I'm going to put some gas in the Escalade and then see what kind of luck I have meeting Reverend Jones," I announced.

"You be careful," Martha said as she got out of her chair, came over to me, and gave me a big kiss.

"If you ladies decide to stay over night and aren't home in time for supper, don't worry. I can feed myself," I said.

"From the size of your gut, it looks like you can feed yourself quite well," Martha replied as she gave me another kiss.

I slapped her butt and headed towards the front door.

I left the house and drove to the Kum N Go in Jonesborough, where I filled the Escalade with gas. Although I used a credit card at the pump for my gas, I went inside the building. I thought maybe someone who worked there might have heard from Angel. As I walked inside the building, I noticed the counter located to the right of me. The top of the counter was piled with several racks of merchandise and various advertisements. There was just a big enough space between all the stuff for me to see the young woman clerk.

I walked over to the woman standing behind the counter. She was about five foot eight inches tall and looked to weigh about one hundred twenty-five pounds. From the looks of the buttonholes stretching on her uniform blouse, she must have at least size 40D boobs. She had smoky dark eyes that glistened in the light and long hair the color of coal, which flowed down to the middle of her back. Her name badge was pinned on the front of her right boob, making sure you would see her name as you looked over her body. The badge read *Rhonda*.

"May I help you?" she asked as she smiled at me.

I don't need anything right now. I already paid for my gas with a credit card," I replied.

"I know."

"My name is Butch Brogen. I'm a private investigator looking into the disappearance of Angel McCoy. I was told she worked here," I said.

"She worked here for awhile, but then she disappeared. The sheriff has already talked with me and I have already told him every thing I know," the woman replied as she pulled at her hair.

"Well, I was just wondering if you could tell me everything you know about Angel. Maybe you forgot to tell the sheriff something important," I said.

Before she could answer, a male customer dressed in tattered blue jeans and a soiled green tee shirt walked up behind me. His sandy brown hair was as unkempt as his clothes. He showed several days growth of beard and had a chew of tobacco tucked between his lower lip and teeth. Tobacco juice stained both sides of his mouth. I quickly stepped aside.

"Go ahead. I'm just chatting with the lady," I said to the man.

Giving me a hound dog look, he walked up to the counter.

"Twenty dollars of gas on pump five, babe," he said as he handed Rhonda a twenty-dollar bill.

"I'm not your babe," Rhonda coldly said as she took the money from the customer and rung up his purchase.

"With the price of gas the way it is, you only get fumes for twenty dollars," I said as I smiled at the customer.

He glanced at me, gave a grunt, and turned to walk out of the store.

"Didn't seem too friendly," I said to Rhonda as I walked back to the open space on the counter in front of her.

"And doesn't know how to talk to women either," Rhonda replied.

"Now where were we? You were going to tell me everything you know about Angel," I said.

"Like I told the sheriff, I don't really know anything. Angel worked here for a while. She seemed happy and we chatted about various things whenever we worked the same shift," Rhonda said.

"What did you chat about?"

"How lucky she was graduating from college and getting a job right away. Nowadays it's hard to find a job that you went to school for," she said.

"I graduated two years ago with a elementary teaching degree, but the jobs are just not there right now, so I work here to try and make ends meet," she added.

Elementary school teacher! My grade school teachers sure didn't look like Rhonda. All my teachers were old spinsters with shriveled up bodies, grey hair piled up on their heads held in place by long pins, I thought to myself.

"This place pays well enough to make ends meet?" I asked.

"Oh no. I'm a professional dancer also."

"Professional dancer, huh. Ball room, line dance, square dance, ballet?"

"None of them. I'm a professional pole dancer," she replied as she smiled.

"Pole dancer. That seems like quite a different line of work than being an elementary school teacher," I replied as I looked up and down her body one more time.

Imagine that naked body wrapped around a pole, I thought to myself.

"Yes it is, but it's money. I work three nights a week at a place just out of town called the Ace of Spades," she said.

"How did you ever get into that line of work?"

"I was at the local swimming pool one day soaking up some sun when the owner of the Ace of Spades brought his son to swim."

"We struck up a conversation and he said that with my body and looks, I should come to work for him as a dancer," she added.

"Did you know anything about pole dancing?" I asked.

"Of course not."

"I went out there when they were closed and a couple of the girls showed me what I should do," Rhonda said.

"Weren't you nervous dancing naked in front of strangers?" I asked.

"The first couple of times, sure. But after that it seemed fairly natural."

"Isn't that line of work kind of dangerous?"

"Not really. I'm a free lancer so I don' have a promoter to worry about. The guys who come into the Ace of Spades are usually very polite," she said.

"Every once in awhile one of them might get a little frisky, but the bouncers take care of that," she added.

"Besides, I make a lot more than I do here, so what little risk there is in my pole dancing is offset by the money I earn."

"On a good night, I can earn close to one hundred dollars in tips alone," Rhonda added.

"You should come out some Monday, Tuesday, or Friday night," she said as she smiled at me and slightly arched her back making her already ample boobs jut out farther, almost popping the buttons off her uniform shirt.

"I don't think my wife would like that," I quickly replied as I tried not to be too obvious as I starred at her chest.

"Bring your wife along."

"I don't think that would be such a good idea," I said.

"Why, hasn't your wife ever seen a naked woman?" Rhonda asked.

"I'm sure she has," I said.

"She has never seen me ogling any naked women except her. She might not like me staring at you," I added.

"You wouldn't have to stare," Rhonda replied as she grinned.

"From what I imagine your body looks like, I'm sure I'd stare, even though my wife has a great body also," I said.

"I would like to see you sometime if you change your mind," she said as she smiled once again.

Trying to quit thinking of what she looked like naked, I asked her, "Did Angel ever talk about her fiancé?"

"Only a couple of times. She said that she had made a mistake and had an affair while away at college and her boyfriend broke off their engagement."

"Did she say he seemed mad enough to cause her harm?" I asked.

"No. In fact, Angel said they had recently started talking again and trying to patch things up," she said.

192

"What about Grandpa Hatfield? He seemed to really hate McCoys. Did she ever worry about him harming her?"

"No, she didn't worry about him. She said he was old and just a little off, but she never said anything about him harming her," Rhonda replied.

Just then, another customer came in and I once again stepped aside so they could get to the opening in the counter. The customer finished their business and left the store, so I started talking to Rhonda again.

"I was told Angel was seen talking to a stranger several days before she disappeared. Do you know anything about that?" I asked.

"All I know about her and the stranger is what Lucie told me. She was working the shift when Angel was seen talking to the stranger," Rhonda said.

"What did Lucie tell you?"

"She said it seemed like Angel knew the man although Lucie had never seen him around here before," Rhonda replied.

"Why did Lucie think Angel and the guy knew each other?" "Were they touching, hugging, kissing or something?"

"Lucie said that as the man and Angel talked, he put his arm around her shoulder," Rhonda said.

"In a threatening manner?"

"I don't think so. Lucie said they seemed to be enjoying each others company."

"They were both smiling and nodding their heads as they talked," Rhonda said.

"So, this guy might be someone that Angel knew."

"Seems like it."

"Did Lucie tell you what this guy looked like?" I asked Rhonda.

"No she didn't, but I'm sure she gave the sheriff as good of a description as she could," answered Rhonda.

"Why don't you ask the sheriff?"

"The sheriff and I aren't exactly on the best of terms, if you know what I mean."

"So you pissed him off, huh?" asked Rhonda as she smiled.

"I guess. I just questioned several things about his investigation in regards to Angel's disappearance."

"Could you give me Lucie's address so I could talk to her?" I asked.

"I guess that wouldn't hurt anything. You are a private investigator, so you said."

"Yes I am," I said as I retrieved my PI identification from my money clip and showed it to Rhonda.

"You look a little younger in this picture," she said as she smiled.

"And a little lighter," I answered as I smiled back at her.

Rhonda returned my ID and gave me Lucie's full name and address. I wrote it down on a piece of paper Rhonda gave me.

"Thanks. I should get going now. I have several other places I want to get to today," I said as I turned and started walking towards the front door.

"I still say you should come out to the Ace of Spades some night when I'm working. I'll give you a special dance," Rhonda said as she grinned and swayed her body in a sexy fashion.

"I just might do that," I said as I neared the door.

I sure would like to see Rhonda dance sometime, but I'm sure Martha would have shit fits, I thought as I neared the Escalade. Although, I could tell Martha that going to the Ace of Spades was part of my investigation. Fat chance she'd believe that, I thought as I got into my vehicle.

194

I left the lot of the Kum N Go and started driving towards the Family of our Lord compound.

As I drove towards the compound, I started to think. I doubted that Reverend Jones would see me, but I wanted to ask him several questions. Who was the stranger Angel had been seen with at the Kum N Go? According to Rhonda, he seemed friendly. Was he a family friend? Was he the person Angel had an affair with? Did he have anything to do with her disappearance? Was I ever going to discover anything that would lead me to find Angel?

# Chapter Twenty One

As I approached the entrance to the Family of our Lord, I slowed down. I was still thinking about what I would do if the Reverend Jones refused to see me. What could I do? I couldn't get a search warrant, only the sheriff could and I doubted that he was to serious about helping my investigation.

When I approached the gate to the front entrance, a guard emerged from inside the guardhouse located near the gate. He was a different guy than the one who had been in the guardhouse the first time I had visited the Family of our Lord.

He looked to be in his mid thirties, had short, cropped hair, and was clad in a khaki shirt, which had the arms cut off, and khaki pants. He had a tattoo on his right arm depicting an open bible and the words *Family of our Lord* circling the bible.

"What do ya want?" he asked gruffly as he approached the open window on the driver's side of my Escalade.

"I'm here to see Reverend States Rights Jones," I replied.

"He expecting you?"

"No," I answered.

"Well, then you can't see him. He only sees folks who have an appointment."

"Could you just call him and tell him Butch Brogen wants to talk to him again," I said.

"Ain't gonna do no good. Like I already told you, he only sees people who have an appointment."

"Just try, would you please?" I asked.

"OK," the guard replied as he turned and walked back to the guardhouse. I watched him through the window as he picked up a cell phone off the counter inside the guardhouse and made a call. I could tell he was talking to someone because he was motioning his arms and looking out of the window at me while he talked to someone. The Reverend Jones, I presumed. After several minutes of arm waving, he put the cell phone back down on the counter and came out of the building, walking towards me.

"So?" I asked as he neared the window of the Escalade.

"I got no clue what's going on, but Reverend Jones said he would speak with you."

"Thanks. I told you he would talk to me."

What I really meant was, I'm glad he would talk with me.

The guard walked back to the guardhouse, reached inside the door, and pressed a button allowing the crossbars blocking the entrance to the compound to slowly rise.

I put my vehicle in gear and slowly proceeded through the front entrance and gave the guard a slight wave of my hand and a nod of my head.

He returned neither.

"I wonder what the hell that snoopy private investigator wants," growled Reverend States Rights Jones to the two men who were standing next to him at the entrance to his office building.

"I don't know," answered one of the men.

"You said he had gone to the sheriff and said we had bootleg cigarettes and booze here," the other man said.

"That's right. I still don't know how he knew that. There is no way anyone could have got in and out of here without us knowing," replied the Reverend.

"The shipments have been moved, right?" asked Reverend Jones.

"Yes sir, Reverend," said one of the men.

"The latest shipment has been processed and delivered," replied the other man.

"Good. If I show this Brogen some empty buildings, maybe he will quit snooping around," Reverend Jones said as Butch's Escalade neared the spot where the three men stood.

As I neared the building where I had met Revered Jones previously, I saw the Reverend standing along with two other men. Reverend Jones was dressed exactly as he was the first time I had met him, although it looked like he had more bling hanging from his neck this time. I saw that the two men where the same two who I had been introduced to before. Brother Matthew and Brother Mark. I stopped my vehicle, got out, and approached the three men.

"Hello again, Mr. Brogen," said Reverend Jones as he walked towards me with his hand extended.

"Hello, Reverend Jones."

"I'm sorry our first meeting ended so roughly," Reverend Jones said as he clasped my hands in his.

"No problem. As Leviticus 19:18 says, 'Do not seek revenge or bear a grudge, but love your neighbor as yourself'."

"You surprise me Mr. Brogen. You almost recited that verse correctly," said Reverend Jones as he flashed me one of his wide, white toothy grins that revealed the gold caps on his upper front teeth. This time, each of the two gold caps contained a diamond! Business must be good, I thought.

"All do to the diligence of one of my Sunday school teachers as a youth, Mrs. Roberton."

"She must have been quite the teacher for you to remember an obscure passage like you just recited."

"She was as much of a task master as a teacher. She insisted we read our bibles. We would then study various verses of scripture each Sunday," I replied.

"She sounds like one of God's wonderful children," the Reverend answered.

"Now, what can I do for you?" he asked.

"I'm still investigating the disappearance of Angel McCoy and in the process of my investigation, I was told by someone that you were running some illegal sales out of your compound," I lied as not to tip off the Reverend that I had been inside his compound and saw for myself what I was talking about.

"First let me say I'm appalled that someone would accuse me of such dealings. Second, I don't know what this has to do with Ms. McCoys disappearance," said the Reverend.

"I'm sorry about your feelings."

"You dealing in contraband merchandise might not have anything to do with Angel's disappearance, but I figure if you're involved in one criminal activity, you might be involved in another," I said as Brothers Matthew and Mark, who were standing behind the Reverend suddenly rushed around Reverend Jones and stepped right in front of me.

"Brothers, just relax. I'm sure Mr. Brogen didn't mean what it sounded like he said," said the Reverend.

"Oh, I meant it,"

"If you're so innocent, let's take a look in your out buildings," I added.

"Being an ex homicide lieutenant, you should know that a search warrant is needed to search my buildings and seeing as you're retired and now a private investigator, you can't obtain a search warrant."

"I know I can't, but Sheriff Hatfield can."

"The sheriff and his men have already been out here investigating the disappearance of Ms. McCoy. They inspected all our buildings at that time to determine if she was here."

"But, if it will make you happy, we'll check out the buildings you were so wrongly informed contained illegal cigarettes and whiskey," added the Reverend.

He gave the two men a nod and one went to each side of me, but didn't touch me. I was in no mood for the two goons to try anything funny, but I really didn't want anything to start. I was sure the two of them could have put some serious hurt on me.

Reverend Jones turned and started walking towards the two building, which I had broken into. I followed as the two men walked along, one on either side of me. No one was speaking as we walked along.

About half way to the first building, a light bulb went off in my head. How did the Reverend know that I was a retired homicide lieutenant? In addition, I don't remember saying anything about what was in the buildings, other than contraband merchandise. Reverend Jones just mentioned cigarettes and whiskey. How did he know these details?

I was still trying to figure out these two details when we reached the first building. The Reverend stopped and the man to the left of me walked towards the door of the building as he reached into his right front pants pocket and removed a key.

You don't need a key, I thought to myself and smiled as I remembered how easy the padlocks were to pick.

Brother Matthew unlocked the padlock, opened the door, and then stood aside. Reverend Jones walked part way through the door and reached inside to hit the light switch which was located on the wall left of the door.

"After you," said Reverend Jones as he waved his right hand towards the open door and stepped aside.

I walked through the open door, followed by the Reverend and his two henchmen. Looking around, I was stunned to see nothing but a huge vacant area. There were no pallets of cigarettes. In fact, the room looked cleaner than a freshly washed babies butt.

"See any contraband?" asked Reverend Jones as he stood along side of me with his ever present shit eating grin.

"Nope, I don't see anything."

"I told you that your supposed snitch didn't know what they were talking about."

"Let's check out the other building and see what you can find there," said the Reverend.

The Reverend and I left the first building, while the two men shut off the lights, closed the door, and snapped the padlock shut in the hasp. They caught up to the Reverend and me just as we approached the second building.

Once again, one of the Reverends men unlocked the padlock on the door with a key he retrieved from his pocket. Once again, the Reverend went part way inside the door and turned on the light switch. Once again, I walked into a huge empty building, no crates of booze like I had seen earlier.

"See any whiskey, Mr. Brogen?" asked Reverend Jones.

"Nope, this building is as empty as the other one."

"I think in the future, you should make sure that your sources are correct before you accuse someone of illegal activities," said the Reverend as he smiled and walked out of the building.

The lights were shut off, the door padlocked and we started walking back towards where I had parked.

"Anything else I can show you?" asked the Reverend.

"Angel McCoy."

Reverend Jones eyes turned into dark slits, his shit-eating grin disappeared, and Brothers Matthew and Mark once again walked up along side of me, almost brushing against me.

"I don't find that amusing," said the Reverend curtly.

"It wasn't intended to be."

"I just find it funny that in my two visits here I have never seen another living sole other than you and your two bodyguards," I added.

"Brothers Matthew and Mark are not bodyguards. They are servants of the Lord and me."

"And why is not seeing anyone else so surprising? The members of our flock have chores to do. They have fields to attend. They have bible lessons to attend. They are not just idle people sitting around," replied the Reverend.

"As it says in Romans 12:11, 'Never be lazy, but work hard and serve the Lord enthusiastically'," added Reverend Jones.

"OK," I replied.

We walked the rest of the way to my vehicle in silence. I wonder what Reverend Jones was thinking about? It seems that I hit a nerve when I mentioned Angel's name. Where had the cigarettes and booze gone?

"I hope you are satisfied, Mr. Brogen. As you saw, we don't have contraband merchandise here. And, I can assure you that Angel McCoy is not here either," Reverend Jones said as we reached my Escalade.

"I guess you got me there, Reverend."

"No cigarettes or booze. No Angel McCoy," I said as I started to get into my vehicle.

"I would appreciate it, if you would stop harassing me," said the Reverend.

"I'm not harassing anybody. I'm just a private investigator running down leads," I said as I smiled at him.

He showed me another of his golden toothy grins.

"All the same. I think we are done seeing one another unless you have concrete evidence of the things you have accused me of," he said.

"Then you should let the sheriff do his work," he added as he turned and started walking back towards the door leading back into the building to his office.

Brothers Matthew and Mark stood their ground with arms folded across their chests.

I closed the door of the Escalade, started the engine, and slowly started driving towards the front gate. As I drove, I kept looking around trying to see another soul. Where are all the people that are supposed to be members of the Family of our Lord and live here? I thought.

I reached the front gate and stopped. The crossbar slowly started to rise. Before the crossbar was totally erect, the guard slowly ambled out of the guard house towards me.

"Get everything you needed to get?" he asked.

"Yep. I was given twenty cartons of cigarettes, ten bottles of prime Tennessee whiskey and the promise that if I come back tomorrow, I'll get three virgins also."

"What?"

"Just kidding buddy," I said as I slowly drove past him onto the gravel road leading back to town.

I looked at the clock in the dashboard of the Escalade and saw that it was only 4:30 p.m. I could get in a quick round of golf before I went back to Kenny's place.

As I drove to the golf course, I once again started to think.

What had I learned? The cigarettes and booze were no longer in the building where I had seen them. Reverend Jones knew more about me than I had revealed. How did he get his facts? Did Sheriff Hatfield inform the Reverend? Were Sheriff

Hatfield and Reverend States Rights Jones both involved in the bootleg enterprise? Was the Reverend truthful when he said he had no idea what happened to Angel McCoy? Was Angel a captive in the compound of the Family of our Lord? What do I do next?

I'm running out of ides and still have not discovered what happened to Bertha's sister. Should I just say the hell with it, pack up, and go back to Minnesota where I could be golfing with all my buddies? That would be letting Bubba and Bertha down, but I never promised I would find Angel, only that I would try.

As I neared the golf course, I was developing a splitting headache. I had never been so baffled in my life. In all my cases, while on the force or as a private investigator, I always come up with one or more ideas that helped solve the case. Right now, after two weeks, I don't know jack shit!

# Chapter Twenty Two

I pulled into the parking lot of the Jones Valley golf course and once again noticed that there were not many cars in the parking lot. At this time of the day, people should be showing up for evening golf league. Just a sign of the times, people don't have the money to spend on recreation, I thought as I stopped the Escalade at the parking blocks near the clubhouse.

I removed my golf bag from my vehicle, slipped on my Foot Joy Dry Joy golf shoes, grabbed my SkyCaddie GPS, and closed the rear door of the Escalade. I hit the button on the clicker in my hand, the car beeped once and the doors locked. I picked up my bag and walked to the door of he clubhouse. I glanced out on the golf course and couldn't see a soul!

I set my bag down, opened the door of the clubhouse and walked in.

"Hello. Can I help you?" asked the young man standing behind the counter.

"Like to get in eighteen holes if you have room," I replied.

"Oh, we got plenty of room, but I must warn you that this is not a good time to be going out golfing."

"Why, is it going to rain?"

"Nope, no rain, but there have been some strange happenings going on out here this time of night."

"What strange happenings?" I asked.

The clubhouse attendant shuffled his feet, looked at the ground and scratched his head before he answered.

"We've had four cases of people going missing on the golf course," he said.

"Going missing?"

"Yep, four times in the past two months single golfers have teed off around five o'clock and then just disappeared."

"Disappeared?"

"Yep. They just left the face of the earth without leaving a trace."

"They didn't leave a trace?"

"Nope. I was working all four times and when it started getting dark and the golfers hadn't returned, I got a little worried. I closed up the clubhouse, grabbed a flashlight, jumped in a golf cart and started going around the course to see if I could find them."

"Did you find them?" I asked.

"No. That's what I'm trying to tell you. I never found hide nor hair of them. I did find their golf cart and golf clubs sitting in the rough along side of hole number sixteen."

"You found the golf equipment of all four sitting along the same fairway in the same spot?" I asked.

"Yes. All four times, I found the golf cart and their equipment, but there was no sign of them. It's as though a UFO came down and sucked them up," he relayed as he started to get more excited.

"A UFO sucked them up?"

"Sure seems like it. The sheriff searched the entire course and surrounding woods with dozens of people and tracking dogs. They didn't find a thing."

"No landing gear pad marks in the grass or burned areas from the space ship blasting off?" I asked as I smiled.

"No. No evidence was found and I don't think those folks disappearing is funny," the attendant said as he scowled at me.

206

"Sorry, I wasn't trying to be funny. It's just that I've never encountered a UFO on a golf course."

"You've seen a UFO someplace other than a golf course?" he asked excitedly.

"No, I've never seen a UFO."

"Maybe the golfers just got tired of golfing and decided to just go home," I added.

"That don't make no sense. If they wanted to quit golfing, why not just quit and drive the golf cart back to the clubhouse. Why leave the cart and all their equipment out there?"

"You got me there. I guess my thought of them quitting and going home doesn't make much sense," I replied.

"I'm telling you, those golfers must have been beamed aboard a space ship and hauled off to god knows where," he replied as he got more excited.

I didn't know what to make of the attendants' thoughts of UFO's, but time was passing and I needed to get golfing or I wouldn't get my eighteen holes in.

"I'll keep my eyes open for space ships," I said as I smiled and handed him my credit card.

"This ain't no laughing matter. What else could have happened to them?" he said as he swiped my card, handed me a receipt to sign along with a key to a golf cart.

"I believe you that the golfers disappeared, but I have a hard time believing they were sucked aboard a space ship."

"You just be careful and keep your eyes to the sky," he replied.

I grabbed my receipt, the golf cart key and started out of he clubhouse door.

"Maybe you should just golf nine, then you wouldn't have to go down number sixteen," he said as I started opening the door.

"I'll think about it," I replied as I turned and smiled at him before I walked outside, picked up my golf bag and walked to the nearest golf cart.

I was hitting the golf ball great, so I played the front nine in less than one hour. As I teed my golf ball up on the tenth tee box, I thought about what the clubhouse attendant had told me. There's no way those golfers could have been taken away by a space ship, but what happened to them? The kid said the sheriff had searched the woods with people and dogs, but couldn't find anything. What happened to them?

I golfed holes ten through fifteen just as good as I had on the front nine, drives straight down the middle of the fairway, great second shots into the green and so-so putting. As I teed my golf ball up on the sixteenth tee box, I found myself scanning the entire area in front of me along with looking skyward. There's no truth to golfers just disappearing, I thought as I proceeded to hit my tee shot. I hooked the ball left into the woods along the sixteenth fairway!

"Shit!" I exclaimed as I saw my Pinnacle hit one of the massive Maple trees lining the fairway.

"The only time I've hooked a drive all day and it has to been on the damn sixteenth hole," I muttered as I walked back to the golf cart.

I placed my driver back into my golf bag, got into the golf cart and started driving down the fairway to where I thought my golf ball had went into the woods. As I neared the spot I thought my golf ball had gone into the woods, I stopped my golf cart and got out. I quickly looked skyward for space ships, saw none, and then started to walk towards the woods. I removed my HD Blue Ray sunglasses and placed them on the bill of my golf cap.

Because the sun was slowly sinking, the woods were starting to become an eerie dark shade of grey and black. Small flecks of sunlight filtered through the trees revealing shimmering shadows as it landed on the forest floor. Leaves rustled from the slight breeze that had picked up on hole fourteen.

Sure hope there's enough light to find my golf ball, I thought as I entered the woods.

I was suddenly startled by a rustling sound coming from within the woods. Because of the hour, the daylight was dimming and I couldn't see what was causing the noise.

I entered a small opening in the woods and was instantly set upon by two huge men. They both came at me like charging bulls. Neither one of them looked like they were there to show me where my golf ball had landed, or to give me hugs and kisses. I suddenly wished I had brought a golf club with me into the woods. I could have used it for protection!

My situation didn't look so appealing, so I figured I might as well get into action and ask questions later. As the first man got close to me, I swung my right fist and smashed him right in the face. Although my hand started to hurt instantly, he never slowed down. He swung and landed a crashing left along the side of my head. My golf cap and sun glasses flew off my head! I was instantly stunned, but managed to deliver another blow to his face. I hit him full on the nose and was at once showered in blood as his nose spurted blood everywhere. By now my head was clearing a little bit, when I caught movement out of the corner of my left eye just before I felt a sledgehammer like blow to the side of my head. I instantly saw several lighting flashes in the darkness before everything went totally black!

"You dumb shits," hissed the unsmiling Reverend States Rights Jones through clenched teeth. The veins on the sides of his neck were bulging as he addressed the two men standing next to him while he looked through the open door at the unconscious man lying on a bed.

"Do you know who that is?" he asked the two men, still through clenched teeth.

"No, Reverend Jones," one of the men meekly answered.

"It's just another golfer," the second man said.

"He's not just another golfer," the Reverend almost screamed while he closed the door.

"The man you two imbeciles kidnapped is that nosey private investigator, Butch Brogen," the Reverend snapped.

"Whatever," said one of the men.

"Whatever," screamed the Reverend as sweat started forming on his brow and his eyes bugged out! His hands clenched and unclenched as he tried to regain his composure. He finally reached his right hand up to his neck, loosened his necktie, and unbuttoned the top button of his shirt.

"He has been snooping around here and somehow found out about one of my outside activities."

"The cigarettes and whiskey?"

"Yes, the cigarettes and whiskey, dumb shit."

"He was here with his wife, so now I'm sure she will go to the sheriff and demand that he finds Brogen," said Reverend Jones.

"We didn't know who he was. We just thought he was another golfer we could pick up," said the second man.

"That's your problem, you two morons tried to think," the Reverend quickly snapped as he removed a handkerchief from his rear pants pocket and wiped his sweaty brow. Areas of sweat started to form on the front of the Reverends ecru polyester shirt.

"From the looks of his face, you hit him more than just enough to knock him out," the Reverend said as he continued to wipe his face with his handkerchief.

"He damn near broke my friggen nose," said one of the men as he reached up and gingerly touched his nose.

"So you needed to beat the snot out of him?" asked Reverend Jones as he put his handkerchief back in his pants pocket.

"No, I just wanted to make sure he was out cold," replied the man as he tried slowly moving away from Reverend Jones.

"Go get the Salvia Divinorum and give him a shot. Then take him to the barracks while I try to figure out what I'm going to do to rectify your screw up," Reverend Jones spat.

"Yes sir, Reverend," said one of the men as he turned and hurried off to get the Salvia Divinorum as he had been directed.

"I still can't believe this shit," the Reverend said as he once again took his handkerchief out of his pants pocket and wiped his brow.

"I have to give Virgil a call to let him know what has happened. I want him to be prepared when Brogen's wife contacts him," the Reverend said to no one in particular.

I slowly started coming to. I opened my eyes and discovered that the left eye didn't seem to open. I slowly lifted my left hand and gingerly touched my eye. It was swollen shut! I tried to focus my right eye on my surroundings, but could only see darkness. As I tried to set up, I felt a lump along my right leg. I reached down to the side pocket on my shorts and discovered my cell phone. Who ever had brought me here, hadn't taken my cell phone from my side pocket. Not knowing what was going on, I removed my cell phone from my pocket and squinted through my right eye as I tried to see the off button. Because the off button was illuminated, I managed to press it, turning off my cell phone. I placed it back into my shorts pocket. I wanted to save the battery in case I got a chance to use my phone.

My head still hurt, so I laid back down, wondering where I was and what had happened. The last I could remember, I hit my drive into the woods along fairway sixteen and was attacked by two huge goons as I went into the woods to find my golf ball. I remember hitting one directly on his nose, causing blood to spurt from it. Then I felt a couple of crashing blows to my head and then darkness.

I heard some noise coming from outside of the room I was in, so I closed my right eye. The left eye was already closed! I heard the door to the room slowly open and sensed someone entering the room.

"Here, you give him the shot," I heard someone say.

"OK. Is he still out?" another voice said.

"Looks like it."

I felt someone take a hold of my right arm and felt a prick.

"That's done," I heard.

"Let's get him to the barracks like Reverend Jones told us to."

I don't know what was injected into me, but all of a sudden flashes of light appeared, even though my eyes were closed. My head started swimming, more lights flashed and a dark hole appeared to me. It felt as if I was being sucked into this dark hole. I expected my head to start hurting, but didn't feel any more pain than was coming from my swollen face.

I had smoked my share of rope in my younger days, but had never felt any sensation like this. I wonder what I had been injected with?

As my head kept spinning while I spiraled towards this black hole, I felt someone grabbing each one of my arms and lifting me up.

"Come on. Lift him up, so we can get him to the barracks," I heard.

As I was lifted up, a floating sensation overcame me. I couldn't tell if I was being carried, pulled, dragged, but knew I was being moved.

I felt myself spiraling into the black hole and once again was overcome by flashing lights. My entire universe was spinning out of control. I tried to grab onto something to stabilize myself, but felt only air.

I was now being shot out of the black hole at what felt like the speed of light. Crazy colorful lights streaked by my head as I was pushed out of the black hole. I still felt as though I was floating on air, when all of a sudden I felt a thud, but still only saw blackness and flashing lights!

## Chapter Twenty Three

"You dumb shit. You almost dropped him," said the man holding onto my right arm.

"Well, I didn't," spat the second man.

Although I could hear talking, I couldn't make out what was being said. At least the black hole and lights had disappeared!

I once again woke up in a strange place and tried to remember what had happened. I felt like I was lying on my back in a bed. I slowly opened my eyes, but the right eye was the only one that allowed light to be perceived. I lifted my left hand to my left eye, tenderly touched it, and found that it was still swollen shut. I slowly raised my head and tried to see where I was. Through the blurry right eye, I saw I was in a large room with many beds lined against each wall. The room started spinning, so I slowly lowered my head and tried to figure out what was going on.

I don't know how long I was lying in the bed, drifting in and out of consciousness, but at least the black hole and lights were gone. I now heard what sounded like peoples voices around me. I slowly opened my right eye a slit and was surprised to discover a human face several inches from mine.

"Wow, his face is sure swollen."

"Looks like his one eye is swollen shut."

"Who is he?"

"I don't know. Just another person the Reverend has brought to join us."

I tried to make out more of the conversation, but drifted back into unconsciousness.

More time passed and I came to once again. By now my head was beginning to clear and I could focus fairly well through my right eye. Without raising my head, I tried to see as much of my surroundings as possible. I now saw men sitting on the beds that sat along two walls. They were dressed in gray tee shirts and brown pants. They were all reading something from a book. I couldn't make out what the book was, though. I was feeling well enough to get acquainted with my room mates. I slowly sat up in the bed I was laying on and held myself up with my arms propped on the bed.

"Hello," I mumbled through swollen lips.

Instantly, everyone quit reading and looked over at me.

"I'm Butch Brogen," I again mumbled.

Everyone kept staring at me except one guy who slowly laid down his book, arose from his bed, and slowly started to walk over towards where I was.

"Hi Brother Brogen," the gentleman said as he neared me.

"Looks like you met Brothers Elijah and Hiram," he said to me with a slight smile.

"Feels like I met the end of a sledge hammer."

"They have a tendency to make a person feel that way," he said as he smiled and sat down at the end of my bed.

"I would get you something for your pain, but we don't have anything here that would help. We get all our medicines from the infirmary," he said.

Meanwhile, the other men in the room picked up their books and began to read once again.

"Where am I?" I asked the man sitting on my bed.

"The male barracks of the Family of our Lord compound."

"Family of our Lord?"

"It's a religious compound run by Reverend States Rights Jones."

"I know. I've met the Reverend several times," I said.

"You were trying to join the family?" he asked.

"Nope, I was looking for a young lady who disappeared and thought she might be here," I replied.

His eyes darkened into small slits and he quickly glanced around the room.

"You were looking for a missing girl?" he asked.

"Yes. Her name is Angel McCoy. She's about five foot four, a buck twenty, long dark hair and hazel eyes. Have you seen anyone like that around here?" I asked as my head got clearer and I began to feel stronger.

"No," he quickly replied.

Just then, the door to the barracks opened and two guys walked in.

"Lights out brothers," one of the men said.

The man sitting on the edge of my bed quickly got up and started walking backs towards his bed.

As he walked back to his bed, I thought I saw a faint tattoo of a rose and the word *MOM* on his right arm.

I lay back down on my bed as the two men who had entered the room slowly walked up and down the rows of beds. They looked like the two men I had seen the night I had snuck into the compound. The men turned off the room lights and exited the building. I lay still and tried to fall asleep in spite of the throbbing of my eye, lips and head.

As I lay in bed trying to fall asleep, I started wondering about the guy who had talked to me. He didn't look real familiar, but could this guy be Spike, who had owned Your Uncles Place? I had only seen him a couple of times, so I wasn't sure what he looked like. Spike had disappeared, though. Spike

216

also had a rose tattoo on his right arm. This guy seemed friendlier than the other men in the room did. Why had I been beaten, kidnapped, and brought to the Family of our Lord's compound? The final thought I had before I drifted off was that I needed to get in touch with Martha and let her know where I was.

"Psst, psst," I heard in a hushed voice.

Although I had finally fallen asleep, I opened my one good eye and tried to focus in the darkness.

"Psst," I heard once again as I felt a hand on my shoulder.

"Butch."

"Yes," I quietly replied.

"I don't know if you remember me, but I remember you. You were here several years ago investigating a murder."

My thoughts went to the rose tattoo I had seen on the man's arm.

"Spike?"

"Yep."

"What's going on?" I asked.

"I can't talk much now, but I'll try to connect up with you in the morning before I go out to work in the fields."

"We have breakfast in the chow hall at 7:00 a.m. I'm sure they will let you go to eat. Don't let on that we know each other. I'll try to get a seat next to you and maybe we can talk," he added

"OK. Sounds good," I replied as he quietly disappeared into the darkness of the room.

As I tried to get back to sleep, I kept thinking about my short conversation with Spike.

"Up and attem!!"

I slowly shook the cobwebs out of my head and tried to remember what was going on.

217

"Chow in one half hour," I heard.

As I slowly rose up from the bed, I saw everyone getting up and making their bed.

"You need to get up Brother Brogen," one of the men who had come into the barracks said to me.

"I need to shower and brush my teeth," I replied through lips that were less swollen than the day before.

"Just follow everyone else to the shower and I'll give you a tooth brush," the man said.

I did what I was told and got out of the bed. I was surprised that my head didn't hurt as much as I thought it would. As I started walking towards the door of the barracks along with the other men, I noticed Spike glancing backwards towards me as he walked out the door along with the other men.

I did get a shower, but had to put my same clothes back on. My tee shirt was covered in splattered blood that had dried, but it had dried and looked like dark brown blobs on my shirt. I was given a toothbrush and some tooth paste. Although it hurt my swollen lips to brush me teeth, I enjoyed the fresh taste in my mouth. I wasn't given a razor, so I had stubble on my face. After the shower, we were led to a building that I assumed was the mess hall.

As we walked along, I felt the small bulge in my shorts pocket reveling my cell phone. I couldn't believe that nobody had searched me thoroughly enough to discover my cell phone! I knew I couldn't use my phone right now, so I left it in my pocket, turned off.

We reached the mess hall and were escorted in. I saw that already there were a large gathering of women sitting at long wooden tables. Was Angel one of these women? As we walked along towards some empty tables, I tried to focus my working

218

right eye on the women to see if any of them looked like Angel. I saw no one matching her description.

We reached the empty tables and I sat down in one of the empty chairs. Quickly, Spike slid into the chair to my right.

"Good morning, Brother," he said quietly as he smiled at me and looked around to see if anyone was looking at us.

"Good morning," I replied and nodded.

We sat in silence as three men emerged from a door at one end of the room and walked over to the first man at the table closest to the wall. One of the men removed a pill from a bottle he was carrying and handed the pill to the man, who promptly put it in his mouth and washed it down with a drink from his milk glass. This ritual was continued along each table until the men came to me.

"You will get your vitamin later, Brother Brogen," the man with the bottle said as he moved next to Spike. He handed Spike a pill and watched as Spike drank a swallow of milk to wash it down. After every person, except me had been given a pill, the three men retreated through the door they had emerged from.

"What was that about?" I said to Spike as I noticed him spit something into his hand.

"Drugs to keep us quite and obedient," he quietly answered.

"The Reverend drugs everyone here? I asked.

"Sure. How else do you think everyone would be so willing to do the Reverend's work," Spike said.

"The drug doesn't seem to be affecting you," I said.

"That's because I developed a great knack for placing the pill under my tongue while I take a drink without swallowing the pill," he said.

"They just think I take their stupid pill."

We continued to talk while a crew of people came around with serving carts containing the morning meal on plastic trays.

After we were served and started to eat, I asked Spike, "Were you kidnapped and brought here?"

"Damn right I was. I sure wouldn't join a bunch of crackpots like this on my own."

"Have you ever tried to get away from the compound?" I asked.

"Yeah, a couple of times. I tried to sneak out on one of he trucks, but was caught."

"Solitary for one month each time," Spike added as he smiled.

I checked out the perimeter fence, but I couldn't figure out how to get over that damn barbed wire," he replied.

"Oh, there's a way," I said as I smiled at Spike.

"Huh?"

I then told Spike how I had scaled the fence to get into and out of the compound.

"I'll be damned!" he said after I had finished my story.

By now, we were instructed to pick up our trays, take them to the long counter at the end of the room and go outside and form into the work groups. As we stood around, I kept looking to see if any of the women looked like Angel, but I still didn't see anyone who matched her description.

Just then two men started walking towards Spike and I as we continued to talk.

"Come with us, Brother Brogen," one of the men said to me as they stopped in front of me.

I gave Spike a quick glance and started to walk along with one man on each side of me. Neither guy said a word until we reached the Family of our Lord office.

"Reverend Jones wishes to speak with you," said one of the men as he gently pushed me up the steps towards the door of the office building. The door opened and out stepped Brother

Matthew or Mark, I couldn't remember what each one looked like.

"This way," the Brother said as he swung his hand inside the door.

I walked through the doorway and was joined by the Brother, who started walking down a small hallway towards more doors. We walked past three closed doors before we stopped. He opened the door and once again gestured for me to enter the room. The room was quite large and had various religious pictures hanging on every wall. I instantly noticed a large walnut desk at one end of the room. Behind the desk sat Reverend States Rights Jones!

"Ah, Brother Brogen," the Reverend said as he rose to his feet and started walking out from behind the desk.

"It looks as if you've had a small accident," he said to me as he flashed his gold toothy grin.

"Beat up, you mean," I replied.

"I wouldn't know anything about that. All I know is that two of my people found you unconscious along the road leading to the Jones Valley golf course," he said.

"Have a seat,' he said as he pointed to one of the leather stuffed chairs located next to a large table to the right of his desk.

"That's all Brother," he said to my escort who turned and walked out of the room, closing the door behind him.

"Have you been given any medical attention for your wounds?" asked the Reverend.

"Not that I'm aware of. I think I was unconscious for most of the night," I replied through swollen lips.

"We'll take you to the infirmary and have your face looked at," he said.

"So why am I really here?" I asked.

"As I said, you were found unconscious and being the good samaritans we are, you were brought here by two of our flock," he replied.

"I'm sure that you are aware of the parable of the Samaritan Jesus told about in Luke 10, versus 30 – 37. We pattern our lives after the good Samaritan," added the Reverend.

"Why not just call 911?" I asked.

"We believe in taking care of matters ourselves. We don't like to involve outside people," he replied and smiled.

"Whatever," I said.

"I'm ready to leave," I said as I started to rise from the chair I was sitting in.

"Of course. Of course," replied Reverend Jones.

"The sheriff has found your vehicle in the parking lot of the golf course and one of my men will take you there immediately," he said as he also started to get out of his chair.

"But first, we should have your face looked at by our doctor," he added.

"Forget it, I'm OK."

"I just want to get out of here now," I added.

"If you wish, but I still think our doctor could help you."

We exited his office, walked down the hall towards the front door, and exited the building. A silver Chevrolet pickup was parked by the steps leading from the building, with a man sitting in the driver's seat. Reverend Jones opened the passengers' door and I got into the cab of the truck.

"Have a safe journey," the Reverend said as he closed the trucks door.

My chauffeur started driving down the driveway leading out of the compound. He didn't speak and neither did I. As we continued out of the compound towards the Jones Valley golf course where my Escalade sat, I once again started to wonder.

Is this the silver Chevrolet pickup the men who were watching Martha and I driving?  Why had I been attacked? Were my attackers the Reverend's men?  Why had I been let go? Am I actually going to be delivered to my vehicle?  How did the Reverend know Sheriff Hatfield had found my vehicle at the golf course?  Now that I know Spike is in the compound, can I help him escape?  I need to call Martha, but not until I'm alone. Where is Angel?

# Chapter Twenty Four

It took about twenty minutes to get to the entrance of the golf course. Neither one of us had spoken a word the entire trip. I looked at the parking lot near the clubhouse and was glad to see my Escalade sitting there! My chauffer pulled his truck close to the back of my Escalade, put the truck in park, and nodded towards the passenger door. I took that as a signal to get out of his vehicle, so I did. I then realized that my keys and money clip were in my golf bag where I always put them at the beginning of my golf round.

Before I went into the clubhouse to see if they had my golf clubs, I thought I had better call Martha. I retrieved my cell phone from my shorts pocket, turned it on, and was delighted to see I had plenty of battery left. I also saw that I had five messages. Probably from Martha, I thought. Sure enough! Even though she wasn't going to be at Kenny's last night, she had tried to contact me. She'll probably be pissed I had my phone turned off, but once I explain the reason, I'm sure she'll understand.

I selected contacts, scrolled to Martha's cell phone, and pushed send. Two rings later I heard, "Hello. Where have you been? I left you five messages!"

"Hello. Glad to hear your voice also," I replied through swollen lips.

"Where have you been? Why didn't you answer your phone?"

"Just calm down and I'll explain everything."

"You're damned right you will explain!"

This ain't good, I thought to myself. Martha just swore at me for the third time in the past week.

"Please take a breath and let me tell you a little bit of what has been transpiring," I pleadingly said through swollen lips.

"OK, OK. But it had better be good," came her calmer answer.

"You better not have been watching any strippers if you know what's good for you," she quickly added as her voice started to rise once again.

"Calm down. I wasn't watching strippers," I quickly said as I tried to soothe her ruffled feathers.

She didn't know that I had met Rhonda, so why did she bring up strippers?

I wanted to tell her that I had been damn near beaten to death, but knew that would only make things worse at the moment.

"I'll fill you in on all the details when I get back to Kenny's," I said.

"We're not at Kenny's yet. We're still visiting some of my relatives."

"I guess you really care about my safety. You're not even home waiting with open arms and a kiss for me," I said and instantly realized I should have kept my mouth shut. Too late!

"You can stop that trying to be funny shit, Mr. Larry Brogen," Martha barked into her phone.

"Just tell me what is going on," she added.

"And, why does your voice sound so mumbled?" she asked.

Fourth time Martha has swore at me now! I had better just explain what I can and try not being such a smart ass. I gave Martha the highlights of my past eighteen hours, assured her I was alright, and would fill her in on all the details when we got together after she got back to Kenny's house.

"We'll be home sometime early this afternoon. Just go back to Kenny's and wait for me," she instructed.

I was ready to give her another of my smart-ass comments, but realized I had better just say, "OK."

I hung up my cell phone and realized I was still wearing my bloodstained tee shirt. I had another change of clothes in my Escalade in case I ever was caught in a downpour while I was golfing, but my vehicle keys were in my golf bag. I hoped! I started towards the door of the clubhouse. I walked inside the clubhouse and saw that the person behind the counter was the same guy I had talked to yesterday.

"Hi," I said as I reached the counter.

"Hi," he replied as he raised his head from looking at the tee time sheet.

"Holy crap! You didn't get abducted by aliens," he excitedly exclaimed.

"When you didn't come back last night, I went looking for you and all I found was your golf cart and clubs. Just like the other golfers who have disappeared," he added.

"No, I didn't get abducted by aliens," I answered as I chuckled, trying not to hurt my swollen lips.

"What happened then?"

"Your face looks like crap!"

"It feels like crap also," I replied.

"Looks like old blood stains on your tee shirt, too," he said.

"Could be," I replied as I looked down at the stained front of my tee shirt.

"What the hell happened?"

I explained only the part about being attacked by two guys and that I was fine. I didn't go into details about Reverend Jones.

"Do you have my bag, clubs and SkyCaddie GPS?" I asked.

"Sure do. Got em back in the office," he said as he walked around the counter towards an open door to my left and entered the room. He emerged from the room carrying my Bag Boy golf bag and sat it at my feet. He handed me my GPS still locked into the device that attaches it to the golf cart.

"Here ya be," he said as he smiled.

"All your golfing equipment, except your golf shoes," he said.

I looked down at me feet and realized that I was still wearing my Foot Joy golf shoes.

"Got the golf shoes on," I replied as I lifted my right foot to show the attendant my golf shoe.

I immediately unzipped the top pocket of my golf bag and was relieved to find my keys and money clip.

"I was hoping these were here," I said as I removed the keys and money clip from the pocket.

"I could use a change of clothes which I have in my Escalade," I added.

"I never touched anything in your bag. I just brought the bag into the clubhouse in case you ever returned. We still have the golf bags from the other four golfers who disappeared," he said.

"So you say two guys jumped you in the woods along the sixteenth fairway," he said to me.

"Yep."

"Know why?"

"I have no idea," I sort of lied. I knew they were tied in with Reverend Jones, but never did get a good explanation why I was attacked.

227

"You had better report this to the sheriff," he said.

"I'm sure he already knows," I mumbled.

"What?"

"Ah nothing. I was just mumbling to myself."

"And you're right. I'll go see the sheriff as soon as I leave here," I replied.

"Thanks again for retrieving my golf equipment," I said as I picked up my golf bag and started for the door of the clubhouse.

"No problem. Glad you're alright and be sure to come back here to golf," he said.

"If I do, I'll stay away from hole sixteen," I said with a small laugh that hurt my swollen lips, and he laughed with me.

I unlocked the Escalade and put my golf bag inside. I removed my golf shoes and put on my loafers. I retrieved a clean tee shirt from a backpack I always carry in case of emergencies on the golf course. I always figured my emergency would be getting wet from rain, not a blood splattered shirt! I took off my bloodstained tee shirt, put on the clean one, and put the soiled one in the backpack. I closed the rear door, got in the drivers seat and started to drive out of the golf course parking lot.

As the bright sunlight shown through the windshield, I realized I didn't have my HD Blue Ray sunglasses. They along with my golf cap must still be in the woods along hole number sixteen where they flew when I was attacked. I still couldn't see very well out of my swollen left eye, so the bright sunlight was an even more strain on my good eye. My lips also hurt when I smiled, but other than that, I was good to go.

I'll just have to squint as I drive back to Kenny's and buy a new pair of sunglasses tomorrow, I thought.

As I drove back to Kenny's place, I started once again to think about what I should do next.

I'm sure the sheriff is in cahoots with Reverend Jones, so it wouldn't do any good to tell him about my experience. Spike is at the Family of our Lord compound and it seems like he has resisted being drugged enough so he doesn't want to remain a member of the family. I should get Spike out of there. I didn't see Angel. Spike said he doesn't remember seeing anyone who matches her description, either.

Although I'm finding out information on the workings of the Family of our Lord, I'm not any closer to finding out what happened to Angel than when I first got down here. By the time I turned into Kenny's driveway, my head was throbbing. I don't know if it was from the beating I had received or was because I couldn't figure out what happened to Angel.

## Chapter Twenty Five

As I neared Kenny's house, I saw him sitting out front in a lawn chair sucking on a long neck. I parked the Escalade on the apron to the garage, got out, and started walking over to where Kenny sat. He gave me a nod of his head as I got nearer to him.

"Holy shit! What happened to you?" he exclaimed when I was finally close enough to him so he could see my face.

"Had a little accident," I replied as I tried not to smile too much.

"You had better grab a beer or Tangueray to help ease the pain," Kenny said as he smiled.

"Neither one would be a bad idea. Still got some Tangueray?"

"You bet. Need help?"

"Nope, I'm good."

"Does Martha know about what happened to you?"

"Kinda," I replied as I reached the house door and went inside. I made myself a strong Tangueray and tonic and went back outside to join Kenny.

"So, what the hell happened?" asked Kenny as I pulled up a lawn chair next to him.

I took as big a swallow of my drink as my swollen lips would allow before I replied.

"I got attacked on the golf course by two big galoots."

"You hit into em or something?"

"No, I didn't hit into them. I yanked my drive on hole sixteen and when I went into the woods to look for my golf ball, they attacked me," I replied.

"You know what I think?" asked Kenny.

"No, what?"

"You should hit your golf shots straight down the fairway the way the game was invented," Kenny said with a big shit-eating grin.

"Thanks a lot, ass hole. I knew I was doing something wrong," I replied.

I then proceeded to tell Kenny as much of the entire story I knew. All about being taken to the Family of our Lord's, meeting Spike and not seeing Angel.

As I was finishing my tale, Marcie's car came driving into the yard. She opened the garage door with the car remote and drove inside.

"You're gonna catch shit now that sis is back," Kenny said as he stood up and started towards the front door of the house.

"Gotta grab another long neck," he said as he smiled and disappeared inside the house.

"Butch," is all that I heard as Martha came running out of the garage towards me.

"Hi Hon," I said.

"What happened to you?" she exclaimed as she neared me.

"Why does everyone have to ask me what happened to me?" I said.

"Because we want to know," Martha replied as she bent down and gave me a kiss on the lips.

"Ouch. Be careful."

"I was being careful," she replied as she gave me another kiss, only gentler this time.

"Let me take a look at your injuries. You might have to go to the emergency room," Martha added.

"I'm not going to the doctor. I just have a swollen eye and lips. I'm not going to die," I replied.

Just then, Marcie and the girls emerged from the garage saving me from more doctor talk.

"Oh Uncle Butch, you look terrible," one of the girls said as they both stared at my swollen face.

"What happened to you?" asked Marcie.

"I fell off a bar stool," I replied.

"He did not. Don't be such a smart ass, Butch," Martha said.

"I want to know the entire story," she added.

"Me too," said Marcie.

"Just let me put these packages in the house before you start," she added.

"What the hell is this? Story time with Butch," I said in a disgusted tone.

"Don't you swear in front of the girls," Martha admonished me.

"OK, I'm sorry," I replied as Marcie and the girls went inside the house just as Kenny appeared with another cold beer.

By now, Martha had retrieved another lawn chair and pulled it up along side of mine.

"As long as I need to wait for Marcie before I start story time, I might as well make myself another Tangueray," I said as I rose from my chair and started towards the front door.

"Do you know what happened to him?" I heard Martha asked Kenny as I walked into the house.

I made myself another drink as Marcie sent the girls to their rooms to watch television and joined me walking back outside. Marcie grabbed another lawn chair and pulled it over next to where Kenny sat. I sat back down in my chair, took a nice long drink of my Tangueray, and said.

"I'm only going to do this once. If you have questions, feel free to ask them."

"Butch, this is not some police interrogation. Just tell us everything that happened to you since yesterday," Martha said in a chastising tone.

I began my story by telling everyone I had gone to the local Kum N Go, where I started talking to one of the clerks to see if she could shed any light on Angel's disappearance. During our conversation, I discovered she was a pole dancer at the Ace of Spades three nights a week.

"Good lookin?" asked Kenny.

"She sure is," I replied before I realized what I had said and looked towards Martha who gave me one of her looks.

"And she invited me to a special performance," I added.

"I'm sure she did," Martha said coolly as she rolled her eyes.

"I told her that I have a beautiful wife at home and didn't need to watch a naked woman gyrate around a pole to be happy," I said.

"Smart thinking," said Marcie as she glanced at Kenny.

"So, you weren't watching a stripper, grabbed her and her pimp beat the piss out of you?" Kenny asked as he grinned and looked towards Martha.

"Thanks for the help, dumb shit," I said to Kenny who was laughing by now.

Quickly changing the subject, I related how I had gone to see Reverend States Rights Jones and then decided to get a round of golf in. How I hooked my drive on hole sixteen into the woods and was attacked by two huge guys as I looked for my golf ball. About waking up in the Family of our Lord's compound and talking with Spike. About Reverend Jones talking with me and having me escorted back to my Escalade, which was still at the golf course.

"I retrieved my golf equipment and vehicle keys, and here I am," I said as I finished my story.

By now, I noticed Kenny's beer bottle was empty as well as my glass.

"So, what are you going to do now?" asked Marcie.

"Make another Tangueray."

"Need another beer," I asked Kenny as I rose from my chair the same time he was getting out of his chair.

"Does a dog have fleas," he replied as we both walked into the house.

We got our drinks and returned to where the ladies still sat.

"Seriously, what are you going to do now?" asked Martha as Kenny and I both sat down in our lawn chairs.

"I honestly don't know," I replied in a sincere voice, because I didn't have a clue what my next move would be.

"You think Sheriff Hatfield is working with the Reverend," Kenny said.

"I have no proof, but some of the things going on around here make me suspicious about where the sheriff's loyalty lays," I answered.

"You didn't see Angel inside the compound?" asked Marcie.

"Nope and like I said, Spike doesn't remember seeing anyone fitting her description either."

"What are you going to do about Spike?" asked Martha.

"I've been thinking about that. I believe I should get back inside the compound and try to get Spike out of there," I said.

"You're not using those stupid stilts, are you?" asked Kenny.

"I'm not sure what I will do," I replied.

"Kenny will help you if you don't use those stupid stilts," Martha quickly said.

I looked over at Kenny, who shrugged as if to say, whatever my sister says.

"Is anyone getting hungry?" asked Marcie, who had gotten tired of our conversation involving the Reverend Jones.

"Sure," replied Martha.

"And I'll help you," she added as she rose from her chair and started towards the house door.

After the women left, I started thinking about what my next move would be. Kenny detected that I was in deep thought, so he quietly sat and nursed his beer.

"You know I'm supposed to be finding out what happened to Angel," I blurted out and startled Kenny.

"Huh?"

"I've been hired to find Angel McCoy, but this Reverend Jones has gotten under my skin. I need to figure out a way to bring down his little empire," I replied.

"Oh, yeah. You and whose army is going to march into the Family of our Lord compound and confiscate all the contraband cigarettes and booze you say he is dealing in," replied Kenny.

"I don't know. I think my old partner on the Rosecrest police force, Ben Johnson, was in tight with a couple of guys in the Bureau of Alcohol, Tobacco, and Firearms," I said.

"So you think he could get the ATF boys to search the Reverends compound?" asked Kenny.

"Don't know. It's just a thought. I'm grasping at any small straw I can find right now," I said.

"Would the ATF come into Sheriff Hatfield's jurisdiction without telling him?" asked Kenny.

"If what you think about the sheriff is correct, he would warn the Reverend about the ATF," Kenny added.

"I know. That's why I'm not certain of what I should do," I answered.

"None of this helps find Angel though, does it?" asked Kenny.

"I don't know. I still have a feeling that the Reverend had something to do with her disappearance," I said.

We continued talking and sipping on our drinks until Martha opened the house door and stuck her head out.

"Soups on," she said.

Kenny and I rose from our chairs and walked into the house. After washing up, we joined all the women at the kitchen table for what looked like a wonderful meal of Swedish meatballs, mashed potatoes, and whole kernel corn. I didn't think these southern folks knew about Swedish meatballs!

Thank goodness we have something soft I can get between my now half-swollen lips, I thought to myself as we eat supper.

We enjoyed a great meal and as the women cleaned the supper table, Kenny and I retired to the family room to watch some television while we each had another drink.

My swollen eye and lips were now starting to feel better, due to the gin I was putting into my body!

Martha and Marcie joined us while the two girls went to their rooms to watch something on television that adults wouldn't like.

Kenny tuned the television to one of my favorite shows, *Swamp People*.

Although I enjoyed Troy, Elizabeth, Junior and Willy my mind kept drifting off as I thought about what I should do next.

Should I call Ben? Would he think calling the Bureau of Alcohol, Tobacco and Firearms be a good idea? Would the ATF boys be interested in what I had discovered? Would they be willing to bypass Sheriff Hatfield? Would they enter the Family of our Lord compound? Should I try to get Spike out of the Family of our Lord compound? Where was Angel?

"Shoot em Elizabeth," I heard as I was jolted from my thoughts.

"Shoot who," I exclaimed aloud as I jumped in my chair.

"What?" Martha said as she, Kenny and Marcie looked at me as if I was nuts.

"Nothing. I guess I must have been daydreaming," I replied.

"You must have. What you heard was the television show. Troy was telling Liz to shoot the gator," said Martha.

"I thought you liked this show," she added.

"Why aren't you paying attention to it?"

"I don't know. I guess I've got too much on my mind right now," I replied and tried to refocus on the television show.

# Chapter Twenty Six

Saturday, May 28, I awoke to a bright beam of sunlight shining through the slit between the two curtains covering the window of the bedroom where Martha and I were sleeping. The beam of light was shining on Martha's pillow just above her head, making it seem like she had a halo over her head. She looked so serene and peaceful that I decided I would quietly get out of bed and not wake her. My swollen eye was now completely open although I'm sure it looked like crap. My swollen lips were almost back to their original size and didn't hurt too much.

As I came out of the bathroom, Martha was sitting on the edge of the bed, ready to get up.

"Morning," I said as I walked over and gave her a kiss.

"Your lips must not hurt too much," she said as she returned my kiss.

"Getting better," I replied as I got dressed while Martha went into the bathroom.

Kenny and Marcie were already sitting in the family room having their coffee as I entered the kitchen. I poured myself and Martha a cup of coffee before joining them. Martha's coffee would be the perfect temperature for her by the time she joined us. The girls were still in their rooms.

"What's on the agenda for today?" asked Kenny as I walked into the family room.

"I don't know. I hadn't really thought too much about it," I replied, even though I had been thinking about what I was going to do quite a bit.

"Seeing as it's the Memorial Day weekend, Marcie and I thought we could all just relax and enjoy some down time," Kenny said.

"That sounds like a great idea," Martha said as she joined us and sat down in one of the chairs.

"Down time won't help me find Angel," I replied.

"You haven't found her even though you've been working hard at it," Martha blurted out.

I took a couple sips of my coffee, trying not to say anything as Martha looked over towards Kenny and Marcie, knowing she had just pissed me off with her statement.

"I'm sorry honey," Martha quickly said.

"I didn't mean you aren't doing the best you can."

"I just meant I thought it wouldn't hurt to take a couple of days and just relax. You need your bruises to heal," Martha said.

"Sure, and what's a couple of days lounging around. You always told me you came up with your best ideas while you where relaxing with a Tangueray," Kenny quickly interjected.

"Besides, you said you wanted to call Ben, but because it's a holiday weekend, he won't be at work until Tuesday. Right?" Kenny added.

"Yeah, you're right. Even if he was working a hot case, he wouldn't be in his office, so I couldn't get a hold of him," I replied.

I didn't bother to mention that I had Ben's home phone and cell phone numbers in my cell phone. Or that, I knew his email address, so I could get a hold of him if I wanted to.

"What did you have in mind?" I asked Kenny as I still glared at Martha.

239

"Marcie and I thought one day we could go over to Lake Champlain, rent a pontoon boat and just cruise around the lake. We could do a little fishing, a little drinking and a little swimming," Kenny said.

"The cruising, fishing and drinking I could do, but the swimming is out. I swim like a rock," I said.

We continued to talk about things we could do during the Memorial Day weekend. I kept thinking about what Martha had said. She was right. I had been working on this case for almost a month and still had no clue as to what happened to Angel.

I decided that the best way to find out if Angel was at the Family of our Lord compound was to get a hold of Ben and see if he could talk to his ATF buddies. If the ATF would be willing to investigate the Reverend and search the compound, we would know for sure if Angel was there or not.

As the four of us sat and talked, we decided that we wouldn't do anything today, but go for a boat ride on Sunday. I suggested that I could cook up a supper of grilled shrimp and grilled stuffed jalapeno peppers. The meal seemed to excite every one except Martha who wrinkled her nose at the idea of grilled jalapenos.

"We don't have any shrimp or jalapenos," Marcie said.

"No problem. I'll just go into town and get the items I need for supper," I replied.

"And as long as I have to go into town, I could probably get in eighteen holes of golf," I added.

"Do you feel well enough to golf?" asked Martha.

"What do you think," I replied.

"Do you want to go golfing with me?" I asked Martha.

"Go ahead and go golfing," Marcie said.

"I don't want to leave you folks all alone, when we're supposed to be your guests," Martha said.

"Go."

"OK."

To be on the safe side, I called the golf course to see if they were busy and if I could get a tee time around 10:00 a.m. I was informed I could have a 10:08 tee time.

"We got a 10:08 tee time," I informed everyone.

"Why so early?" asked Martha.

"So we can get done golfing, have time to buy the fixings for supper and get the shrimp marinating while I prepare the stuffed jalapenos," I replied.

We sat around and talked for awhile and then Martha and I headed to the golf course. It was a beautiful sunny day with a slight breeze. I golfed great and Martha golfed good.

After our round, I drove into Jonesborough to buy the items we needed for supper.

"Before we go to the grocery store, I should buy some gas," I said to Martha as we neared the Kum N Go.

I pulled in next to a vacant gas pump and proceeded to fill the Escalade with gas.

"I want to go inside and see if Rhonda is working and if she's heard anything about Angel," I said to Martha.

"Wanta come along?"

"Sure, I want to see this pole dancer you've told me about as you drooled," Martha said as she grinned at me.

"I didn't drool. I just told you she had a good build. I never said she was built better than you," I replied.

"Smart man," Martha replied as she pinched my butt as we walked towards the door of the Kum N Go.

Upon entering the store, I looked over towards the counter and saw that Rhonda was placing some candy bars in racks sitting on the counter.

"Hi, Rhonda," I said as we approached her.

She looked up from her work, answered, "Hi" and did a double take "What happened to you?"

"It seems like everybody nowadays asks me that question," I said.

"I hit a golf ball into the woods and ran into a tree branch as I was looking for my golf ball," I lied.

"I'd like you to meet my wife, Martha," I quickly added.

"Pleased to meet you," Rhonda replied.

"So, this is the woman who keeps you from coming to the Ace of Spades and see me perform," Rhonda said with a smile on her face.

"Yep, she's the one."

"I still think you and your husband should stop out some time. We do put on a good show," Rhonda said.

"Oh, I'm sure you do," replied Martha as she glanced at me.

"I just stopped in to see if you or anyone here has heard anything about Angel," I quickly said trying to thaw the tension that had suddenly developed.

"No, I haven't heard anything. Lucie hasn't said anything about Angel either," Rhonda said.

"I figured as much, but as long as I was here, I thought I would ask," I said.

"No problem," Rhonda replied as a paying customer started walking towards the counter where she stood.

"See ya later, Rhonda," I said as I turned and started walking towards the door.

"I hope you do," she replied and flashed a big smile.

I don't know if the smile was for my benefit or Martha's, but Martha huffed as she walked past me through the door I had just opened.

"I still don't see any reason to go watch some naked bimbo flop her big boobs around a brass pole," Martha said as we were getting into the Escalade.

"I never said the pole was brass," I replied with a smile.

"Don't get funny with me, Mr. Brogen. You know what I mean," Martha snapped.

"All I know is that both of you are teachers and both of you have great bodies although I have never seen Rhonda naked," I said.

"And you can just keep it that way. Now let's get to the grocery store so you can buy whatever you need to make supper," she said as I started the vehicle.

I drove to Bill's Country Market while silence enveloped the entire inside of the Escalade. We went into the grocery store to buy the items I needed for the evening meal and as we got back to the Escalade with our sacks of groceries, Martha had mellowed out a little and was now ready to talk as we drove back to Kenny's.

"You're not really going to the Ace of Spades and watch her dance, are you?" Martha asked.

"Only if you will come with me," I replied.

"Why would I want to see some naked woman dance around?"

"It wouldn't be that bad," I protested.

"So, if I went to a Chippendale show, you would be willing to go with me?" Martha asked.

"Hell no. I ain't going to watch a bunch of guys who shave their bodies and grease themselves down to get you women excited," I instantly replied.

"That's no different than some woman who shaves herself and rubs up and down on a pole," Martha said.

"You got me there. I guess I won't go watch Rhonda dance and you won't go to a Chippendale show," I said.

"I never said I wouldn't go to a Chippendale show. I just said that I bet you wouldn't be willing to go with me," Martha said as she gave me one of her smiles.

We continued a friendly banter back and forth all the way back to Kenny's place. By the time we had reached the house, I knew I wasn't going to go watch Rhonda and I thought Martha wasn't going to watch the Chippendales.

Over the next several hours, I started marinating the shrimp in garlic and lemon juice. I cleaned, stuffed the jalapenos and wrapped them in bacon slices. I managed to have a couple of Tangueray and Tonic's while I was slaving in the kitchen.

"What time do you want to eat?" I asked as I emerged from the kitchen with a drink in my hand and a smile on my face.

"When will your masterpieces be ready?" asked Martha.

"About one hour from when I start grilling them."

"Do you have something good to eat along with the shrimp?" Martha again asked.

"Yep. I have some Uncle Ben's wild rice ready to steam for the people who don't enjoy my jalapenos," I said.

"Not everyone likes their insides eaten away by your hot food," Martha said.

"Let's eat around seven thirty," Marcie said.

"We had a good lunch today and I'm sure the girls won't be too hungry until then."

"What about me?" Kenny asked.

"You ate more than any of us."

"If you get hungry, go grab another beer."

"Ah, I'm beginning to love you more and more, Marcie," I said.

"I wish Martha would tell me to go have another drink," I added.

"You don't need any encouragement," Martha said.

Around six o'clock, I fired up the gas grill and commenced to grill my shrimp and jalapenos. At 7:15 p.m., all the food was ready and we sat down to eat. Everyone ate the items they were comfortable eating and the meal went great.

After watching a couple of television shows and the evening news, we all retired for the night.

Sunday, May 29, we went to Lake Champlain, rented a pontoon boat which Kenny had reserved and spent almost the entire day floating around the lake. The swimmers swan and I stayed planted firmly on the deck of the pontoon, playing captain and sipping on a cold Tangueray.

"We should be going before everyone gets too sun burned," Marcie said around 5:00 p.m.

"Sounds good to me," I replied as I started the pontoon towards the rental dock.

"How does Kentucky Fried Chicken sound for supper tonight?" I asked.

"Martha's buying," I added.

"Yummy," said both girls.

"Sure beats cooking," Martha said.

"As if you've done tons of cooking since we've been here," I replied.

We made our way back to the dock and I helped the women retrieve all of our items from the pontoon while Kenny went and settled up the days' expenses.

Martha and I stopped at the local KFC on the way back to Kenny's and purchased the evenings meal. Regular chicken, extra crispy chicken, cold slaw, baked beans and rolls.

After supper, we all went outside to enjoy some more of the nice weather. None of us had gotten too sunburned today due to Marcie's diligence of applying sun screen on every square inch of bare skin she could find.

As we sat around talking, I was thinking about calling Ben. He probably would be done grilling steaks for the family, so I shouldn't disturb him.

"I'm going to call Ben," I said as I got out of my lawn chair, took my cell phone out of the front pocket of my shorts and started walking away from everyone.

"It's Sunday. You already said he wouldn't be in his office," Kenny said.

"I know. I'm going to call his cell phone."

I scrolled through the contacts register on my cell phone until I found Ben's cell number. I punched send and waited as I heard ringing. After several rings, I heard, "Hello."

"Hi Ben. Butch here," I said.

"Well, why am I blessed with this call?" Ben asked.

"You're not busy, are you?" I asked.

"Never too busy to talk to the best partner I ever had on the Rosecrest Police Department," Ben replied.

"I'm the only partner you ever had, dumb shit," I said.

"I know, that's why you're still the best."

"How's Mary and the girls?" I asked.

"Every one is just great."

"How about you and Martha?"

"We're fine."

"So why the call?" Ben asked.

"You got a few minuets?" I asked.

"Sure."

I explained that I was in Tennessee looking into the disappearance of a young woman and had stumbled across a stash of what I thought were bootleg cigarettes and whiskey in a religious compound. I knew that Ben was in tight with several of the head guys at the ATF, so I was wondering if he could contact them and have them check out my thoughts. Ben listened attentively to my story before he spoke.

"Tennessee is way out of my jurisdiction. You know that."

"I know, but I think the local sheriff here just might be involved with the Reverend at the religious compound," I said.

"I don't want to ask him for help, because he might just tip off the Reverend," I added.

"Even though we were only partners for several years, I've learned not to doubt your hunches," Ben said.

"Thanks partner," I replied.

"Tomorrow is a holiday, so I'll give my buddy Wayne at the ATF a call on Tuesday and see what he has to say," Ben said.

"Great!"

"But you know just as well as I do, if the ATF is going to get involved, they would need months to do their research," he added.

"Yeah, I know how they work. It's just that I'm at a point in my investigation where I have no solid leads as to what happened to the missing woman. I also know that there are some people inside the compound who have been brought there against their will," I said.

"How do you know that?" Ben asked.

"I was told."

"By whom?"

"A little birdie told me," I replied.

"I see. Still up to your old tricks, huh?"

"What are you inferring?" I asked.

"You know what I'm talking about. There were times when you were on the force that you didn't always follow correct police procedures," Ben said.

"Ah, you hurt me," I replied.

"I never did anything illegal."

"I didn't say you did anything illegal. I just said that you skirted the rules sometimes."

"You somehow got inside the religious compound, didn't you?" Ben asked.

"Could be."

We bantered back and forth for another fifteen minutes before I decided I had better hang up.

"I should quit disturbing you," I said to Ben.

"No problem. It's been great hearing from you. I'll give Wayne at the ATF a call on Tuesday and get back to you as soon as I hear what their response is."

"OK."

"Say hi to Martha for me," Ben added as he hung up.

I walked back over to where everyone was still seated, sat down in my lawn chair, and picked up my Tangueray.

"Is Ben going to help?" asked Martha.

"He said he would make some calls, but he knew the ATF would want to spend time doing an investigation even if they thought my hunch was right," I replied.

"Well, we can't do anything about that. How about another drink?" Kenny said.

"Sounds good to me," I replied as I finished off my Tangueray and followed Kenny into the house to make another one.

It was finally time for the evening news to come on, so we all went into the house to see what had happened this day. The girls came out of their rooms to give everyone a good night kiss before they retired for the night.

After the news was over, the rest of us headed towards our bedrooms, ready for a good nights sleep. As I lay in bed trying to fall asleep, I thought about my request of Ben. I knew it was a long shot for the ATF to be involved very soon. How could I get Spike out of the Family of our Lord compound? Was Angel inside the compound? If not, where was she?

## Chapter Twenty Seven

The weather on Memorial Day was fantastic as usual. We all went to Johnson City to view the big Memorial Day parade, and then took the girls to the water park. I grilled some of my famous wild rice stuffed Cornish hens, which we ate with fresh grilled sweet corn for supper and spent the rest of the evening watching television.

Tuesday, May 31 found me sitting in Kenny's living room when my cell phone rang. Looking at the caller ID, I saw it was Ben calling me.

"Hello," I said as I answered my phone.

"Hi, Butch," Ben said.

"Did you have a good holiday weekend?" asked Ben.

"Yeah. We did some boating, swimming and watched a big parade on Memorial Day," I replied.

"You went swimming?" asked Ben.

"I thought you swam like a rock," he added.

"I do. I was the skipper of the pontoon boat," I answered.

"Ah, that makes sense," he replied with a chuckle.

"I got a hold of my buddy at the Bureau of Alcohol, Tobacco, and Firearms," Ben said.

"And?"

"And he said that they were more than interested in checking out your Reverend States Rights Jones, but," Ben paused for effect.

"But what?"

"But they would need to spend months with surveillance, investigation and the like," Ben said.

"Kinda like we thought, huh?" I said.

"Yep, just like we thought."

"I'm sure if what you told me is true, they will be able to nail the Reverend," Ben said with encouragement.

"I know. However, I want to know what's going on inside that compound right now. I need to help Spike and find out if Angel is in there," I replied.

"I told Wayne that you were concerned about someone whom you believed was kidnapped and being held in the compound against their will. I also told him you thought Angel might be held by the Reverend," Ben replied.

"He was very sympathetic, but they can only move so fast and that won't be fast enough to help you right now," Ben added.

"Ok, I guess there's nothing they can do for me right now. I'm going to have to figure this out on my own," I replied as I sighed.

"Sorry I couldn't be more help, partner," Ben said.

"I know how bad you want to figure out what's going on down there," he added.

"Thanks for letting the ATF know what is going on at the compound. If they need any info from me, have Wayne give me a call," I said.

"Will do. Good luck and I hope you find Angel real soon," Ben said.

"Thanks again for your help. We'll have to get together for a beer after I get back to Minnesota," I said.

"Sounds good to me," said Ben as he hung up his phone.

I closed my cell phone and stuck it back into the front pocket of my shorts as Martha walked into the room.

"Was that Ben?" she asked.

"Yep."

"Can the ATF help you?"

"Yeah, but it will take them months of investigation before they are ready to do anything," I replied.

"That doesn't help me find Angel or get Spike out of the compound," I added.

"I know," Martha said as she walked over and sat on the arm of the lounge chair I was sitting in. She gave me a hug and a kiss and quickly looked around to see if the girls were present.

"I'm going to Wal-Mart in Johnson City to do some shopping. Want to come along?" Martha said.

"You know I hate shopping," I replied with a whine.

"I know you do, but I thought it might be nice if you took your mind off Spike and Angel for a few hours," she replied as she gave me another kiss.

"The reason we're here is so I can find Angel," I said.

"I know that, but I thought you would just like to be with me for awhile," Martha said as she gave me another kiss.

"If you two don't quit your necking, I'm going to have to show you to your bedroom," said Kenny who was sitting in his favorite recliner.

"I have two young girls who don't need to see their aunt having sex on the family room floor," he added with a smile.

"Oh, shut up," Martha snapped at Kenny.

"So, are you going with me?" asked Martha.

"I guess I could."

"I could just sit outside on one of their benches watching people instead of shopping, couldn't I?" I asked.

"That's fine. You can watch people," she said as she got off the arm of my chair and started walking towards our bedroom to get ready.

As I drove to Johnson City, Martha and I talked about my dilemma in regards to Spike and Angel. As usual, she had several suggestions about some little things I hadn't thought about.

We reached the Wal-Mart parking lot and I parked in the first open parking stall I found.

"You really enjoy having me walk five miles to the front door, don't you," said Martha as we exited the Escalade. She is always complaining about me not driving around the parking lot looking for a parking stall closer to the door.

"Quit your whining. We haven't gone on our morning walks since we've been here. The exercise will do you some good," I said as I slapped her on her butt.

"Are you insinuating I'm getting fat?" she instantly asked.

"No, I never meant such a thing. I just said we haven't been getting our morning walk in," I quickly said.

As we neared the entrance to Wal-Mart, I spied a bench sitting along the front wall of the building in the shade of a canopy.

"Here's my spot," I said as we got to the bench.

"Have fun shopping," I added.

"Of course I will," replied Martha.

"Do you have your cell phone with you?" I asked her just before she walked through the open sliding doors.

"Yes."

"Is it turned on?"

"Of course."

"Good, because if it gets too long, I'm going to be calling you and telling you to get your butt out here," I replied as I sat down on the bench and Martha walked into the store.

It was a nice day and the people of all sizes, shapes, and nationalities were streaming into Wal-Mart. Doesn't anyone work? I thought to myself.

As I mindlessly watched just about every age group, social group, race, and sex walk past me into the store, I was startled by a voice.

"Gotta a cigarette, buddy?"

I looked up to see a man whom I assumed to be around fifty years old, but actually looked more like seventy. His face was lined, weathered, and leathery from years of being outside in the elements. His hair was shoulder length, shaggy and dirty. He sported an eight-inch graying beard. He wore a tattered tee shirt, cut off blue jeans made into shorts and a pair of sandals of which one had a broken strap.

"Huh?"

"Gotta smoke?"

"Nope. I don't smoke," I replied as the man stopped directly in front of me.

"Gotta couple of bucks?" he then asked.

"What for?" I said as I squinted up towards his face looking directly into the bright sunlight.

"Gotta eat," he replied.

By now, because I was wearing a new pair of HD Polaroid sunglasses, which deflected the bright sunlight; I could clearly see this gentleman did indeed need some nourishment.

"There's a Subway inside Wal-Mart. I'll buy you a foot long sub, chips and drink," I said as I started to rise.

"I don't eat that shit. Just give me some money," he snapped at me.

"If you're so hungry, why won't you take up my offer?" I asked as I stood up and faced the guy.

"I said I don't eat that shit. I just want some money," he snapped.

"You just want money so you can go buy some rotgut booze or drugs, don't you?" I asked.

"What's it to you," he snarled.

"I'm willing to buy you some food, but not booze or drugs," I replied as I started to sit back down on the bench.

"Asshole!" he exclaimed as he flipped me the bird, turned and started to shuffle away looking for someone else to try to scam some cash from.

After my visitor left, I continued to sit on the bench and watch people as I waited for Martha. I saw numerous women in various stage of pregnancy as some walked, some waddled, and some leaned on a shopping cart for balance as they walked towards the store.

I saw several women coming towards the store with two little kids in tow. They might be hollering as mom drug them along or they might be going peacefully. I empathized with the ones being drug along while mom shopped. I knew the hell they were facing! I saw some women and men pushing a shopping cart they had retrieved from the cart corral with one or two kids seated inside.

Boy, there are sure a lot of people with kids around here, I thought to myself.

Just then it hit me! I think I know what happened to Angel!

I quickly grabbed my cell phone from the front pocket of my shorts and called Martha.

"Hurry up and get done shopping," I loudly said before she had a chance to say hello.

"What's wrong?" she asked.

"I've got an idea of what happened to Angel," I excitedly said.

"Can't it wait until I'm done shopping?"

"No, we need to get somewhere right away."

"Ok. I'm almost finished so I'll go check out and see you in a few minutes," Martha said.

"Great. Just don't take too long," I said as I hung up my phone and placed it back in the front pocket of my shorts.

I paced back and fourth in front of the bench waiting for Martha to appear. If what I was thinking was true, I had just figured out what had happened to Angel!

After what seemed to be an eternity, Martha appeared from inside the store with a shopping cart almost full of bags. I was too excited to even comment on all the unnecessary items I'm sure she had bought.

"Come on. Let's get going," I said as she got next to me.

"Just slow down and tell me what's going on," Martha said.

"I'll tell you as we drive. Now, let's get all your booty into the Escalade," I said as I grabbed the shopping cart and started to trot through the parking lot towards our vehicle.

"You wouldn't have to run, if you would have parked closer to the entrance," Martha said as she jogged along side of me.

"Whatever," I said half winded.

We reached the Escalade; I opened the door and started tossing Martha's packages inside.

"Take it easy. There's some items in those bags that are fragile," she scolded me.

"Ok," I replied as I slowed down.

I got her shopping cart emptied, wheeled it back to the cart corral, ushered her inside the Escalade, got inside myself and started out of the parking lot.

"Where are we going and why so fast?" Martha asked as she was fastening her seat belt.

"I'll tell you on the way," I replied as I drove through a red light.

"Watch out! You're going to get us killed," Martha exclaimed as she grabbed the *Oh shit* handle located over the passenger door.

"Now just slow down Butch and tell me what you are thinking," Martha said as we made our way onto Century Street.

I slowed down and slowly started telling Martha about sitting on the bench watching the people as they entered the store. I explained just what my idea was and what was up with Angel.

"OK. That's kind of makes sense," Martha said after listening to my tale.

"But where are we going?"

I told her where and once again she said my idea made sense.

"I sure hope you're right, honey," she said as we drove along towards my destination.

# Chapter Twenty Eight

Twenty minutes later, I pulled up along side of the curb in front of Burton House, on the Spartan College campus.

"I want you to go up to the house with me," I said to Martha as I started to exit the Escalade.

"What for?"

"Because if my hunch is correct and Angel is here, she might be more willing to talk to you," I replied as I shut the drivers' side car door.

Martha reluctantly also got out of the vehicle and joined me on the sidewalk leading to the front door of the house. As we started walking towards the house, I noticed the curtain on the front window being pulled back just as I had observed before.

"Somebody's looking out at us from behind the curtain on the front window," I said to Martha as we neared the door to the house.

"You think it's Angel?" asked Martha.

"Hope so," I answered as we reached the front door of the house.

I knocked sharply on the door.

No answer.

I knocked harder a second time and still no answer, but I could swear I could hear someone moving around inside the house.

"Angel," I yelled.

"Not so loud," Martha said as she looked around.

"I want her to hear me, if she's in there," I replied.

"I know, but you don't need to get the neighbors excited about some guy yelling at the front door," Martha replied.

"Angel, I know you're in there," I loudly proclaimed as I once again knocked sharply on the door as I ignored Martha's request to be quiet.

"Angel, my name is Butch Brogen and I've been hired by Bubba and Bertha to find you," I said in a slightly lower voice.

"Angel, everyone in your family is so worried about you. Please open the door," I said in a pleading tone.

The door remained closed.

"Angel, I know that you know that I know you know that I know you're in there," I said.

"What did you just say?" asked Martha.

It's not a Yogism, but a Butchism," I replied with a smile on my face.

"Whatever."

"Angel, I can call the police and tell them that I see someone lying on the floor inside this house. They won't need a search warrant to break down the door and find you. Let's just keep this between us," I said.

I was about to knock on the door once again when it started to slowly open. I stepped back a little bit as the house door opened wider until it was completely open. The person in the doorway pushed the screen door out towards me to open it. The open doors revealed a dark haired woman dressed in shorts and large tee shirt. She looked exactly like the woman in the picture with Bertha, except for one thing. This woman looked to be about six months pregnant.

"Angel?"

"Yes."

"Like I said when I was yelling through the door at you, I'm Butch Brogen and this is my wife Martha," I said.

"Can we come in?" I asked.

"I guess there's no reason not to now," she replied as she sighed and stepped backward into the house.

Martha and I followed her as I shut the door. We entered the living room where she said, "Have a seat."

Angel sat on a sofa and I nodded to Martha to sit next to her. I sat on a stuffed chair across from them.

"I'm so sorry," she said as we sat down.

"I didn't want everyone to be worried about me, but I was embarrassed about my situation and didn't know what to do," she added as she wiped a tear with the back of her hand, which had appeared in the corner of her right eye.

"The main thing is now we know where you are and that you are safe. You need to get a hold of your family," I said.

"I suppose, but I'm scared. I know everybody will be mad at me," she replied.

"Can't I just stay here and you tell everyone I'm OK?" she asked.

"You know I can't do that. Even if I did, Bertha would come here looking for you," I replied.

"I guess so," she said as more tears started to form in her eyes.

"Tell you what. We're staying at Martha's brothers' place. Let's the three of us go there and try to relax for a while. I don't want to disturb Bubba or Bertha at work, so I'll wait until they get home and then give them a call," I said.

"You can leave your stuff here and we'll come back tomorrow or some other day and pick it up," Martha added.

"You'll help me," Angel said in an almost surprised voice.

"Most certainly. That is if your family doesn't want to do everything for you and kick me out of the way," Martha replied.

That's when the waterworks erupted. Angel started to sob loudly and her shoulders shook as she cried. Martha slid next to her, put her arms around Angel, and hugged her.

"There, there," Martha said as she held the sobbing Angel.

"Everything is going to be alright. Try not to get too overwrought. You're in charge of two people now," Martha said as she patted Angel's stomach.

After several minutes of watching the two of them hug and cry, I finally said, "OK, let's get going."

"Here's my handkerchief," I said as I got out of my chair and walked over to the two women.

"Don't be so gross, Butch. Nobody wants to use your old snot rag," Martha said in a chastising tone.

"Let's go find some Kleenex," Martha said to Angel.

They both got off the sofa and started walking towards another room as I stood holding my handkerchief.

"It ain't gross," I muttered to myself as I looked at a couple of yellow splotches on my hanky and put it back into my pocket.

The women returned after several minutes and Angel had quit crying. Her eyes were bright red and she sniffled every once in a while, but she wasn't blubbering.

"Do you need to leave Olivia and Ahron a note letting them know what's going on?" I asked.

"No. I'll just text them as we drive to Martha's brother's place," Angel replied.

"I can barely dial one of those cell phones to say nothing about texting," I said.

"Butch is one of the older generation," Martha said as she smiled and put her arm around Angel.

"Texting isn't hard," Angel replied as a small smile actually formed on her face.

We left Burton House, got into the Escalade, and started our journey to Kenny's. Martha had crawled into the back seat with Angel for the trip. As I drove along I could hear snippets of muted conversation between the two of them. By the time we had reached Kenny's, Martha and Angel were conversing, giggling and seemed to be having a good time.

I pulled onto the approach to Kenny's garage, stopped the Escalade, and got out. Martha and Angel were still seated in the back seat.

"Are you two coming?" I asked as I shut the door.

Just then, the two girls came bounding out of the house.

"Hi Uncle Butch," they said in unison as they usually do.

"Who's the lady with Aunt Martha?" Kayla asked.

"She's a friend of ours," I replied.

By now, Martha and Angel had gotten out of the Escalade and were walking towards the girls and me.

"Oh look! She's going to have a baby," Karla excitedly said.

"Can we touch the baby?" asked Kayla.

"Girls," Marcie said in a scolding voice as she arrived on the scene.

"You don't ask ladies if you can touch their baby."

"That's OK," said Angel as she smiled at the girls and walked over to them.

Each girl took turns placing their hands gently on Angel's stomach and giggling.

"I felt something," Karla exclaimed.

"Me too," chimed in Kayla not wanting to be outdone.

By now Angel seemed more relaxed and she seemed to have her mind off the forthcoming meeting with her family. The five women went into the house and I plopped down in a lawn chair.

Kenny was no where to be seen, so I got out of my lawn chair and went into the house to make myself a Tangueray, which I carried back outside and sat back down in the lawn chair. The inside of the house had turned into a chicken house, there was so much cackling going on in there you would have sworn eggs were being laid.

I sat and reflected on what had just happened and what was still ahead. At 5:15 p.m., I took my cell phone out of my shorts pocket, selected contacts, and scrolled to Bubba. I pressed send and waited as I heard ringing coming through the earpiece.

"Hello."

"Hi Bubba. It's Butch."

"What's up?"

"I found Angel."

"What the hell you talking about!" Bubba almost screamed into the phone.

"I found Angel and she's fine," I said.

"Where's she at?" Bubba asked as I heard Bertha ask him something in the background.

"Butch found Angel and she's alright," Bubba said to Bertha even though he was talking to me.

"Where's she at?" Bertha asked as she grabbed the phone from Bubba.

"She's with Martha and me out at Kenny's place," I replied.

"We're coming right out," Bertha blurted.

"I know she would like that," I said.

"Here you talk to Bubba. I gotta pee," Bertha blurted and handed the phone back to Bubba.

"Where was she and what was going on?" asked Bubba.

"We'll explain all of that when you two get here," I said.

"And Bubba, all this disappearance stuff has to do with the fact Angel is pregnant," I added.

"Pregnant."

"Who's pregnant?" I heard Bertha asked in the background.

263

"Angel," I heard Bubba reply.

"Hot damn! I'm going to be an aunt!" I heard Bertha say.

"We'll see you as fast as I can get to Kenny's," Bubba said.

"No reason to speed. Angel is not going anywhere but with family," I replied as Kenny came driving up the driveway.

"OK. See you shortly," Bubba said as he hung up the phone.

"You look like a hog who just found a new slop hole," Kenny said as he approached me.

"I found Angel," I proudly proclaimed.

"The hell you say. Where was she? How did you find her?" Kenny asked.

"Bubba and Bertha are coming here, so I'm going to wait until then to tell everyone about my excellent detective work," I said as I smiled at Kenny as he walked towards the front door of the house.

"I'm getting a beer. Want one?" Kenny asked as he neared the front door.

"Nope. But I'm going to have another Tangueray," I replied as I rose from the lawn chair and followed Kenny into the house.

## Chapter Twenty Nine

About twenty-five minutes later, Bubba's big dark green Dodge Hemi pick up came roaring up Kenny's driveway. Kenny and I sat in our lawn chairs as Bubba wheeled in behind my Escalade and slammed on the brakes.

"Good thing his brakes work," Kenny said as he smiled at me.

Bubba's pick up had barely come to a stop when the passengers' door flew open and Bertha bounded out.

"Where is she?" Bertha hollered as her feet hit he ground.

"She's in the house," I replied as Bertha headed towards the front door.

"I wouldn't want to get in front of her," Kenny said as he smiled once again.

"You got that right," I replied as Bubba came hurriedly towards us.

"Where's she at?" he said.

"Just follow Bertha," I said as I nodded towards Bertha who was already going into the house.

"Might as well go in and make sure nobody gets hurt," I said as I rose from my lawn chair.

"I could use another beer, so I might as well follow along," said Kenny as he also got out of his chair.

We walked into the house in time to see Bertha grab Angel and give her a big bear hug.

"Hey be careful Bertha. You don't want to hurt my nephew," Bubba said as he walked over to the two women.

"I'll be careful. I don't want to hurt my niece," replied Bertha as she still clung to Angel.

"Get outta my way," said Bubba as he grabbed Bertha by the shoulder and tried pulling her away from Angel. It took several attempts, but Bubba finally got Bertha away from Angel so he could give her a hug. His hug was gentler than Berthas!

"How are you? Where have you been? Why did you disappear?" Bertha was asking Angel as Kenny and I walked into the kitchen to retrieve our drinks.

"We might as well go back outside and sit by ourselves," I said to Kenny as I mixed my drink and he uncapped another beer.

"That's for sure. I don't know how anyone can hear what each other is saying in there," he replied.

We grabbed our drinks and walked back into the living room where Bubba and Bertha had Angel cornered on the sofa, while Marcie and Martha sat in the recliners. All five of them seemed to be talking at the same time!

Kenny and I walked outside without being noticed by anyone. We sat in our lawn chairs, enjoying our drinks while watching the golden setting sun slowly disappear behind the huge oak trees that grew down by Kenny's workshop.

"So, what happened with Angel?" Kenny asked as the last of the sun slowly disappeared.

"She had a one night stand with a guy from her college and got pregnant," I replied.

"She was so ashamed of cheating on Frank and getting pregnant on top of it, she decided to just disappear," I added.

"She thought that was going to solve everything?" Kenny asked.

"I don't know what she was thinking. All I know is that she was scared."

"She keeping the kid?"

"I have no idea, I want to stay out of the whole thing. I'm just happy I found Angel," I replied.

"Right on."

We had each finished our drinks and were debating whether to go back in the house or not, when the front door opened. Bertha emerged from the house with her arm around Angel, who had no choice but to follow. Bubba was behind them, followed by Marcie, Martha and the girls, who seemed to have joined in the family fest.

"Angel's coming home with us," Bertha said as she neared Kenny and me.

"That's great," I replied.

"And we're going to have a big family outing tomorrow to celebrate Angel coming home," Bubba added.

"Tomorrow is Wednesday, don't you have to work?" I queried.

"I'm calling in and taking the rest of the week off," Bubba said.

"Me too," replied Bertha as she continued to have her arm around Angel.

"We'll plan on eating around 5:00 p.m. You can come over anytime you want to," said Bubba.

"Bring Kenny, Marcie and the girls," Bertha added as she opened the passenger door of Bubba's pick up.

Before Angel climbed into the cab of the pick up, she turned and mouthed "Thank you" to me.

Bubba turned his truck around and drove down the driveway about thirty miles per hour slower than when he had arrived.

"There goes one happy family," Kenny said.

"Thanks to Butch," Martha said as she walked over to where I was sitting, bent down and gave me a kiss.

"Yuk," one of the girls said.

"I'm glad we have a happy family," Marcie said as she walked over to Kenny and gave him a kiss.

I instantly glanced at Martha, who shot me one of her 'shut up' looks.

"Is it quiet enough in the house so I can go in and watch some television?" I asked.

"What do you mean quiet enough?" Martha instantly asked.

"Well, for the last couple of hours, it sounded louder than a hen house at egg picking time in there," I replied.

"You are such a jerk. Bubba and Bertha were happy to see Angel," Martha instantly spat out.

"And Angel was happy to see them too," added Marcie.

"I don't know why you are so insensitive," Martha added as she turned and followed Marcie and the girls back into the house.

"Didn't make many points there, did you?" Kenny said with a chuckle.

"Guess not."

Kenny and I followed the women into the house and started to watch television.

"I know it's late, but I made some bean and ham soup for supper tonight, not knowing we were going to be talking with Angel," Marcie said as she walked back into the family room where Kenny and I sat.

"Does anyone want a bowl?"

"You bet," I replied as I started getting out of my chair.

"Sure," Kenny responded.

After eating two bowls of Marcie's bean soup, Kenny and I went back to the family room where we started watching the evening news.

"You should be on the news now that you've found Angel," Kenny said.

Nope, don't need that."

Martha and Marcie came into the room, followed by the two girls, who gave everyone a kiss and headed off to bed.

The evening news got over and some stupid talk show started.

"See everyone in the morning," I said as I got up and started towards the bedroom.

"Hope so," Kenny replied as he grinned from ear to ear.

Martha had simmered down by the time we went to bed, so I had a restful night.

Wednesday, June 1 started out as a nice sunny day. The girls were walking into the kitchen as Marcie was making omelets filled with cheese, onion, green pepper, and real crumbled bacon for breakfast. I stuffed myself and retired to the living room along with Kenny to read the newspaper.

"What are you going to do today?" Kenny asked as we sipped our coffee and glanced at the newspaper.

"I don't know. Now that Angel is home, I'm trying to think of some way to get Spike out of the Family of our Lord compound," I said.

"I think you're screwed on that idea," Kenny offered.

"Why?"

"Because, I drove around the compound the other evening around dusk and saw that the Reverend had armed men walking around the fence. Even on the back side where you went in," Kenny said.

"Why would he have armed guys walking around now?" I mused.

"Because you told him about his contraband stuff. I'm sure he has no idea where that information came from, but I'm also positive he wants to make sure it wasn't from someone sneaking into his compound," Kenny said.

"I guess you're probably right," I sighed.

"I don't want to just sit around before we go to Bubba's, so maybe I'll go golfing," I said.

"Want to come with?"

"You're shitten me. I've never swung one of those clubs and have no desire to," Kenny quickly responded.

"I'll see if Martha wants to go," I said.

Martha did agree to go golfing with me, so I got a 1:00 p.m. tee time. That would leave us plenty of time to get eighteen holes in before we went over to Bubba and Berthas.

Kenny agreed to go to Bubbas with us, so around 5:00 p.m., Martha, I, Kenny, Marcie and the girls arrived at Bubbas. The place was already a beehive of activity. There must have been over thirty vehicles parked around the place. We parked our vehicles on the grassy slope of the road in front of Bubba's house, got out, and started walking towards the house. As we neared the front door, Angel came bounding out of the house.

"I'm so glad you came!" she exclaimed as she gave both Martha and I a hug.

"Why wouldn't we?" It's not every day I get to celebrate the homecoming of an expectant mom," I said as I gave her a kiss on the cheek.

"Everyone's out back watching Bubba grill his world famous ribs. Let's go join them," Angel said.

"You do have a sweet spot in you, don't you," Martha whispered to me as we followed Angel around the house to the back yard.

"Hey, everybody!" Bubba loudly exclaimed as we walked around the corner of the house.

"This is the guy who found Angel and convinced her to come home!"

Several people clapped, a couple people walked over to me and shook my hand.

Kenny and I managed to find the beer, while Marcie and Martha talked to Angel.

Angels return was celebrated in fine fashion. Everyone was enjoying Bubba's cooking and beer. They also were happy that Angel was back. Several people came up to me and wanted me to tell them just how I had figured out where Angel was. I told them several of the details of my investigation, but left out everything concerning my thoughts about Reverend States Rights Jones.

Around 9:00 p.m., Bubba and Bertha came walking over to where Martha and I were sitting with Kenny and his family.

"Butch, we're so glad you found Angel," Bertha said as she bent down and gave me a hug.

"I suppose you will be going back to Minnesota," she added.

"Yep. I'm kinda missing the old place," I replied.

"You leaving tomorrow?" asked Bubba.

"Tomorrow or the next day."

"Well then, I need to get our debt settled," Bubba, said as he took his checkbook out of his back pocket.

"How much do we owe you?"

"Put that away. You don't owe anything. I won't accept your check," I said.

"You might as well take it or I'll mail you a check," Bubba replied.

"Won't do you any good. I'll just rip up the check and throw it away."

"I'll mail another."

"Won't do any good, I'll just rip it up also."

"All you'll be doing is pissing away good postage," I added.

"You're not getting by without getting paid," Bubba said.

"That's damn right! You found my sister and I think everything is going to work out good. You need to be paid for all your hard work," Bertha said.

"I'm not taking your money," I protested.

"OK. I'll just transfer some money into your PayPal account," Bubba smugly said.

"Won't work. I changed our email address. Martha doesn't even know it now," I said with a big grin on my face.

"Ass hole," Bubba said.

"I agree," Bertha said.

"At times, I do too," Martha added.

"Alright let's forget about this payment stuff. You folks get back to your relatives and enjoy yourselves. We're going to be going shortly so the girls can get to bed. I'll give you a call before we head back to Minnesota," I said.

Both Bubba and Bertha reached down and gave me a handshake before they returned to the festivities. My hand hurt so much after their handshakes; I didn't know which person put the most pain on me.

"Did you really change our email address?" Martha asked me after Bubba and Bertha left.

"No. I just told them that so they didn't try to put some money into my account," I replied as I grinned at Martha.

"Some time you can be so sweet," Martha said as she leaned over and gave me a kiss.

"Other times......"

## Chapter Thirty

Thursday, June 2, started out as a beautiful day. The sun was peaking over the top of the pine trees located on the southern edge of Kenny's property. A slight breeze was blowing, causing the tops of the tall maple trees to sway in the wind.

The weather was beautiful, but there was a pall in the kitchen as the six of us sat around the kitchen table eating a baked egg soufflé Marcie had risen early to bake.

Marcie, Martha and the girls sat glumly staring at the food on their plates. Every once in a while, one of them would take a small bite and begin staring again.

"Why is everybody so down? You girls should be happy that school is over," I said.

"Whatever," Kayla responded.

"Angel was found and reunited with her family," I added.

"So."

"I'm just saying that I think everyone should be happy and not acting like they are at a wake."

All four of the women lifted their heads and looked at me, but not a word was uttered.

Kenny and I conversed with each other between bites of the egg soufflé, the English muffins that accompanied the eggs and a drink of coffee.

"I don't know how you two can seem so happy," Martha finally said, breaking her silence.

"I'm eating. Therefore I'm happy," I responded as I shrugged my shoulders.

"I know you're eating, but how can you be so happy?" Martha asked.

"Why not," I said as I shrugged my shoulders again, took another fork full of the eggs, and stuck it into my mouth.

"We're leaving today!" Martha exclaimed.

"And?"

"I'm going to miss Marcie, Kayla, and Karla," Martha said.

"What about me?" asked Kenny as he smiled.

"Of course I'll miss you! You know what I mean!" Martha snapped at Kenny.

"We'll miss you also, Aunt Martha," the two girls said in almost unison.

"I'll miss you too," Marcie added.

"So that's settled. You'll all miss each other after we leave," I said.

"Don't be such a jerk," Martha snapped at me.

"Better shut up and just eat, bro," Kenny said to me as he once again smiled.

Following Kenny's advice, I shut up and continued to eat my breakfast. After polishing off two large slabs of the egg soufflé and three English muffins, I excused myself from the table with my coffee cup in hand. I went into the family room followed by Kenny.

"Oh, I shouldn't have eaten so much. I'm going to be miserable for the first few hundred miles," I said to Kenny as we both sat down.

"Better make sure you take a good dump before you head out," Kenny advised.

"You got that," I replied.

We sat in silence and sipped on our coffee. We could hear voices coming from the kitchen, meaning the women must have been coming out of their funk.

"I sure wish I could have gotten Spike out of the Family of our Lord compound," I said breaking the silence between Kenny and me.

"I know you do, but I don't know what you could have done," Kenny said.

"Like I said, the Reverend has armed men walking the perimeter of the compound day and night. It would be almost impossible to get in or out now. Besides, you couldn't put Spike on those damn stilts so he could try to scale the fence. He would break his neck just like you almost did," Kenny added.

"I know."

"There's no way you could use ladders to get over that fence and conceal them. You would need to use two and removing and hiding them would be almost impossible," Kenny said.

"I know."

"I doubt if you could even get to the barracks without being caught," Kenny said.

"I know."

"You know what?" asked Martha as she walked into the room.

"That he can't do anything to get Spike out of the Family of our Lord compound," Kenny said to her.

"Don't feel bad," said Martha as she came over and sat on my lap, giving me a kiss.

"You came down here to find Angel and you did. You should be happy," she said.

"Isn't that what you were just telling us as we ate breakfast?" Martha asked as she gave me another kiss.

275

"Yuk, Aunt Martha," Kayla said as she and Karla came into the room and plopped down on the sofa.

Marcie followed the girls and joined them on the sofa. The mood had lightened somewhat, so we talked about the trip back to Minnesota and what each of us were going to be doing.

Finally, Martha suggested we get our things packed up and start for home.

"Sitting around would only make the leaving harder," she said.

Martha and I spent the next twenty minutes gathering our things together and packing them in the Escalade.

"I have one more thing to do before we leave," I said as I headed towards the bathroom.

"What's that?" Kenny yelled at me and smiled at the women.

"I know," Martha said.

"What's that?" asked Karla.

"Just never mind," replied Martha as she gave Kenny a dirty look.

After finishing my work, I joined the others who where seated in the family room.

"I wish you didn't have to go. I've enjoyed having you two around so much," Marcie said.

"Well you know why they say relatives and dirty underwear are alike," I said.

"No," replied Marcie as she gave me a strange look.

"If you're with either one of them for more than a week, they both began to stink," I said as I smiled.

"Oh, gross," said Kayla.

"That's awful, Uncle Butch," added Karla.

"OK, time to hit the road," I said as I started walking towards the front door.

Everyone followed, but I could tell leaving would be hard for Martha. We gathered at the Escalade, gave hugs and kisses and Martha and I started to get into the vehicle.

"I'll save those stilts in case you might need them the next time you are down here," Kenny said.

"You just destroy them. He won't ever again get on those stilts," Martha said as she gave me one of her glances.

"You be sure to come up to Minnesota and visit. We have plenty of room and a nice swimming pool you can use," I said just before closing the Escalade door.

"Oh, I'm sure a trip to Minnesota is already in the works," Kenny replied as he looked at Marcie and the girls.

I started the engine, put the vehicle in gear, and slowly started driving down the driveway. I looked in the rear view mirror and saw Marcie and the girls waving. I looked at Martha and noticed her dabbing several tears from her eyes. The first forty-five minutes, I drove in silence with only the SiriusXM radio channel fifty-six, *Willie's Roadhouse* keeping me company.

The trip back to Minnesota was nothing special. Martha and I talked about finding Angel. How she was glad she had come with so she could see Kenny and his family. And, how I was looking forward to golfing with the guys back home.

After a nice leisurely drive back to Minnesota, we pulled into the driveway to our house at 1:00 p.m., Sunday, June 5. We unpacked the car, checked over the house and yard. Everything seemed to be in order, so Martha decided to go swimming, while I sent Don an email stating I was back and ready to golf. I called Babe to see if he wanted to golf on Monday if we could get a tee time. I called Donk to let him know I was ready for a Thursday golf outing.

# Chapter Thirty One

The temperature was eighty-two degrees, the sun was shining, and the humidity was almost zero as I pulled into the parking lot of Southern Ridge Golf Course. As I pulled into an empty parking spot, I saw Don and Joe getting their golf equipment out of their vehicles. I parked, got out of the Escalade, and walked over to where they were.

"Hi. My name is Butch Brogen," I said as I extended my hand towards Don as if it was the first time we had met.

"Hi, I'm Don. Would you care to join us for a round of golf today?" he answered as he smiled.

"Sure would."

"Hi, I'm Joe. Glad to meet you," Joe said as he came over and grasped my hand as he also smiled.

We bantered back and forth, as we all got our golf equipment out of our vehicles, ready for the days round.

"Is Dick Weed golfing?" I asked using one of Karl's many nicknames.

"Who knows. He never responds to my emails," Don said.

The three of us started walking towards the clubhouse to check in. Me holding the remote of my electric golf bag kaddy cart, Don pushing his three-wheel Sun Mountain golf bag cart and Joe carrying his bag.

"You can sure tell who the young pup is around here," I said as I nodded towards Joe.

"My back hurts just watching you carry that bag," I added.

We checked in, grabbed a score card, and went back to the putting green to practice. Why I don't know. I putted the same way whether I practiced or not. Around ten minutes later, Dick Weed, and Timmy came walking towards us.

"Who the hell is this guy?" Karl yelled as he walked to where we were standing.

"A better golfer than you," I replied as I grabbed his hand as he extended it towards me.

Because there was just the five of us and the course wasn't very busy, we decided to golf as a five some. This meant that I had to put up with both Timmy and Karl as we golfed. The five of us teed off with nobody going into the woods or number two fairway.

"So, how was Tennessee?" asked Karl as we walked down the fairway to where our golf balls laid.

"The weather was real nice and I got some golf in," I replied.

"Don said you went down there to find a sister of some friend," Karl said as we reached my golf ball.

"That's right. I had met Bubba and Bertha several years ago when I was in Tennessee searching for the killer of Martha's Dad," I said.

"Bertha's sister Angel had disappeared and the local law enforcement hadn't been able to locate her," I said.

"Did ya find her?" asked Karl.

"Does a bear shit in the woods?"

"Don't know. I don't go around looking at bear butts to see if shit is coming out," Karl replied as he grinned.

"You're such a dick head," I replied as we reached where my golf ball had ended up after my drive.

"Not too bad of a drive for an old fart," Karl said before I had a chance to answer his question.

I hit my second shot and it landed just short of the green, bounced three times and rolled to what looked like three feet from the hole!

"Great shot. At least you didn't screw up your second shot," Karl said as we continued on to where his golf ball lay against a small maple tree.

"Nice lie," I said.

"It ain't stopped moving yet," Karl said as he deftly kicked his golf ball away from the tree allowing him a shot at the green.

"Nice foot wedge."

"Best club in my bag," replied Karl just before he hit his approach shot very close to the pin.

We walked towards the green as Don, Timmy and Joe were hitting their shots to the green. We finished the first hole with Karl and me getting pars, while the other three got bogies.

Holes two and three went just as good for me as the first hole, two pars!

"Looks like the golfing in Tennessee helped your game," said Joe as we stood on the fourth tee waiting to tee off.

"It must be nice to have a summer vacation in Tennessee," Timmy said.

"It wasn't a vacation. I was down there trying to find a young woman who had disappeared," I replied.

"And just happened to be able to get in numerous rounds of golf," Joe said.

"It wasn't all fun and games. I got the shit beat out of me on a golf course," I said.

"Hit into someone?" Karl asked.

"No, I didn't hit into anyone. I was attacked by two thugs who kidnapped me and hauled me off to a religious compound," I quickly replied.

"Holy shit! You sound just like Hogg, coming up with a story like that," Timmy said.

"Up yours!" I said.

"I even walked on eight foot stilts," I added as I puffed up my chest.

"Now I know you're full of shit," Don said.

"Yeah, you ain't coordinated enough to walk on two foot stilts, to say nothing about eight footers," Timmy said.

"I ain't shitten. I'll tell you clowns about my entire ordeal sometime over a cold beer," I said.

"Based on the amount of bullshit in what you've told us so far, it will take more than one beer for you to get your story out," Karl said.

"It ain't bullshit! What I've told you so far is the truth."

Just then, Mary Jo, the beer cart woman, came driving up to where we were standing. As she got out of the cart, I noticed she was wearing short shorts and a tank top that emphasized her ample breasts. She was a tall, long legged woman who had a tattoo of a snake wrapping around her right leg. The tail of the snake started at her ankle and wove its way around her leg until it disappeared under her short shorts.

"You guys need anything?" she asked as she stood facing us, allowing all eyes to be fixated on her chest and snake tattoo.

"Nope."

"I'm good."

"In another couple of holes."

"OK. See you guys later," she said as she got back into her cart and drove off.

"Who's she? I don't remember her," I said.

"Me neither," said Don.

"Must be new," added Timmy.

"Did you see that snake tattoo spiraling up her leg?" asked Joe.

"Sure did," I replied.

"I wonder where the head is?" asked Karl as he grinned.

"I'm surprised you didn't ask her," Don said as he prepared to tee off.

"I don't ask embarrassing questions," Karl said as he grinned.

My game fell apart over the next five holes, but I still managed to shoot a forty. As we were putting out on hole nine, Mary Jo showed up again.

"Need anything yet?" she asked as she got out of her beverage cart and stood along side of it, once again reveling the snake tattoo curling up around her leg,

"Sure, I'll have a Gatorade," I replied as I dug in one of the pockets of my golf bag to retrieve some money.

"I'll have a water," Joe said.

"I'll have one of those cheap beers," Timmy replied.

"I want to know where the snake's head is," said Karl as the other four of us tried to turn away and ignore him.

"You'd be surprised," replied Mary Jo as she pulled up the right leg of her short shorts as high as it would go and smiled.

"Does it bite?" asked Karl.

"Nope. It just tickles a little bit," replied Mary Jo as she smiled at Karl.

"Let's get golfing, Dork," Don said to Karl.

"Yeah, we don't need to get a sexual harassment charge filed against us," I said as I teed my ball up.

"I wasn't harassing her. I just wanted to know where the snakes head was," replied Karl as he flashed one of his shit eating grins.

282

"Thanks for the tips, guys," Mary Jo said as she got back into the beer cart and started driving down number ten fairway.

"I still didn't see the snakes head!" Karl hollered at Mary Jo as she drove away.

We finished our round of golf, compared scores, and headed back to our vehicles.

"See everyone next week," Joe said.

"Yep."

"Yeah."

"That's if Butchie doesn't have go off and save the butt of some damsel in distress," Karl said.

"I sure wouldn't save yours," I said as I neared my Escalade and Karl chuckled.

"I still want to see that snakes head," Karl replied as he started loading his golf clubs into the trunk of his car.

# Chapter Thirty Two

Friday evening October 11, found Martha and I sitting in the family room of our house. We had gone out for supper instead of me cooking and now were watching an episode of *Pawn Stars* when the telephone rang. The caller ID showed Gottfried Butz 657- 555-4567. Knowing it was Bubba, I picked up the cordless telephone that was laying on the lamp stand next to my chair.

"Hello, Gottfried," I said.

"Gottfried your ass! This is Bubba," he said.

"I know. I just get a kick out of rattling your chain," I replied.

Although Bubba is big enough to squash me like a small bug, I felt safe giving him crap since he was in Tennessee.

"So what's up?" I asked.

"I thought I'd give you a call and let you know what is happening down here," he said.

"Sounds good. Let me turn the television down and put you on speaker phone so Martha can hear what you have to say also," I replied.

"Hi Bubba," Martha hollered across the room before Bubba started to talk and I had the speaker phone turned on.

"Hi Martha," came Bubba's voice booming out of the telephone speaker after I had turned it on.

"As I said, I wanted to let you folks know how things are going here. Angel had her baby on September 19. It's a boy and he weighed a little over eight pounds. She named him Gavin Edward McCoy," Bubba said.

"Hey, the little guy was born on my birthday," I said.

"Must make him special," I added.

"If you say so," Bubba replied and continued.

"Both Angel and Gavin are doing fine. She is living with her mom and dad right now until she can get back on her feet. She found a job in Jonesborough so she has some income. It's not as good of a job as she had lined up, but it's a job. Her mom is babysitting little Gavin to save on expenses."

"How are she and Frank doing?" asked Martha.

"Well, they're talking to one another. Frank has visited her and the baby several times and seems to enjoy little Gavin. We're hoping things will work out between the two of them, but I'm trying to convince Bertha to stay out of it," Bubba replied.

"She's acting like a big, bossy sister trying to patch things up between Angel and Frank. I figure if it's meant to be, it will be," he added.

"Anything happen at the Family of our Lord compound?" I asked Bubba.

"Yep. The ATF spent the past several months watching Reverend Jones and the activity around the compound. Last week they raided the compound and found the bootleg cigarettes and whiskey just as you had described.

"While the ATF men were making their way around the compound, several of the flock came forward and claimed they were kidnapped, just as Spike told you. Reverend Jones has been charged in federal court with bootlegging and kidnapping along with some of his top henchmen," he replied.

"The feds are also investigating Sheriff Hatfield. There is talk that they have a pretty good case against him of being a partner in the Reverend's illegal activities. If nothing else, they can get him with aiding and abetting Reverend Jones," Bubba added.

"What happened to the other people at the compound?" I asked.

"The feds let whoever wanted to stay on the compound, stay until the courts decide what is to become of the property. All who wanted to leave were allowed to leave."

"What about Spike?" I asked.

"He is alright. He's working with the feds on purchasing his bar back. After the Reverend was arrested, a federal judge put all of his holdings in a court trusteeship, so who knows how that will shake out. The court did appoint Spike manager of the bar for the time being, so at least he's back doing something he loves."

"I'm glad to hear Spike is OK. I don't feel quite so guilty leaving him," I said.

"I talked to him a week or so ago and he told me he realizes there was nothing you could do to help him. In fact, he said the first two Tangueray and Tonics are on him the next time you are down here visiting," Bubba said.

"You still there Martha?" asked Bubba.

"Yes I am."

"You'll be happy to know that Rhonda got a teaching job and no longer works at the Kum N Go or doesn't pole dance. You don't need to worry about Butch making another trip down here to check her out," Bubba said giving a hearty laugh.

"I wasn't worried, because he knows what's good for him," she replied as she gave me one of her looks.

"I guess that's all I had to tell you folks other than come on back down and visit sometime when you're not working on a case," Bubba said.

"Bertha wants to say hi before we hang up," he added.

We talked to Bertha several minutes and she thanked me numerous times for finding Angel before we hung up.

"So, another case successfully solved," Martha, said as she got out of her chair, came sat in my lap and gave me a kiss.

"I guess," I replied.

"I just wish I could have helped Spike more," I added.

"You did everything you could. It would have been stupid to try and get back into the Family of our Lord compound," Martha said.

"Besides, you might have tried to use those stupid stilts again and probably broke your fool neck," she added as she gave me another kiss.

"I think I'll build another pair of those stilts so I can practice on them in the back yard. You never know when that ability might come in handy again," I said as I returned her kiss.

"So you think," replied Martha as she got out of my lap, returned to her chair, and sat down. We continued to watch what was left of *Pawn Stars*.

As I watched Rick, Corey and the Old Man strike deals, rag on Chumlee and bicker between themselves, I found myself wondering if I would get involved in solving another mystery some day?

## About The Author

Larry Pedersen is the author of the Butch Brogen novels. Larry was employed by the Minnesota Department of Transportation in various positions for thirty-seven years until he decided to retire to pursue his two hobbies, golf, and woodworking.

Although Larry has no formal training in manuscript writing or book publishing experience, he decided to try his hand at writing mystery novels to help pass the time during the cold Minnesota winters when he could not golf.

With the help of his wife Ruth, Larry has written and self-published three Butch Brogen novels.

Larry resides in Kasson, Minnesota where he has lived since 1975.